Debbi Bedford
PASSAGES

Harlequin Books

TORONTO • NEW YORK • LONDON
AMSTERDAM • PARIS • SYDNEY • HAMBURG
STOCKHOLM • ATHENS • TOKYO • MILAN

D0010714

Published November 1988

First printing September 1988

ISBN 0-373-70333-3

A day, a time

that rushes back
 to be again
 in me again

I wonder
 if you

 remember,

 if you hold me
  in your mind,
 if you feel
  sad and sorry
  that the

  passages

  we travel
  lead us
  forever

  away.

    —D.

To Jack, who leads me, follows me, holds me.

Acknowledgments

*To Steve Martin,
who explained the currents of
the Snake River,
and to Harvey Atkin,
who explained the currents of
the television industry.
Thank you.*

CHAPTER ONE

THE SNOW-COVERED FIELD stretched before him in a vast expanse of diamonds that shone in the intense mountain morning sun. Each breath he took cut into his nostrils and froze there. The thermometer on the north side of the house had only climbed to twenty-three degrees by the time he had set off on cross-country skis just after breakfast.

The snow was dry, a fluffy talcum that dusted his leather ski shoes and his gaiters. *Schuss crunch schuss crunch*. The unaccompanied rhythm of his skis on powder filled the meadow with sound.

If the temperature had been warmer, the snow would have been wet enough to impede his pace. Peter Barrett did not mind the exertion of skiing wet snow. But today he was running a race with himself. Today he was striving for speed. Solitary speed.

Peter squinted behind his sunglasses against the glare of the snow and the sun. Each time he crested a rise on the path, the shimmering jeweled vastness swept away from him, a mirage, and it occurred to him that his life was the same way, forever sweeping beyond his grasp.

A tiny, aimless, mittened hand fluttered against the wool scarf at Peter's neck. The weight in the Gerry pack on his back shifted slightly.

"Are you waking up back there, little wump?" The human voice would have sounded harsh in the silent snowy field if not for all the gentle love that registered there.

The child in the backpack was a baby boy, although he was almost a toddler. His first birthday was only three weeks away. He didn't talk much yet. But the boy and his father had been through a great sadness together, a sadness that the baby would have to relive someday, and Peter already looked upon his son as a tiny man.

It was nearing lunchtime. Perhaps, Peter thought, it was time to take him in out of the cold. He and the baby had been skiing almost two hours. Taylor was bundled well, in a goose-down baby bag Lorilee had ordered for him from the L. L. Bean catalogue. Even so, Lorilee wouldn't approve.

Lorilee. How many times did Peter have to remind himself not to think of her as if she was alive? How many times did he forget she wasn't still sharing his life?

Every time he walked into the bedroom they had shared, Peter wanted to strike out at something. Every time he surveyed Taylor's miniature features—the innocent gray opallike eyes, the lacy web of lashes, the close-lipped grin that so perfectly duplicated hers—Lorilee was with him again, standing beside him in the stillness, admiring her son through the eyes of his father, haunting him.

Peter turned toward the house and let his own determination push forward with his skis. He was gliding now as if he was running, every muscle tuned, pumping, straining with the motion, as if the sheer effort of his exercise would erase the grinding pain he was still feeling.

The house was in view now, on past one more rise in the meadow, just south of a clump of stark winter-dead aspen. Peter glided toward it. When he reached the moss-rock patio, he popped the ski bindings open and left his long skis propped upright beside the door. With Taylor still on his back, he trudged into the stone entryway, trailing snow.

The house was not as hollow, as darkly cool, as he had expected it to be. A fire burned in the family-room fireplace. Peter smelled ginger snaps baking in the kitchen. For an instant his heart shot into his throat. This was the way his home once had been. Warm, the fire crackling, Lorilee waiting for him.

Peter had let the last housekeeper go the same week Lorilee died. He hadn't wanted her around, running his household on remnants of Lorilee's instructions. So he'd hired a new woman, a woman named Camille who reminded him of a bantam rooster. His parents had known her for ages and she'd proved a godsend. Peter tugged off his wool cap and ran a disgruntled hand through his hair. Now he couldn't get rid of her. Today was supposed to be Camille's day off. But secretly he was glad she had come.

"Peter Barrett—" she clucked at him from the kitchen "—did you have that baby out in this weather?"

"Go home, Camille," he said in a teasing tone.

"Two red, cold noses." She stood on tiptoe and kissed Taylor's cheek when Peter brought him into the kitchen. The child's flesh was icy. "Did you think of putting a muffler around this boy's face?" It was the way Camille most often lectured him, by asking questions in a motherly tone.

"The kid has to breathe," he said, grinning at her.

Peter shrugged the pack off his shoulders and lifted Taylor out of it. When Camille saw how warmly the child was dressed, her disapproval faded. She was a mother herself to three healthy, full-grown children and she couldn't help mothering this baby a bit. God knows, the child needed it. But when she looked at Peter, at how much he loved his son and how thoughtfully he cared for him, she was almost sheepish about her concern. Peter Barrett was a fine, loving father.

"So tell me," he commented as he watched her unzip the baby's tiny snowsuit, "is your husband thrilled you've decided to shirk your duties at home so you can come to my house to bake cookies on Saturday? I didn't know weekends were a part of our agreement."

"They aren't." She handed Taylor a warm ginger snap and kept an eye on him while he took tiny nibbles. "Robert is ice fishing on Jackson Lake today. I decided I needed a little kid to appreciate my cookies."

Peter realized, as he took one of the cookies, that he was utterly dependent on her. Camille was a grandmotherly dynamo, just heaveyset enough to have a cuddly lap for Taylor, and she did everything for him on the weekdays when he had to be at the bank. She cared for his son and she organized his clothes and she cooked each evening. A hearty meal was always waiting for him in the oven when he arrived home. And Taylor was always bathed, dressed in overalls or a little pair of jeans, waiting to play with his daddy.

After supper, Peter would lie on his back in front of the fire Camille had built for him at dusk and he would hold Taylor high above him, his tiny limbs flailing like seaweed in an ocean current. Peter would tickle him in the stomach with the top of his head and he would whistle and the baby would hiss until the two of them were wild with laughter. Those were the times Peter felt as if he had almost found his sanity again, lying on the dust-blue Indian rug on the floor, grappling with his son and with reality.

"You need lunch." Camille eyed him with conviction. She had already made his decision for him.

"Ginger snaps would have been fine. What else did you make?"

"Tuna sandwiches. Although I don't know if Taylor will want lunch after that cookie."

"It's all in the timing, Camille," Peter teased her again. "Most people serve the tuna first and save the cookies for dessert."

"But the cookies are so *good*. I hated for the two of you to have to wait for them." Camille screwed up her mouth in challenge and Peter had to laugh at her.

"You are past the point of being motherly, Camille. You are being grandmotherly." He reached across the kitchen cabinet and touched her hand. "But I'm glad you are." He didn't know exactly what to say to her to make her understand how he felt about her being here today. She was saving him. But he didn't want her to come again on a weekend. It was too much for her to give.

"It's time for sleeping." Possessively, Camille lifted the baby from the high chair and carried him to the sink. She ran a dishcloth under a stream of warm water and used it to wipe Taylor's hands, his mouth, his one tuna-splotched eye. "You ought to sleep, too," she said to Peter without turning toward him. "You look worn out. You always look worn out." Camille did not skirt issues. She shouldered his son the same way she would have shouldered a weapon. Peter watched after her helplessly as she marched out of the kitchen. Then he climbed the stairs to his study where he knew he could rest.

Peter's study was a homey, masculine room with a
deeply slanted ceiling and an open log railing, a loft that
opened above the family room and the fireplace. In ad-
dition to the bank, this study was Peter's domain. It was
one of the few places in the house he was not contin-
ually plagued by thoughts of his wife.

Lorilee had not ventured up the stairs to his loft
often. When Peter secured himself in the loft behind his
oak desk, his mind was strictly set on financial business. This same place was a haven to him, a secret room
where he belonged to no one but himself. The walls were
lined with a decoy collection Peter had started as a boy.
Now he displayed decoys of every duck species that
frequented the Northern Rockies—scaups, a male and
female mallard, the Common Goldeneye, several teals
and loons and an American Wigeon. Lorilee had
laughingly called this place his "wildlife room."

The ducks were what remained of his boyhood. Peter still hunted with his father every autumn, on the
ranch where his parents lived now, in Idaho. This collection of decoys bounced him back to an innocent time
in his life, a time when his father had taught him to believe in miracles, a time when he had fearlessly expected
happy endings. Happy endings. How easy they had
once seemed to come by.

Peter lazed behind his desk, rummaging through the
mail, and he finally dozed off after reading the last three
pages of yesterday's *Wall Street Journal*. When he
awoke, the vibrant light of midafternoon slanted in
through the study window. A fire cackled in the fireplace below. The popping and the spitting of the hot
pine tar seemed, in a way, like the sound of a familiar
voice. But Peter realized, as a massive weight bore down
on him, that he was alone.

He rose from his desk and made his way down the log steps. "Taylor went to sleep at 1:30." Camille had written him a note. "See you Monday. C."

Peter took a ginger snap from the cookie jar and then padded down the hallway to Taylor's room. Slowly, so as not to make a sound, he turned the doorknob and peered into his son's room. Camille had drawn the shades, and despite the sunlight outside, the room was dusky. Peter could barely see the stuffed cow and the teddy bear and the fat red dinosaur on the shelf beneath the window. From across the nursery, Peter heard the faint rhythm of his son's breathing.

Without approaching, he could not see Taylor sleeping in the little bed. The baby was ensconced in things made to protect him, bumper pads and pillows and assorted hand-knit blankets in splashes of primary colors. Peter slumped against the doorjamb, his mind traveling back to the year before, to this very same time, just a month after Christmas, when everything in his home had been so joyous, so hopeful.

Lorilee had gained almost thirty pounds during her pregnancy. At this time last year, she had been waddling around the house like an overfed bird. He had taken to teasing her then, telling her she was another duck decoy and he had gotten her with child so he could add her to his collection of fowl in the wildlife room.

She had pretended to be furious with him, she had pummeled him with her fists, but his wife had been so huge and so happy about the baby, so expectant, that she hadn't been able to stay mad at him. Instead, she'd collapsed into his lap with laughter and Peter had chuckled, too, until tears had streamed down Lorilee's face and they were both breathless.

Peter shifted in the nursery doorway, half hoping the rustle of his movement would wake Taylor. Peter was desperate with sadness and with feeling alone. He moved toward the bed and gazed down at the upturned side of his son's sleeping face. "Oh, little wump." His words were just a touch louder than a whisper. Taylor didn't move. Peter stretched one tentative finger toward the baby and traced the velvet outline of his son's ear. "Oh, how I wish..." But then he didn't know exactly how to finish his sentence.

"I WATCH TELEVISION every day," the lady sitting in the bulkhead of the DC-10 whispered to the woman seated beside her. "I know that's her." She only meant to confide the information to her seatmate but she was so excited that she couldn't control the volume of her voice. "That's Lisa Radford from 'Wayward Hopes.' This is so exciting. I wonder where she's going." She was talking to anyone who would listen. "Do they film those daytime soaps in New York? Maybe she's going to the Rocky Mountains to make a movie."

"Did you see 'Wayward Hopes' Thursday?" The seatmate made an effort to conceal the remark behind her hand. "That horrible man she's married to is having an affair. I wonder if she'll divorce him when she finds out."

"Why don't you ask her?" the man across the aisle couldn't resist asking smugly. "She's sitting right there."

"We wouldn't know what to say to her." The two women glared askance at him.

The man turned away from them. This flight from New York to Denver was going to be a long, interesting one. He managed to hide his amused grin by staring at the jagged seams of tar on the runway.

"It *is* in the script." Another woman sitting on his side of the plane jumped to his rescue and that amused him even more. "*She* knows what will happen. You should ask her."

"The only thing I'm going to ask Lisa Radford for is her autograph. Imagine being on the same plane. Maybe I'll get one for Aunt Maude, too. Maude lives for 'Wayward Hopes'." The woman settled back victoriously in her seat just as the aircraft's engines roared to life. "That's what I'll do. I'll get her autograph." And she barely waited until the plane had risen into the sky before she reached above her and pushed the button to hail the stewardess.

"I'M SORRY to disturb you, Miss Eberle," the flight attendant apologized. "It seems our passengers have recognized you. Several of them have requested your autograph. Do you mind?"

"No." The dark-haired actress flashed a smile that didn't reach her tired eyes. This was only the beginning of a very long journey. She took the cocktail napkins and the pen and scrawled a salutation on each of them while the flight attendant waited. "Best Wishes. Shannon Eberle." Beneath her own name, she added her character's name on "Wayward Hopes." Lisa Radford.

Shannon had grown accustomed to identifying her character during her four years on "Wayward Hopes." The admirers who requested her autograph didn't care about Shannon Eberle. They wanted Lisa Radford. It was something Shannon had gradually come to terms with, always playing understudy to another woman, a

woman who didn't exist, a character who was an intimate companion to millions of American television
viewers. But there was more to Shannon than all of Lisa
Radford's designer gowns and diamonds, more than the
character's glamour and chic style. Shannon was earthy
and steadfast, and she cared about the people around
her. Her huge, penetrating dark eyes reached out to
people.

The casting director for "Wayward Hopes" had noticed Shannon immediately when she'd walked into his
office to audition. The show's writers had instructed
him to find someone fair to play Lisa. He had been in-
terviewing blondes all morning. But when Shannon read
for the part and the casting director recommended her,
Mark Troy, the show's executive producer, knew he had
to have her. Physically, she was wrong for the role. The
script called for someone diminutive and light com-
plexioned. Shannon's olive skin had the texture of
honey and combined with her chestnut-colored hair, she
looked exotic, almost swarthy.

Al Jensen, the show's director, sensed Shannon's
honesty, her hold on reality, and he had known immediately she would bring vitality and complexity to the
role. And he had been right. Lisa Radford received
hundreds of fan letters each week. Viewers couldn't get
enough of her. Every place Shannon went, complete
strangers stopped her and talked to her or asked for her
autograph. Every part of her life was a delicate balance
between reality and the illusion she created on the television screen.

Shannon handed the autographed napkins back to
the flight attendant. She sat perfectly still, thinking of
her own life, so precious and simple, compared with

Lisa Radford's life and the relentless, destructive storyline it necessarily followed.

It had been eleven months since she'd visited her family. Going there now made her feel as if she was thrusting herself onto a different path. But she was traveling to a world she loved, one she often longed for when she was sweating beneath the glaring set lights at the studio or when she was battling crowds shopping on Fifth Avenue. And despite her fatigue, she was excited and preoccupied. Tonight she would be sitting on the porch at the old house, bundled into one of her father's worn goose-down parkas, listening to a thousand head of sheep bleat in the distance.

She changed planes at Denver's Stapleton Airport. The Metroliner that would take her northwest into central Wyoming seated nineteen passengers. The aircraft was too small to approach a boarding gate. A shuttle bus transported Shannon and the other passengers from the concourse, across the runway, to the tiny plane. "I've survived this trip before," Shannon whispered to herself as she steadied herself against the aluminum railing and then climbed the shaky steps. But she felt as if she was flying off to the edge of the earth. For a fleeting moment, she wondered if she should have come. Perhaps it was unfair of her to cling to a past she had wanted so desperately to leave behind.

But fifty minutes later, when the Metroliner banked off and then came in low to land at the Wind River airport, Wyoming, Shannon knew she had been right to come home. The familiar red Dodge pickup was parked on the shoulder of the highway. The plane crossed the highway at the same time every day, at the same altitude, just before it landed. Shannon's two brothers were standing beside the truck. A white butcher-paper sign

that read Welcome Home in huge hand-painted red letters lay flat in the pickup's bed. Shannon could even see
Wiley, her father's old sheep-herding dog, standing in
the truck just beside the sign.

"Somebody in this plane has quite a welcoming
committee," the man across the aisle commented with
a smile.

Shannon laid her head against the smooth glass of the
window and drank in the old feeling of belonging that
was welling up inside her. She smiled at the man across
the aisle. "They're mine," she told him quietly.

As the little airplane passed overhead, Shannon's two
dark-haired brothers jumped into the truck and raced
toward the terminal, the dog barking, the tires spray-
ing gravel as they went. They were waiting for her at the
baggage claim by the time the aircraft landed and tax-
ied to the gate. When Shannon saw them there, looking victorious and sheepish, she didn't know whether
she should shake her head at them in reprimand or fly
into their arms. She stood there, laughing and speech-
less, shaking her head, and then she ran to them, hugging them both, as tears pooled in her eyes. "You two
are crazy, you know that?"

"She *did* see it." Seventeen-year-old Tommy winked
at his older brother.

"All right!" Nolan cheered.

"Welcome home, Shannon." There was a hand on
her shoulder as her mother moved to embrace her. Then
her father was there, too, standing beside her and she
stared up at him, at his massive chest, his grizzled
whiskers, his dark eyes that so perfectly matched her
own. "Oh, Daddy."

He swept her into his arms and Shannon felt like a
little girl again, surrounded, as she had always been, by

the textures of her father, the gruff voice, the leathery creases around his eyes, the sandpaper chin. Despite his age, the muscles lining his arms and his torso remained firm. They told the complete story of him and of his days, of the toil he endured on the sheep ranch that had once been his own father's, the land that would some-day belong to his eldest son.

Daniel gazed down at his daughter and his clear, dark eyes shone with pride. "Welcome to Wyoming, kiddo."

As Shannon clung to her father, a great rush of relief coursed through her. She hadn't been wrong to come. The searing confusion she felt each time she tore her-self away from New York City to return to this place was justified once again.

Shannon's memories were painfully precious to her. Growing up here, watching her parents desperately trying to pay the monthly bills and keep food on the ta-ble had taught her the value of choosing a goal and sticking by it. And still her family remained un-changed. It was selfish of her to need that stability, somehow. Even the pickup her father had been driving for a dozen years was a symbol to her. It represented everything that had ever been unfaltering in her life. It was almost a ceremony to her now, watching her brothers pitch her luggage into the pickup bed as Wiley cowered in the corner. Tommy and Nolan jumped in beside her suitcases for the ride. She climbed into the cab between her mother and father and straddled the gearshift.

"You aren't wearing a coat," Daniel Eberle com-mented. "Didn't you expect it to be cold out here?"

"I didn't have one that was—" she hesitated "—suitable." Shannon thought of the full-length crys-tal fox she'd left hanging in her closet in Manhattan. "I

was wishing I could borrow one of yours." She was sad
suddenly, thinking of his huge bulky sweaters, his parkas, his shirts that hung off her shoulders with tails that
fell to her knees. Chunks of her childhood. Gone. She
felt as if she had come from forever away then, and it
made her miss them all, even though she was here with
them, just asking to borrow her father's coat.

"I've got an old parka I'll dig out for you when we
get back from the school meeting."

"Meeting?"

Tommy stuck his head in through the back cab window and grinned at her. He had been dying to tell her
about it ever since she had climbed down the steps from
the plane. "The kids at high school are having an assembly this afternoon. To honor you. So you can talk
about BEAT."

His hair was dancing in the wind as the truck sped
down the highway and his eyes were dancing, too, and
Shannon didn't have the heart to tell him how exhausted she was.

"You just wait," he shouted, still grinning. "It's
supposed to be a big surprise. A bunch of teachers made
cakes. The band's going to play. And you're going to
make a speech...."

CHAPTER TWO

THE BEAT PROJECT—Be Aware of a Teen's Dream—
had been born while Shannon was reading an issue of
the Wind River paper her father always forwarded to
her in New York. She had come across a survey a local
reporter had taken of high school seniors in Wind River.
It was a simple questionnaire asking students about
their plans for after high school—if they could afford
to go to college, if they wanted to leave Wyoming, if
they had any overwhelming dreams they wanted to follow.

The results of the survey frightened Shannon. A large
percentage of the class could not afford to attend college. Most of them didn't think college was worth the
effort. They were coming back to Wind River anyway,
to work on the sheep ranches or to check groceries at
Farmer Jack or to wait tables at the café on Main Street.

Shannon's older brother, Nolan, had worked toward
a degree for two years at the University of Wyoming in
Laramie. He had given up at last and had come back
home to the ranch. It had just been too much, working
forty hours each week at Radio Shack for minimum
wage and trying to do well with his studies.

His girlfriend, Melissa, had stayed in Wind River to
wait tables at the café while he was gone. Now that Nolan had come back to town and had married her, she
was doing the same thing, taking orders for cheesebur-

gers or chicken-fried-steak dinners, coming home ecstatic with extra change in her pocket when the tips were good. The baby, P.J., stayed with Melissa's mother every day while Melissa worked.

It had been Tommy who had cemented the idea of BEAT and a teen center firmly in Shannon's mind. She had watched her younger brother grow up working several hours each day at the five-and-dime on Main Street, doing his best to save enough to attend college. Shannon wanted to pay for his college education. It would have been easy for her, and Tommy had already been accepted at the University of Wyoming. But she didn't dare offer. Tommy was much too proud and she knew her family would never accept financial help.

There had been two other articles in the newspaper that day to command Shannon's attention. One was a front-page story about the slumping economy in central Wyoming because of slumping oil prices. The second article, almost hidden on page seven, told the story of two fifteen-year-old girls who had run away from home within days of each other. Shannon knew one of the girls. She read the story through as a great lump of helplessness rose inside her.

It was then, while tears coursed down her cheeks for Tommy, for the two girls who were gone, that her idea had taken form. It would begin with a recreation center, a place for teens to gather and talk, with pool tables, maybe a skating rink, VCR viewing rooms and audio-recording rooms and studios for performing plays and maybe practicing the piano. The organization would be governed by the students, giving many of them a chance to become leaders among their peers. Teachers and volunteers would supervise "dreaming sessions," sessions, which Shannon pictured as heart-to-heart sharing times laced with advice, encouragement and support.

Scholarships and loans would be available from BEAT for qualified students. Shannon had mailed the Fremont County School Board a synopsis of BEAT as she perceived it. She had volunteered to donate money to fund the program. Now, thanks to the Washakie High School Student Council and several enthusiastic staff members, BEAT was finally coming into its own.

Tommy was proud of his sister as he led her into the assembly. Everyone in Fremont County knew of her—the pretty girl who had been a cheerleader once, who had earned enough money waitressing at the café to take drama classes at Western Wyoming Community College.

Shannon had stashed every dime, even her tips, into an account at the Wind River bank. And when she attended classes at Western Wyoming, she knew it had been worth everything. She loved studying and she loved setting up props, and after she performed a myriad of plays, her drama instructor urged her to apply for a grant at the University of Utah.

She performed a monologue for faculty members visiting her campus. It took weeks to find out if she had been accepted after that; she lost eight pounds waiting because she was too excited and worried to eat. When the letter finally arrived, she sat on a bench at the campus post office just staring at the return address on the envelope and crying—she was so frightened of what it might say.

The letter was a rejection. But it was one of the best learning experiences she could have asked for. Because she proved them wrong. She had become a television celebrity despite what the fine arts people in Utah thought of her.

This was the story she told as she stood behind the rickety podium at Washakie High School. No one spoke as she told them how depressed she had felt that night, how she had decided her dreaming was absurd. It had been the first time in her life she had been afraid to face her own future.

The next morning, she'd skipped drama class. That night, she received a telephone call from her drama coach at Western Wyoming. "Don't you ever let anyone's subjective opinion turn you away from what you want," his voice had boomed over the telephone. "I'm sending you the address of a college friend in New York," he had continued, undaunted by the sniffles he could hear on the other end of the line. "Lawrence Wills is a good talent agent. I've told him about you and he thinks he may have something. In my opinion, you have served enough of an apprenticeship."

When Shannon met with Lawrence Wills and read for him, she felt strangely buoyant again, as if her life was out of her own hands. She felt as if she were watching herself perform from a different angle, an angle from which she had never observed herself before. And three weeks later, the contract came for her in the mail. Lawrence Wills wanted to represent her.

While she was still going through the contract, the agent called her. He wanted her to fly to Los Angeles to audition for a chewing-gum commercial.

She took the bus. Larry Wills met her at the Greyhound station and drove her to the studio. She had five minutes to brush her teeth, freshen her makeup and straighten her clothing. Then she was on, auditioning for her first professional role without having time to think of it.

The ad agency's creative director thought she was perfect for it. Never mind her acting ability, she explained to the students at Washakie High School. He hired her because he liked the shape of her mouth.

"MISS EBERLE," James Clarkson, president of the Fremont County School Board, gripped her arm as the students filed out of the gymnasium, "I need to speak with you in confidence. If you don't mind..."

She followed him. "Do we have a problem?"

He nodded. "The ground breaking for the BEAT project is off for tomorrow. Unfortunately, we must postpone it."

"I don't understand."

He waited, uncertain how to go on. She had come all this way. And now, for what? "I know you volunteered all of the money toward this project. And everyone agrees BEAT is a good concept, Miss Eberle. But some of the townspeople don't like the idea of someone from New York coming to Wind River and funding the entire thing. They're afraid you'll try to pull too many strings. Instead, they want BEAT to remain strictly a community project."

"But it will be." Shannon's hands were fists knotted against her sides. "I was born here."

"They're willing to take a donation from you. But nothing more. A group of them presented a petition at the school board meeting Monday night. They want more people involved. Wyoming people."

"But no one around here has that kind of money." Her face had gone white. She felt as if her last lifeline to her past had been pulled away. "What about a loan?

I could give them the money and they could pay me back.''

"It's the same thing, Miss Eberle," he told her. "They would still feel obligated to you. They don't want a loan. The town's tax coffers couldn't support one. They need donations, both local and out of state, to make BEAT work. The townspeople are willing to let you donate the land. Your money has already purchased it. But it has to stop there."

Everything she wanted to do for them was slipping away. Shannon felt inadequate, lost. The community that had once been her home wouldn't take what she most wanted to give it.

"At one time, the Wind River bank could have underwritten such a project," Clarkson continued. "The oil slump has drained this economy."

Shannon felt something horrible and heavy settle inside her. "We can go ahead with the ground breaking, can't we? These kids have worked so hard. We have the land."

"I see no point in incurring expenses we are unable to pay. The school board consists of elected officials. After that petition, we cannot schedule the ground breaking until we know we are representing Fremont County residents. I'm sorry."

"We have to find someone else to underwrite the cost of the construction. Someone the townspeople will find acceptable." She was determined suddenly, when only moments before she had been defeated. "Isn't there someone, another bank perhaps, that might be willing to finance this project?"

Clarkson had been mulling over the possibilities for days. "There is a bank we could approach. It isn't local but it *is* located in Wyoming. The president's name is Peter Barrett. The economy in Jackson Hole is better than it is here. When the price of oil goes down, tourism goes up. The bank there does well in times like these."

"Who circulated that petition?" Shannon was all business again. Her feelings didn't matter. What mattered now were the teens and the town.

"Herbert Budge. He's a sheep farmer. His daughter, Sandy, is a high school senior."

Shannon smiled. "She's on newspaper staff with my brother, Tommy. They're close friends."

"She's applied to an out-of-state college for a full scholarship and her father is certain she'll get it. He was one of the few who could afford to look at your proposal objectively. Then others followed. Over one hundred people signed the thing."

"Does Sandy know of her father's involvement?" If she remembered correctly, the girl was on the BEAT committee at the school. "Do the kids know their parents are doing this? Hiding behind their community pride?"

"No. They'll only be told the ground breaking is postponed because funding fell through temporarily."

"Let's hope it's only temporary." Shannon slung her purse up over her shoulder with one fluid motion. She hated the pride the local people felt. And she loved it, as well. It was as much a part of her as it was of them.

"I'll call First National in Jackson and make an appointment with Peter Barrett if he can see us. We'll do everything we can."

Shannon grasped his elbow. "We'll do more than that," she told him. "We'll find someone to help us."

"Somehow you make me believe that." He took her arm and led her across the room to meet several other staff members. And as Jim Clarkson watched the actress greet his faculty and sign autographs, he knew he was watching an extraordinary woman. He thought of her then, of how she had looked when she had been fourteen, with a red bandana tied around her hair, balancing a tray of café steak dinners on one hand. *Look at her,* he thought. *Look what the girl has done for herself.* She had told the student body that she believed dreams could come true. And as he watched her, as she hugged one of her former teachers, he thought about dreams and about miracles. Just being around Shannon Eberle made him believe in them, too.

FIRST NATIONAL BANK of Jackson Hole, Wyoming, opened its doors to the public in 1870, two years before Yellowstone National Park, fifty-five miles to the north, became the United States' first national park. Peter Barrett's great-great-grandfather opened it with capital of $40,000. His first deposit came in ten days later— $230.75 in gold specie.

The bank was now a silent member of the Barrett family. Over the years it had been robbed by Western outlaws, hammered by the Great Depression, always surviving the tumult of the local economy and the weather and the stock market.

First National Bank of Jackson had been good to the Barretts. It had supported their men for over a century. But, in a way, it had taken the one thing from Peter that mattered to him most. Lorilee. In a way, First National Bank was directly responsible for his wife's death.

Peter was sitting behind the massive desk, his head in his hands, his fingers jutting up through his hair, when his secretary, Barbara, knocked on his door. "Your appointment is here, Mr. Barrett."

"Thank you." He looked very young and very fierce when Jim Clarkson and Shannon Eberle entered his office. He did not rise to welcome them.

"Mr. Barrett—" Clarkson offered him his hand. "Thank you for seeing us on short notice."

Shannon stood there, staring down at him, surprised by his age, and wondering why he looked so angry and so sad.

Peter finally rose.

"Jim." Shannon's voice was soft. They had driven three hours for this meeting. But she sensed this man was distracted and melancholy. It was her job to study faces, emotions, and portray them effectively on camera. It was easy for her, observing people, knowing how they felt by reading their body language and their expressions. "Perhaps we should come again, Mr. Barrett. Perhaps this is a bad time."

"No." Peter held up a hand to stop her. "Wait." When her eyes met his, they seemed to bore into him, as if she could see into his mind and know everything he felt in his soul. And she looked vaguely familiar to him, but he didn't know why. "It isn't a bad time. Stay. Please."

"If you're certain." She watched him intently, taking pleasure in the strong lines of his face. His eyes were large and dark, set deeply above high cheekbones. His mouth was generous, his chin chiseled in a firm square that tightened as he spoke to her. Everything about him—the etched lines around his eyes, the dark hair—was precisely drawn. Nothing about his face was soft or vague. Even his voice was clear and strong.

Jim Clarkson snapped open his briefcase. He presented everything he knew the banker would want to see. Blueprints of the proposed teen center. An artist's

rendering of the exterior. Title papers to the land. And
the constitution that would eventually govern the organization.

Peter surveyed the constitution. "This is impressive.
Very well thought out."

Clark gestured toward Shannon. This was the perfect opportunity to play her up, to use her name to impress the man. "The entire program is Miss Eberle's
idea. It was hard for her to get time away..." He was
going to say "from taping the show," but she gestured
for him to be silent.

"Don't give me so much credit," she interrupted. She
pointed to the document in Peter's hands. "The kids at
Washakie High School came up with that. It's very
good. Wind River's teens have put an incredible amount
of energy and thought into this."

Peter glanced at her once again. He was surprised by
this young woman, someone, a professional administrator perhaps, who had been paid to put this plan into
progress. He admired her for giving credit to the high
school students. When she smiled at him this time, a
tentative, questioning smile, Peter was certain he had
seen her face before.

He faced Jim Clarkson. "I'll set the two of you up
for an appointment with Don Woolsey in the commercial loan department. I'm certain he'll be able to work
out a payment schedule satisfactory to us both."

"That isn't what we want." Shannon was shaking her
head, her long hair twisting at her shoulders, her eyes
sad. "We can't..."

"We aren't here for a loan, Barrett," Jim Clarkson
explained. "We are asking you to underwrite a portion
of this project."

Peter glared at them. *Everyone thinks I can pull money out of a hat.* "I cannot do that." His face was grim.

"Shannon originally agreed to underwrite the cost." Clarkson was doing his best to explain. "It's something so beneficial for the kids. But—"

Peter eyed her. "She backed out on you at the last minute."

"No. The local residents petitioned me out. I grew up in Wind River. But I live out of state now. The townspeople are afraid I will become too involved in the project if I pay for it."

"They presented a petition this past Monday night," Clarkson said. "We never would have gotten this far if we hadn't found firm financial backing."

"And you hope," Peter interjected dryly, "that First National Bank will intervene now." His jaw was clenched and his eyes were melancholy again. He wished he could pull open the vault and shove handfuls of money at them. He wished he could help everyone who came to him. And there had been a time, not so long ago, when he hadn't even been able to help Lorilee.

"Mr. Barrett," Shannon said, and then she stopped. When she called him by name, something tight wrenched in his heart. He hated what he had to tell her. "I cannot do this for you, Miss Eberle." The Jackson High School students would benefit from a teen center and a BEAT program, too. But even if Peter could pry the funds loose, he knew he would have to spend them in his own community, not in a town halfway across the state.

He thought of Taylor then, his own son, and he turned away from them so they couldn't see his face as a great wave of discouragement slashed across it. He still had so far to go with his son, so far to lead him, so far for the two of them to travel alone. "If I had children involved, it might be different." He turned back to them. "It might be worth it to me then."

Shannon stood silently for a moment, thinking of Tommy and the others. "There is no help for us here, then."

"I'm sorry."

Gingerly, she moved forward and touched his arm. Perhaps they had placed him in a precarious position by coming here. Perhaps he would have helped them if it were within his power. She could tell by watching him that his concern was sincere. "Thank you for hearing us out. If you think of someone, an investor for us, will you call?"

"I will." His eyes met hers. "Yes."

PETER GLANCED at his watch. One-fifty p.m.

Camille had been planning Taylor's first birthday celebration for weeks. He hadn't thought of it while he talked to the people from Wind River. And now he was almost late for his son's birthday party.

Taylor's present was stashed in the corner of his office. It had been hidden behind the mahogany desk for days, wrapped in neon orange paper with Snoopy and Woodstock and balloons all over it.

Peter was as excited about the gift as he hoped Taylor would be. It was a little train, with a bright blue seat and red wheels that chugged across the floor, with a loud, airy whistle that sounded almost real. Taylor would be awed by it, maybe even a little afraid. But Peter intended to teach him to ride it. Tonight. Taylor Barrett was not a baby anymore. It was time he started zipping around on wheels.

Peter balanced the package under one arm and closed the door to his office with the other. "I'll be out all afternoon, Barbara," he informed his secretary. "If there's an emergency, I'll·be at home."

Barbara reached for a pen to jot down his schedule, and when she did, he could see her hand shaking. She tried to pull out one red pen and two pencils came out, too. The pencil holder fell over, and as Barbara grabbed for it, she bumped into the desk lamp with an elbow. It wobbled but Peter caught it with his free hand before it crashed to the floor.

"Barbara? Are you okay?" She was obviously flustered.

"I'm *wonderful*." The secretary turned her face up toward his and she was beaming. "I got her autograph. I can't believe she was here, just talking in your office like a normal person. The whole time she was in your office, I sat out here trying to get brave enough to talk to her. And I *did*. She's so nice. She's so *beautiful*." Barbara was clutching a piece of typing paper in her hand and waggling it at him. "My best friend is going to *die*."

Peter had no idea what she was talking about. And then he read the scrawled signature on the paper Barbara was waving. "Best Wishes, Shannon Eberle." And below it, "Lisa Radford."

"Barbara." He was smiling slightly and she almost laughed at him then, he looked so puzzled. "Who *is* she?"

"You don't *know?*" She did laugh then. "Shannon Eberle just spent an hour in your office. I guess the fact that she's a major television star just never came up." She waved the autograph at him once more. "She's the hottest thing in New York, Mr. Barrett. On the soap operas. Now you know my secret. I'm a sworn 'Way-ward Hopes' fan. I videotape it every day and I watch it every night. Lisa Radford has been on for as long as I've watched it. She's wonderful.''

"Lisa Radford." He couldn't help grinning. "Now you know my secret. I don't watch soap operas." But Shannon was obviously famous enough for him to recognize her face. He felt dumb and surprised and more than a little impressed. If he had known, he might have asked for her autograph, too.

He hurried downstairs through the bank lobby and the tellers whispered to one another as he walked by. They were acting as if he had just had an audience with the queen. But the woman wasn't a queen and he hadn't been able to help her with the things she needed. She was only a mortal, after all. And life had a way of playing tricks on mere mortals. He had learned that the hard way.

When Peter arrived home, Taylor's party was under way. Camille was chuckling at the commotion as she warmed hot-dog buns in the toaster oven. There were children everywhere, children he and Camille had decided should be invited as Taylor's friends, kids he played with when Peter took him to Sunday school and bank picnic parties, and even some he liked who lived near Camille's house.

Camille had called Peter one afternoon at the bank to go over the guest list. And Peter had been amazed when he heard how many children Taylor knew. "One little boy," he had said, laughing, over the phone to his housekeeper. He had been secretly proud. "Already collecting so many special friends."

"Hi," he said as he swept Taylor into his arms. "Give Daddy a dinosaur kiss." It was a game they played, one both of them loved, and the baby laughed as he fell forward toward Peter's face until their noses bopped. "Good."

The table was draped with crepe-paper streamers and balloons and a tablecloth with bright red fire engines. A miniature fire marshall's hat waited at each child's place. It was a grand celebration. Peter set his son on the floor and Taylor sat there, in the midst of it all, looking very important and very pleased.

Peter leaned against the stairway, watching his son, while Camille poured lemonade for the children who requested it. He was thinking of this day a year ago, when the celebration had been so different, so quiet and poignant, as he and Lorilee shared the birth of their son. Peter had been running from these memories for months. Now they overwhelmed him.

"This is nothing," Lorilee had told the nurse and Dr. Bricca and Peter when the doctor came into the birthing room to check her progress. They had been at the hospital for hours. She was sitting upright in the rocking chair and she kept talking just so she wouldn't have to move. She was having a contraction. "This is a snap." She turned glimmering eyes toward her husband. "I've filmed a hundred different species of females doing this." And she was right, she had. Before she had married him, she had traveled all over the world with a small film company, taping miles of material on interesting animals. One of her reproduction specials had aired again on the Public Broadcasting station just the week before. She had laughed the entire time she watched it.

"Easy... Easy..." She patted the stretched, fat belly she had grown accustomed to and almost fond of.

"What a show this **is** going to be. Why isn't someone here filming?"

Peter was so proud of her. He loved her so much and he couldn't take his eyes off her—she looked so determined, sitting there, having his child. He saw her face tighten and he saw her grip the chair's arm. He knew it wasn't as easy as she was trying to make it sound.

Taylor was born in the early evening and, after the doctor left, they heralded their son's birth with a toast from a bottle of expensive champagne the staff had sent over from the bank. Lorilee was elated. She had been almost certain the child would be a boy. Peter wanted her to rest, but she wouldn't take her eyes off the tiny new human she held at her breast.

Taylor nursed for a while and then he fell asleep, and when he awoke two hours later, Peter held him and stuck a finger in the tiny mouth so the baby could suck. He threw his head back and laughed when his little son latched on to his finger. "Maybe we should have named him Kirby... after the vacuum cleaner."

They talked and examined Taylor and drank champagne for a long time before they called anyone. The time was just too precious to them, being together, just the three of them, sharing their first moments as a family.

How quickly it had all disappeared. Four months later, Lorilee was gone. Someone came to the house one afternoon and took her. Mercifully, the baby had been out with the housekeeper. Peter was certain they would have taken him, too. It was a very trendy crime, the *Jackson Hole News* reported the following Wednesday. If Peter had known, he would have hired a bodyguard to watch the house. But it still seemed so impossible that it could happen here in Wyoming, where there was nothing but country people and wild game and rugged scenery.

Peter had come home early in the afternoon to find it all—furniture knocked over, Taylor bleating from his crib, the housekeeper in hysterics and a ransom note on the kitchen table. The note demanded three million dollars for Lorilee's safe return.

The kidnappers had assumed he could draw any amount of money he needed from the family's bank. But it didn't work that way. It had taken him precious hours to locate his father and sell stock and accumulate the cash.

His parents had driven in from their ranch in Idaho as soon as Peter had reached them. His mother cared for the baby. Taylor wanted to nurse; he screamed when they tried to get him to take a bottle, but finally, desperate with hunger, he accepted it. He drank his first eight ounces of formula while his father stormed through the house, feeling alternately furious and helpless, begging the telephone to ring.

At 10:45 that night, the telephone call from the Teton County sheriff's department rang through. They had found her. Not bound and gagged on some deserted ranch as they had hoped they would, but in a car, a 1970 Impala that had gone off the side of the road into Hoback Canyon south of town. The sheriff assumed she had escaped from her captors and had taken their car. She had been driving too fast. She had been trying to come home.

Peter dreamed it and lived it over and over again, trying to rewrite the ending, trying to do something differently, anything, that might have saved her. In his dreams he was a rancher or a merchant instead of a bank executive. His position of power had not placed his wife in jeopardy. She was still with him, loving their son . . . celebrating his first birthday.

The children around the table blurred back into Peter's vision. Taylor was opening presents. "This one's from your Daddy," Camille read the card.

I can't do this. I can't stand here pretending to celebrate this day.

Taylor squealed as Camille lifted the train out of its wrapping and held it high so the children could see it. Then she positioned Taylor atop the tiny train. Taylor's legs were an inch too short to touch the ground. One of the older girls jumped up to push him. The whistle blew and Taylor shrieked and children tumbled down from their chairs, begging to be the next one to ride.

No one was watching him as he shrugged into his down parka and closed the front door behind him. He had to get away from the children's joy. It was unbearable.

Peter's telemark skis were waiting for him beside the door. Mechanically, he loaded them onto the ski rack on his Jeep Cherokee and then drove away from the house without looking back, in search of a vast place covered with snow. He had to find somewhere, anywhere, where he could ski away from this relentless, stifling sorrow.

CHAPTER THREE

SHANNON DID NOT KNOW where to turn. She knew she couldn't give up. Giving up was not an option. It never had been.

She was glad she had thought to bring her skis with her to Jackson. Jim Clarkson had business associates to see this afternoon. He had invited her to attend his late luncheon meeting with him but she had declined. She wanted to be alone.

The peaks surrounding Jackson Hole offered some of the best cross-country ski trails in the world. She stepped into her ski bindings and started off, zooming through groves of trees and gliding over crests, stopping every so often to view the valley from the slopes of Teton Pass where she stood.

She stopped again, beside a tree, to turn back to see a man skiing just above her. She had sensed long ago that she was not alone on the trail. And as she watched the figure behind her leaving snakelike tracks in the snow, Shannon was impressed by the control and the obvious agility of the man. His telemark turns seemed an extension of his legs and his skis, timed to perfection. Seeing him ski was like seeing heavy liquid make its way downhill. There were no pauses, no hesitations. He came toward her at an incredible pace, the carved snow flying as he made each of his turns. And when he pulled up short beside her on the trail, she realized who he was.

"Mr. Barrett." It was odd seeing him like this, twice in the same day. Only hours before he had been wearing a business suit, turning her away, refusing to finance a project that, in the past days, had become everything to her. "Hello."

Peter looked at her a full fifteen seconds before he recognized her. Her long, dark hair was stuffed up inside a Ragg wool cap and she was almost lost inside the huge army-green parka she wore. This morning in his office, she had been dressed in an expensive designer suit and, although she had looked lovely, her face had remained impeccably masked. Now her cheeks were ripe with color and she was breathing fast from the exertion of her skiing. She looked like a different woman. The same woman. This was just a different facet of her. "You are a skier."

"I used to be. I don't have time to practice anymore." Shannon's smile was an honest one. She was glad to see him again. She wanted him to know she understood the decision he had handed them earlier in his office. "I do know enough about skiing to know you are very good. I watched you come down the mountain. I envy your control."

"Thanks." It was all he could think of to say. He was still breathless. He had been flying on his skis for miles across the snow. He was surprised to find her on this trail. "You're good, too," he said, "or you wouldn't be here."

"I skied a lot when I was a kid. In Wind River."

"You said you were born there?"

She nodded.

"A Wyoming native." He shot her a polite smile. But she noticed that it didn't reach his eyes. "This is one of the few states where you still find natives. I'm one, too." He surveyed the sky above them. "Did you ski here, too?"

She shook her head. Even if her father had been able to take time away from the sheep ranch when they had been children, he never could have afforded the gasoline to drive so far. "No. We stayed pretty close to Fremont County. The terrain is a challenge there, too. I had to keep up with my brothers. That was good for me."

"I'll bet." He had turned back to her and now he was puzzled by the expression on her face. "I suppose your family still lives there."

"Yes."

"Is that why you came back? To see them?"

She sensed he was asking her more than just this one question. "Partially."

Her pensive expression told him what he wanted to know. She had put her heart on the line in support of the teen program. "Can I ask you something?"

"Yes."

"Why is BEAT so important to you?"

"Because my brother is a senior at Washakie this year. Because I had to fight too hard to follow my career and it shouldn't have had to be that hard."

"The school district isn't paying you to go around and make a big deal out of this?"

Shannon was horrified. "No, Mr. Barrett. Why would you think that?"

"I'm used to striking deals," he said. "I forget people can be motivated by something other than money."

She looked at him wistfully, all the strength gone from her face. "It must be difficult to be responsible for so much."

"It is." He stared into the sky again through the laced branches of lodgepole pine that surrounded them. Peter was surprised someone so successful would be willing to fight a battle she had, in a sense, already won.

The air held a new iciness, and the sun was hovering just above the mountains behind them. In half an hour, it would be nearing twilight.

Peter knew he needed to get back to the house. Camille would be wandering around the family room, straightening furniture while Taylor played, clucking at Peter like a disapproving hen. He had left her with no word, with what seemed like hundreds of toddlers racing around his family room. He turned to Shannon. "I need to get back. Do you want to ski the rest of this trail with me?" He didn't feel right skiing away, leaving her here alone.

Shannon nodded and then said nothing more. She welcomed the company.

Peter pushed off first and she followed. He skied slowly, afraid of pushing her, but she stayed right with him. He picked up his speed then and he could hear her racing behind him. He listened for her carving turns and, finally, he heard her laugh.

"Hey," he called back over his shoulder. "No fair having such a grand time."

"I can't help it." She was breathing hard again. She had been watching him glide in a fluid zigzag ahead of her and thinking he was one of the most graceful, powerful male skiers she had ever seen. "This is good snow."

Shannon's laughter and her childlike verve made Peter smile honestly for the first time in hours. It was okay to be here, more than all right to be alive and flying along through the trees with another human behind him.

They were nearing the end of the descent. Next they would ski a draw, a place where they would both have to work, using the wax on their skis to cling to the snow so they could advance uphill. Peter pulled up and waited for Shannon to stop beside him. When she did, he looked at her nose, red from the cold, and suddenly he remembered the excitement she had caused among his employees at the bank. "Funny, Miss Eberle," he said. "Out here in that enormous parka, you don't look anything like a star of stage and screen."

He was surprised at how startled she looked. She didn't mind his knowing about her acting career. But she had almost forgotten it herself as she skied down Teton Pass with him. She peered out at him from under the wool hat.

"You should have told me. Everyone at the bank thought I was crazy." He was laughing now, and for the first time in a long while, he wasn't thinking of Lorilee. "If only I had known you were 'the hottest thing in New York'." He shook his head. "That, Miss Eberle, is a direct quote from my secretary."

"She asked for my autograph."

"I know that. She waved that piece of paper in my face the minute I stepped out of my office." His expression turned serious. "I felt sadly uninformed."

"I'm certain Jim Clarkson thought you knew. That's why I came here with him. At least I can let BEAT use my name and my reputation to bolster fund-raising efforts."

"So that's why you came all this way from The Big Apple."

This time it was Shannon's turn for a smile that didn't quite reach her heart. "It was a good reason to come home."

"I suppose so."

"Would it have made any difference in your decision? If you had known about me?" She couldn't resist asking. "If you had known I was 'the hottest thing in New York'?"

"No. It wouldn't have."

She watched him for a moment without saying anything. At last she spoke. "It must be very hard to be in your position...to have everyone calling upon you..." Her voice held no anger, only sorrow.

"It is." *If only she knew how hard. It's taken everything from me.*

"I don't know what to say to those kids when I get back."

"Tell them the truth. That it was impossible for me to help them."

"I won't tell them that." Shannon's tone was bitter. "That's what these kids have been hearing their entire lives. That fighting for what you believe in or reaching for what you dream of is impossible. *Impossible.* That being young means nothing. That there's no way out. That's what everyone told me. You can't expect me to go back there and hand them the same ugly excuse. I won't do it."

"Okay. Don't." It was as if she was grieving for someone, her family or her own life, and he didn't know exactly what he should say. "But you can't save them all, you know." Peter was thinking how far she must have come, how hard she must have worked, to think she could help them to do the same.

Shannon speared the snow with a ski pole and pointed her skis toward the trail. She didn't want to talk about it anymore. She wanted to do something about it. Only she had no idea what she could do.

Peter synchronized his movements with hers, and together they made their way through the evergreen forest. Finally he reached one mittened hand toward her and stopped her. She turned to face him.

"What about fate?" he asked her. "You don't believe in fate?"

"No. There is no such thing." She gazed up into the rapidly darkening sky. "I believe in human will. I can't understand people who sit back and let events tumble all over them."

Peter's words were soft. "Sometimes people have no other choice."

"They do."

Peter felt she could be talking about him, telling him she couldn't condone the emotions he was feeling over his wife's death. He grasped her arm forcefully. "You have no idea what you're saying."

"I do. A strong person would fight—"

"Don't say anything more."

Shannon hated herself when she looked up at him and read all the torture in his eyes.

"Maybe fighting works for some people. Maybe I'm just not one of the strong ones."

Something horrible had happened in his life and overcome him. She knew it. For an instant, she saw the defeat on his face. "Mr. Barrett. What is it that has hurt you?"

He turned his eyes toward her and met her determined gaze. He felt vulnerable. He had let her see too
much of him. A glint of caution rose in his eyes, a steel
wall between them. He told her nothing.

Shannon studied the changing emotions on his face.
He was a kaleidoscope, angry, hurt, vulnerable, dis-
tant. "Forgive me." Her voice was so soft that suddenly he could barely hear her. "We aren't even on a
first-name basis. I have no right to force my views of life
on you."

He dropped the gaze. She made him uncomfortable
because she could see so much. "My little boy's first
birthday was today."

It was an odd thing to say. Shannon didn't know if
she should make a comment or if she should let it pass.
Of course he had a family. A wife and children.
"Birthday number one," she said lightly. "The first of
many milestones."

"A milestone." He was mulling over the word, rolling it around in his head. *Not a milestone I wanted to
celebrate without Lorilee.* And then he thought of the
little son he had left at the party at home, Lorilee's
Taylor, his alone now, and Peter wondered if the boy
was riding the tiny train or sleeping or tugging at Camille's legs until she had no time to prepare their supper.
He was angry at himself, more angry than he was at
Shannon Eberle's words. He had missed most of Taylor's birthday party because, once again, he had let his
memories defeat him. How many other days would
there be like this one, when he was too bitter to face his
only son, or too afraid?

He reached out and gripped her shoulders. "You
have done a great deal with your own life." Just by

gripping her, he felt as if he was gripping hope for himself. "I know you can do a great deal for others."

Shannon searched his face, trying to understand why he was grasping her. She only knew that he was desperately sad. "Go home, Mr. Barrett." She backed away from him as his hands released her. "You've got people there waiting for you." She dared herself to think of his son, his wife.

"Will you be okay?" It felt strange leaving her here in the twilight, alone.

"You keep forgetting," she said, "I negotiate New York streets all the time, usually so early in the morning that the sun hasn't come up yet." The studio always sent a car for her but she didn't tell him that. "I think I can handle these pine trees without any problem."

"You're sure?"

"I'm sure." She laughed and the sound rang out like a bell in the stillness before it drifted off to echo in the distance.

"Good luck, Shannon Eberle."

She raised one ski pole and waved it at him in a lighthearted gesture of salutation. "If you come up with an extra million dollars, get in touch."

"I will." Peter stood beside his car and watched her as she skied away across the frozen meadow, one solitary figure clothed in wool against the darkness, and he was lonely suddenly, as if, by letting her go, he had let go of a large chunk of his courage, as well. Finally, when he could see her no longer, he climbed into the front seat of the Jeep and warmed the engine.

He drove back to the house and Camille met him at the front door, cackling at him, demanding to know where he'd been. She made a sandwich for him while he sat quietly by the fire. When she left, it was almost six.

Taylor had been asleep for almost an hour when Peter arrived home. At seven, Peter padded into the nursery to check on him. The boy had rolled out from under his blanket. He was wearing a pair of pajamas Peter hadn't seen—yellow ones with plastic treads on the feet and a grinning snowman on the shirt. They must have been a birthday present, Peter decided.

Taylor's birthday. How much of today he had missed. Gently he bundled his tiny son inside the blanket and gathered him into his arms. "Hey... little wump..." Peter held him close and the two of them went into the living room where they sat for a long time, Taylor just waking up, Peter staring at the flames in the fireplace.

Eventually Taylor began to wriggle. Peter gripped him tightly once more before he set him free to toddle around the room. The little train was parked in the corner. Taylor went to it and did his best to climb aboard. His tiny legs were still too uncontrolled and chubby to swing across the little seat.

"Need help?" Peter asked his son gently.

Taylor looked at him and gurgled. Peter rose from his chair near the hearth and placed Taylor on the toy. His tiny son leaned forward, backward, and the train whistle blew, but the wheels didn't turn.

"Okay. I'll show you how," Peter said softly, his voice the only sound in the room. It was funny, talking to a baby who didn't talk back, as if he was only talking to himself. Peter checked to see if Taylor had a good grip on the handlebars. "Someday you'll be able to push with your feet. You'll be tall enough and strong enough. Just like—" he thought of the woman he had

skied with again, of the things she had said to him about
human will ''—Daddy.'' *Someday I'll walk tall enough
again, strong enough.*

He pushed the train across the hardwood floor as fast
as it would go. ''Hang on, kid,'' he called out to his son
as Taylor squealed with delight and the wheels chugged
and the train whistle blew.

''YOU HAVE TO come back to New York.'' The long-
distance line between Shannon and her agent was
crackling. She could barely hear him. She was standing
at a pay phone at a service station two miles from her
parents' home. The Eberles did not have a telephone.

Lawrence Wills had called the Fremont County
School District that afternoon and had left a message
for her. Now she was sorry she had returned his call.

''Don't ask me to give up what's left of my hiatus,
Larry. I earned this time off. I come back now and I
face another twenty weeks of taping.'' She was doing
her best to sound flippant but it wasn't working. She
knew Larry could hear the despair in her voice. She and
Jim Clarkson had visited five Wyoming banks in as
many days. The ground breaking for the teen center had
been called off indefinitely. And no one was offering
any hope. She couldn't leave Wyoming. Not now.

''You also earned a Viewer's Choice nomination.''
The news had just been announced at a press confer-
ence that morning. ''Best Actress in a Daytime Series,
Shannon. It's the best you could ever do.''

''I know that,'' she sighed.

''Mark Troy wants you back on the set.'' Larry Wills
didn't mention the fact that the network had to pay a
fee for her to even be considered for the nomination.
''Your fans want to see you on the show. The network

publicity department wants new still shots. *Soap Opera Digest* wants a cover shot. This isn't in your contract but they've got you by the ears, anyway. You know that."

"I know that," she echoed.

"You signed a contract with me, too, Shannon. Years ago you trusted me to manage your career. Trust me now."

"I do trust you, Larry."

"You're tired." He could hear it in her voice.

"I'm fine."

"You're exhausted. You sound the same way you sound after you've finished playing a big scene."

"That's what I'm doing." He was surprised by the obvious regret accompanying her words. "I'm out here in Wyoming playing a big scene."

"Shannon. Let go. Come back."

"Okay. *Okay*," she told him. "I'm coming back." She couldn't live two lives. She knew that. "I've been skiing. My face is tanned. Tell Al so the writers can put it in the script." It happened all the time. "Wayward Hopes" writers took things from her own life and gave them to Lisa Radford. Sometimes she forgot what had started out as Lisa's and what had started out as her own.

"A tan will look great in your publicity stills."

"Publicity is all you think about."

"That's all you think about, too," he reminded her, "when you're in the city thinking straight."

He was right. Her career, the show, was her life. It was all she had ever wanted. She should have been overjoyed, astounded, by the Viewer's Choice nomination. But she wasn't. It was only one thing more to tug at her. It didn't seem as real now as the searching she was doing in Wyoming, the speeches, the meetings, the hoping.

Maybe someone in New York *could* help her with BEAT. Maybe someone she knew would find it a novelty to finance a teen center in a state that most New Yorkers thought was somewhere near the edge of the earth. "Okay," she said again. "Okay." Her answer sounded loud and harsh, despite the bad connection. "I'll catch the first flight out tomorrow."

CHAPTER FOUR

PETER THUMBED THROUGH the day's issue of the *Casper Star-Tribune*. He didn't find much to interest him. He read one article about a state representative who wanted to bring an outdoor-skills leadership school to central Wyoming to stimulate the lagging economy there.

He flipped through three more pages. And then he saw it. Shannon Eberle's picture.

Peter gripped the paper with both hands. There was no mistaking her. He read the article while she smiled up at him from the photograph like a glamorous waif, and he felt as if he was prying, suddenly reading everything about her that she hadn't told him, about how her career had started and about her family and about the volumes of mail she received from her fans.

Shannon Eberle, a central Wyoming native, has been nominated Best Actress in a Daytime Series by the Viewer's Choice Award Committee in New York City. The selection, which is sponsored by *Viewer* magazine, is based on votes taken from a random selection of the viewing public...

A Viewer's Choice nomination. Peter laid the paper across his desk. He tried to picture Shannon bounding forward to accept the trophy, her hair twisted to one side in a glamorous style, her backless designer gown glimmering with her every movement.

He couldn't quite accept it. Shannon seemed so down-to-earth to him, so intensely caring. She didn't fit his idea of an actress at all. Even while staring down at the photo, with her huge dark eyes gazing out at him, her hair curled until it became a wild background of froth around her face, he could only envision her as he had seen her four days ago, with her nose red, her cheeks rosy, her face surrounded only by the grey Ragg wool of her cap.

He read on down the page, feeling better now, imagining he was reading about someone he didn't know. But as Peter continued, her entire week began to unfold before him, the trips to various banks, the same speeches she had given him, the same denial he had necessarily had to give her. She had been all over.

Peter reached for his Rolodex and leafed through the cards until he found Jim Clarkson's number in Wind River. He wanted to talk to her, to add his congratulations for her nomination, to acknowledge this one victory for her, although she had probably already received hundreds of phone calls from her fans and her friends in New York.

When Jim Clarkson answered his line at the school district office, Peter asked to leave a message for her. He was hoping she would call him but he heard her voice in the background as he spoke with Clarkson, and he realized she must be there, in the office, still trying to make things work out.

"Yes? Mr. Barrett?" Her voice had a lovely melody over the telephone. It probably did on television, too.

"Hey, that's enough." He felt the urge to be light with her. "Call me Peter. Please." There was a hint of expectancy in her voice and he remembered what she had said to him as they'd parted in the trees just above the valley. *"If you come up with an extra million dollars, get in touch."*

"I haven't found an extra million lying around," he told her. He felt the need to explain his call to her quickly so she wouldn't be disappointed.

"I was so hoping you had, Peter." She tried his name on for size. "So we'll call each other by first names. Now that I'm so intimate with you, let me give you another lecture. Shannon's views on the goodness of life."

"Oh, great." He was laughing.

"But I'm afraid I don't feel like talking about life right now—BEAT is dying, Peter."

"But your career isn't," he said. He felt the need to buoy her with his words. She had seemed so optimistic before, and now she only sounded tired. "I read about you in the Casper paper. You got a Viewer's Choice nomination. Is that one of those award shows on television where people make tearful thank-you speeches?"

"You've seen them." Shannon smiled in spite of herself.

"That's what I thought," he said. "You'll be seen on nationwide television and you'll make speeches about life...."

She was still smiling. There was something about him, the way he poked fun at her optimism, that made her like him. "Should be right up my alley, huh?"

"Right." He was smiling, too, on his end of the line. She had a way about her, of turning desperation to spunk, that challenged him. He wished he could do the same. "I knew that. I called to congratulate you." He paused, thinking. He didn't know if he should tell her how much she impressed him. "It seems so strange. I've never known anyone who was famous before."

"Fame and fortune," she said simply. "Sometimes I wonder if it's worth everything."

"What do you mean by that?" In a way, because of the things he had gone through, Peter thought he understood. But he wanted her to tell him. He wanted to hear someone else say it, that what counted as success sometimes wasn't worth the pain or the things you had to give.

"There are always stipulations," she said, frowning at the last word. "Somebody always knows what's good for your career. Somebody is always willing to hold you to the contract you signed or to tell you what you owe him. Somebody is always wanting things." *Taking me away from the things I want to give.*

From what little Peter knew of her, the bitterness she shared with him seemed uncharacteristic. "You make it sound as if you'd rather get your teeth pulled."

"I'm angry," she said. "They're making me return to New York. And I'm not finished here."

I wonder if she'll ever be finished here. "When are you leaving?"

"The first flight out tomorrow morning. I talked to my agent a few hours ago. The nominee selections went to the press the same time they were announced to us. I'm here now trying to resolve some of the smaller details before I go."

"Shannon. If I think of anybody..." They had talked of it before, she had prodded him, making him promise to call her if money turned up. Until now it had seemed like a casual promise to him, something she cared about, secondary to the life she lived in New York. Now he knew it was more than that. The BEAT project was important to her, maybe too much so, and she was fighting against her career because of it. He made a mental note to brainstorm for her. He did know people who had money to play with.

"I know," she said. "Don't worry. It's impossible to find someone with that much money to spend who doesn't want some sort of a return on it."

His mind was racing. "Do you have a number in New York where I can reach you? Just in case I come up with something?"

Shannon gave him her home telephone number in New York and bade him goodbye. And Peter sat at his desk then, feeling empty, the telephone receiver back in its cradle, while he thought of the things she had said.

There had to be a systematic way to find the answer.

The Rolodex still lay open to Jim Clarkson's business card. He flipped the file back to the As and then proceeded back in the other direction, his finger resting on each card in turn, as he considered each name there.

It wasn't until he got to the Gs that he stopped. Calvin Gleason. Peter glared down at the card, deep in thought. "Calvin Gleason." He said the name aloud. "Of course."

Calvin Gleason served on the bank's board of directors. He had been Jackson's mayor for many years. He ran seven successful tourist establishments in the valley. He was actively seeking a tax shelter. He had been in Peter's office two weeks before discussing the possibility of buying into a troubled business so that he could deduct a loss.

Peter pulled his adding machine closer and began to punch figures into it. If Gleason agreed to mortgage two of his businesses and donate some of the money to finance Shannon's BEAT program, he could deduct the dollars he donated plus the interest he paid toward the mortgage. The bulk of the money could remain untouched in an untaxable retirement account at First National. Although the plan would not cover the entire cost of constructing the teen center, it would be a beginning. A very substantial, strong beginning.

Peter dialed Gleason's number.

"Peter Barrett." The Jackson entrepreneur had a way of growling even when he was being friendly. "How are things in the finance business?"

"On the upswing," Peter answered honestly. And then he decided not to mince words. "Gleason. You're looking for a tax shelter. I have one for you."

"Tell me about it."

It took Peter no more than five minutes to outline the plan.

"I'm interested, Barrett. Would First National be willing to take on my mortgages?"

"I can't see anything standing in the way. We'd need to draw up the paperwork and run it through all the channels. That's it."

"I want to discuss this with my personal accountant," Gleason told him. "I'll have to decide which businesses I want to place in hock. Probably the little motel on Pearl Street and the gift shop on the town square. Can you wait a week?"

Peter's voice held steady. "I'd like to give them a verbal commitment now."

"Fine," Gleason told him. "Give the school district a tentative commitment. Nothing final. But something to get them planning in the right direction." He named a figure over the phone and Peter was only mildly disappointed. The amount was less than he had wished for but acceptable. It was a tangible start for BEAT. Next week, if Gleason's accountant and his lawyer approved the plan, the Fremont County School District could re-schedule the ground breaking.

Peter slammed down the telephone. "Good job, Barrett," he said to himself. And then he glanced at his calendar. His afternoon was free of appointments. Wind River was only a three-hour drive from Jackson.

He felt an almost unfamiliar surge of power. Calvin Gleason had trusted him enough to make a tentative verbal commitment. He wanted to see Shannon's face when he told her the news. But she was leaving for New York City first thing tomorrow morning.

Peter stared at the telephone but he didn't pick it up. "Okay," he said. "I'll just do it." And when he made the decision to go and see her, it was the first time in a long, long time he didn't feel as if his own life was run-ning away from him.

When he did make his second telephone call, it was to Camille. "How about the afternoon off?" he sug-gested mischievously.

"Ah," she clucked at him. "Don't tell me you've decided you need a vacation from your housekeeper."

"Not me, Camille," Peter teased. "It's poor Taylor. He told me last night that you're taking such good care of him that you're driving him crazy. He needs to get away." Peter was laughing now. "Would you mind packing a few of his things? Not much. Just his blan-ket, his red dinosaur and a few hundred disposable diapers. I'll be by to pick him up in fifteen minutes."

"What are you doing?" she asked. Sometimes she seemed more like his mother than his housekeeper.

"Taking my kid on a trip." He hesitated. "A business trip." That's what it was, after all. A business trip. A victory. One he desperately needed.

"Taylor will need to eat lunch."

"No problem," Peter assured her. "We'll stop by McDonald's and share a Kid's Meal. Taylor loves Chicken McNuggets. He eats more of them than I do."

"You let him eat those things? The child doesn't even have teeth."

"He has six teeth. Six teeth are ample to attack McNuggets." Peter loved this conversation. Suddenly he felt as if he was in charge of Camille, too. That was a real coup. "He's *my* son, Camille. When he gets the urge for fast food, he's welcome to have it."

"Yes, sir." Camille laughed then, too, but she was confused. Peter was different today. His teasing, which once had been a tepid excuse to keep from acknowledging the things that hurt him, sounded energetic and wholehearted. He seemed totally in command of Taylor, of himself, of everything around him.

Today he was a Peter Barrett she didn't know, one who didn't need her to care for him. Camille wondered what the catalyst was, what he had found that was powerful enough to stave off his grief.

ELEVEN YEARS BEFORE, when Shannon had been a senior at Washakie High School, the massive gymnasium had stood exactly as it stood now. The same fierce painted warrior stared out from the west wall. The same hollow echoes filled it. Shannon remembered it all—the scuffed floor, the smell of sweat and competition and perfume. The smell of dread.

How she remembered the dread. There had been so many times in this gym when the feeling had gripped her. The cheerleading tryouts the year she made it to the finals. The state volleyball tournament her team had lost by one point. The day before graduation, sitting on these bleachers, telling Marty Hoover she wouldn't marry him, that she was leaving Wyoming.

Marty had been her high school sweetheart. He was a kind, handsome boy who played fullback on the football team. He and Shannon had dated steadily for two years. He escorted her to the senior prom. They had leading roles in *Bye-Bye Birdie*, the senior class play. And after that, almost every girl at Washakie High had had a crush on him.

In a way, Shannon had loved him. She had loved the way she felt when he touched her. But when it came time to make a final commitment to him, she couldn't do it. Marty didn't want to wait for her to finish college. He was afraid if she went away that she might never come back.

Shannon had spent her life watching people afraid to leave or afraid to let go because of the things they might lose. She and Marty had sat together on these same bleachers in this deserted gym and she had tried to tell him of her decision gently, but in the end they had both cried.

"Go ahead and go," he had said finally, not looking at her. "Maybe I'll take my chances. Maybe I'll wait for a while, after all."

"Don't." She'd laid her hand against his forearm as she cried. "I don't want to think about somebody waiting here for me."

He had looked at her with so much pain in his eyes that she'd thought he hated her. Then he'd walked away without turning back, the rubber soles of his shoes squeaking on the polished gymnasium floor.

Shannon closed her eyes and she was there again, fighting against her adolescence. It was not a time she would ever return to. The times she admitted to her own fallibility had always haunted her.

The final bell of the day would ring in fifteen minutes. The members of the WHS Student Council had agreed to meet with her then. In fifteen minutes she would admit to them that her trip had failed and she was leaving. She thought once again of Marty. In a way history was repeating itself. She was deserting people she cared about.

I can't do this for you, she wanted to tell them all. *Don't wait for me. Don't depend on anyone but yourself. It's the only way you'll win.*

Instead, when she stood before them, she told them about her Viewer's Choice nomination. She quietly told them she had been called back to the set, but that she would continue to search for funding for the teen center. Tommy drove her home in the red Dodge truck, and she began to pack her suitcases.

"You can watch her on the television set whenever you want to see her, Mom." Tommy was doing his best to lighten the mood around the house. "She comes on every day."

"Fine, oh, brave one." Agatha Eberle stood to make a late-afternoon pot of coffee for them. "But you aren't happy about it, either."

"She has to go back," Shannon's sister-in-law, Melissa, said absently as she watched Nolan and his father loading supplies into Nolan's truck. "She's a star."

Shannon walked into the kitchen. "I'm finished packing."

"I hope your plane gets out of here tomorrow," her mother said. "It's starting to snow."

Shannon joined her mother at the window. And just as she peered out, a Jeep turned in across the front cattle guard and sped toward the house. She watched as the vehicle parked and a man stood, shut his door and then moved to the other side to retrieve a tiny boy and a bag. The two of them came up the front walk, their heads together at the same angle, one dark, the other one a fragile blond as white as frost when it covered the Wyoming native grasses.

"Peter Barrett," Shannon said. Her heart made one powerful flop inside her chest. Why was he here? She stood frozen only a moment before racing for the door and, when Peter looked up and saw her bounding down the porch steps, her hair pulled into a mahogany mane that bounced at the nape of her neck, she reminded him of colts he had watched grow on his father's ranch. She was all slender legs and expectancy as she came toward him. "Mr. Banker. What are you doing here?"

He couldn't keep from grinning at her. "Do you always have to talk about the bank? All you ever think about is money."

"Right." She grinned back. "Me and a few billion other people. But luckily it usually isn't one of my higher priorities."

"I came because I have good news." Peter didn't say anything more, he just leveled his gaze on her, smiling, a mischievous twinkle dancing there. He reminded her of a grade-school boy trying to befriend her with his pestering. "I wanted to stand here and see the look on your face."

"What? Peter, what is it?" He had been stationary long enough for snow to cover his shoulders and his head. She brushed it off with her hand and then took the baby from him. And as he watched her he was torn between shouting his good news to her or making her wait before he told her. "If you don't say something soon, you and your kid are going to be buried in snow."

"Okay. I'll tell you." His eyes remained locked on hers. "I found an investor for BEAT, Shannon."

She stared up at him, her eyes huge. "Don't tease me. Please."

"I'm not. It isn't final yet. But it will be. The man has already made a verbal commitment. For $180,000."

She stood before him in stunned silence.

"Shannon? What's wrong? I know it isn't enough to pay for the entire thing, but it's a start. The construction company can break ground."

When she spoke at last, her voice was softer than a whisper. "No one has ever helped me like this before." She had fought her own battles for so long.

"It's a good beginning," he said, uncertain of how to react to her emotion. He had expected her to jump around and scream with excitement. "Maybe now someone will be willing to add to it."

"I wish I didn't have to leave now," she said sadly, thinking how kind he was and how handsome and how happy she was that he had helped her. Her trip had done some good, after all. "You've given the kids a great gift." Still, she stood there, gazing up at him. "I've never had anyone do quite so much for me."

"I didn't do that much."

"You didn't have to do any of it."

Peter hesitated. How could he explain to her that he did have to do it, that the success of the BEAT program was a gift of sorts to him, too?

Shannon handed the baby back to Peter and led them into the house to introduce both Barretts to her family. Nolan and her father had come inside for a cup of coffee and P.J., Shannon's niece, was there, too, eager to lead Taylor around the house and show him her toys.

When Shannon told Tommy about Calvin Gleason and the pending BEAT financing, Tommy let out a whoop of satisfaction. "This is it! This is it!" he shouted as he jumped from his chair and danced around the kitchen table. "You did it, big sister—BEAT has funding again! You really did it."

"No. Mr. Barrett did it." She was hugging Tommy and shaking her head at the same time.

"Thank you, sir." Tommy hugged Peter, too, and Agatha Eberle poured coffee for him as Taylor followed P.J. in circles around the table. "Wait until I tell everybody at school."

"Jim Clarkson needs to know," Daniel Eberle said. "We can stop by the district offices on the way to the airport tomorrow. I wanted to talk to him, anyway. To tell him I'd like to volunteer time to put up sheet rock in that building."

"Daddy!" Shannon hugged him. "You don't mind? If we could get volunteer labor, building that teen center will be less expensive than we all planned."

"Perhaps—" he hugged his daughter to him "—I can scare up some other townspeople to help me."

"I can paint." Tommy was still dancing around the table. "I've done a lot of that around here."

"Yeah," his father said with a laugh. "Last time you painted the barn, you got more paint on your face than you did on the walls."

"Dad—" Tommy was laughing "—that was two years ago. I was only fifteen. What do you expect?"

Peter sat watching them all, feeling envious of the camaraderie they shared. They were curious and kind and funny, and they made him want to belong to them.

He sat at the Eberles' kitchen table sipping coffee, grabbing Taylor every so often as he ran by and kissing him. Peter was very glad he had come.

"So—" Daniel Eberle was working to draw him into the conversation "—the tourists continue to keep the economy alive in Jackson."

"Yes, they do."

"Are you one of the bankers who turned Shannon and Mr. Clarkson down for BEAT money this week?" Tommy asked.

"Yes." Shannon nodded. "He is. But he made up for it."

"Thank you, Miss Eberle." He grinned at her again. He loved being included in their bantering.

"Well," Nolan commented. "You'll have to come back when the building is under way."

"You can hammer a few nails," Shannon's father suggested.

"Or paint with me," Tommy said, grinning.

"You've done so much for Shannon and Tommy." Agatha Eberle touched his shoulder. "You're welcome here anytime. Daniel, maybe Taylor would like to go to the barn and see the sheep. Next time you come, Mr. Barrett, feel free to bring your entire family. Your wife is welcome, too."

Peter's face turned to stone.

"Can I go look at the sheep, too, Mom?" P.J. asked Melissa.

"If you'll put on your coat and hold your grandpa's hand."

"Peter?" Shannon was sitting across the table from him, sipping from a huge mug of coffee, and she sensed his change of mood. His eyes were rock hard, his mouth a grim line.

"I'm sorry." His face was expressionless. "I should have said something sooner. I forget that everyone doesn't know...."

"Doesn't know what?" Daniel's eyes had narrowed. The young man was deeply troubled.

"My wife... She died... eight months ago."

Shannon's fist tightened around the handle of the mug.

Daniel Eberle moved around the table to him and placed a reassuring hand on Peter's shoulder. "Son. I'm awfully sorry."

"It's okay," Peter said quietly. "I've had lots of sympathy. Now I just need time. That's what everyone says."

Daniel Eberle stood behind Peter, trying to remember. When Shannon had introduced the man, the name had sounded vaguely familiar. Daniel remembered the newspaper stories now, about Peter Barrett's career at the bank and the kidnapping. He wondered if he should say something more and then thought better of it. He didn't think Agatha would recall the tragedy. And Shannon had been in New York at the time. He was certain his daughter wouldn't have heard about it.

Melissa's watery gaze followed Taylor as Peter helped the boy pull on his coat. "Poor little guy. To be so tiny with no mother."

Peter's heart softened at the compassion in this simple girl's voice. He wondered if she ever thought of dying. Lorilee probably hadn't. She had been so busy worrying about the yellow curtains or the blue...about the vaccination at the pediatrician's that made Taylor's leg swell...about continuing to breast feed him after his gums began to sprout tiny porcelain teeth.

Agatha did her best to make him feel comfortable once more. "Well, Mr. Barrett, consider yourself and your son adopted members of this family. We'd love to have you and the boy visit often."

"Thank you," he said quietly. And then, in desperation, he grabbed his son. "Dinosaur kiss." He did his best to laugh as he nuzzled Taylor's neck. Taylor threw his head back and his laugh made them all smile, as Agatha moved around the table with the coffeepot once more.

Now Shannon knew the reason for the pain that had flooded Peter's face when they were skiing. It had overcome him with such force, like a blow he hadn't seen coming. He had lost his wife. She thought of all the things she had said to him that day...about winning and dreaming and never daring to lose. She remembered the gentle way Peter had told her she was wrong.

"Now—" Tommy poked his sister in the ribs "—everything is happening now. Don't go back to New York. Just tell your dumb agent and director and executive producer and your millions of fans that you aren't going to be there for them right now."

"I can't."

"You probably could."

"Yeah," she said, the irony in her voice evident. "The network pays an exorbitant fee so I'll be eligible for nomination. And I get nominated. Nice. But I'll just stay here. No problem. Nobody will miss me."

"You can't fight a network," Peter commented. "You can't walk away from all those big executives."

"Right," she said. "And I don't think I've walked out on my family, either."

"You haven't." Shannon's mother bent to kiss her on the cheek. "You're a good kid."

As Peter struggled with his own sadness, he saw
Shannon's, too. He finally understood the magnitude
of what she was fighting for. Here was a circle of family that had drawn her in long before she began playing
her role in New York City. This was Shannon Eberle's
life. And as he watched her she seemed so serenely
wistful that he didn't know if it was a life she was trying
to save or a life she was trying to escape.

"Promise me you aren't running away," he said to
her later, when he was out by his Jeep and ready to
leave. Taylor was asleep, tucked inside a blanket in his
car seat. "I love your family. A home like this is something you should always hang on to."

"I always feel like I *am* running from it." Her eyes
reflected the disquiet she felt. She wanted to stay with
them. She wanted to leave. She turned from him and
gazed up into the night. A trillion stars shone above
them. For a moment, the stars seemed so much more
brilliant than any lights Shannon had seen in the city.
Just tonight, just knowing she was going back, made
her feel as if something inside her heart was rending in
half.

"Does it make you sad," he asked her, "knowing life
has given you a beautiful turn when it wasn't quite as
fair to the people you love?" It was a question he often
tried to answer for himself, and he had wondered all
evening, just watching her family and how they lived,
if she ever asked it, too. He couldn't help but look at
their lives and see their hardships. And there was a part
of them in Shannon, too, a part he liked—the earthiness, the energy.

"No." She was shaking her head. "In some ways it's
been easier for them than it has been for me." She was
thinking about how hard she had fought, to come so

far, to be so famous and so alone. Alone. She wheeled back to face him and then she touched his arm with one mittened hand. "You've helped us so much. And I said so many insensitive things to you the other day. About fighting and winning and letting events tumble over you."

"Those weren't insensitive." He gazed down at her.

"They are if you loved someone and she died." She couldn't meet his gaze. She had said so many dumb things. "You should have told me."

"Told you what? What would I have said to make it any better?"

"That I was way out of my league."

"There wasn't anything to say."

"There was. You let me give you my great cheerleader act about life and you didn't bother to tell me what a tremendous loss you'd experienced." She was angry at him and she was hurting for him, too. "I just delved right on in. You let me make a fool of myself."

He grabbed her elbow. "Don't you say that. Don't you blame it on me." He was angry, too. "You're the one who has the glowing reports about life. You're the one who knows how to go to New York and grab on to all of life's glories and victories. Maybe I was keeping my mouth shut so I could learn something."

"I'm sure you absorbed a great deal of it."

Peter hated the cynicism he saw in her eyes. For a moment, she reminded him of himself. He wanted to save her from that. "Shannon. Don't." He silenced her by pulling her toward him. "Listen to me. Do you think I walk into every room of strangers and introduce myself saying, 'Hi, I'm Peter Barrett. Don't say anything stupid. My wife just died'?"

"Oh, right."

"It's a compliment to the Eberle clan that I was able to say anything at all. They made me feel welcome and happy and not quite so alone. I was honest with them because they made me comfortable enough to be so."

Shannon was silent for a long while, standing so close to him, thinking of what he had said, while her breath made little puffs of condensation in the night air. "You're right," she said finally. "They do that for me, too." She turned her eyes away from him to look at the white clapboard ranch house with the rickety steps and the wide front porch. She could see her mother working at the sink inside the lighted kitchen window. "They always have." She looked back at him. "This place has given me so much. All my family just plodded along, working and loving me, and they gave me enough faith in myself to go out and conquer the world."

"So go out and conquer it," he said softly. "Or is that what you came back to Wyoming for?"

"I don't know, Peter." She felt more fragile than Taylor as Peter bundled her up to him, her defeated voice almost lost and buried inside his warm jacket. "I would have flown back to New York empty-handed if it hadn't been for you. Now BEAT has a beginning."

"It had its beginning a long time before you met me." Peter stroked her satiny hair with a firm hand. "You'll be back. I can already see you painting and hammering nails. And something tells me you might teach a drama workshop, too."

He felt her body relax against him. "That's what I want to do. And someday I'd like to get my director here and some of the other actors. I want these kids to learn so much more than I ever had a chance to."

As she spoke, Peter grew vibrantly aware of her body against him. She smelled wonderful, like soap and roses, and clean, like the snow. It had been so long, almost a year, since he had held a woman in his arms. And, as he stood beside the Jeep, just holding her, he felt something warm rise and curl within him, a need he had buried deep inside himself, eight months ago, when he knew Lorilee wasn't coming back. He stared down at Shannon, uncertain of what he was feeling. He was astonished by his own body...ashamed and angered by it. He was furious with himself for his disloyalty to his wife. And guilty because, despite it all, he didn't want to pull away.

"Shannon." He whispered her name.

She tilted her chin back and met his eyes. It was the first time in her life she had felt so serene, so protected. She didn't question his arms around her. She accepted his touch the same way she had accepted his help. She stretched one finger gingerly toward his face and, with it, she traced the firm set of his jaw. "Thank you."

"You're welcome." The humor was fleeting as it crossed his face. "You know, I never can resist a damsel in distress. I knew I was going to help you the minute you walked into my office and said 'Hi, I'm Shannon Eberle. Don't say anything stupid. I'm the hottest thing in New York.'"

"You hush," she said, giggling. "I'm not the hottest thing in New York."

Maybe not. But you certainly feel warm in my arms. The humor was gone now, replaced by the tumult of other emotions within him. This time, when she looked up at him again, the serenity dissipated as she read the darkness in his eyes. "You are to my secretary," he said slowly. Shannon knew he wanted to kiss her. "And maybe to me, too."

"No," she said softly, her eyes locked on the blackness in his. "There are lots of us in that crazy city, crazy people trying to make it, trying to be famous..."

"You are."

"What?"

"Famous."

She said nothing more and stood silently, watching him, waiting for him, daring herself to absorb all the strength that his touch gave her, the deep seated strength she needed to return to the city. "Peter." She whispered his name as he lowered his mouth to hers, as if there might be a great barrier between them. But there wasn't, not now, as he slowly came closer. His fingers wrapped around her arms where they met her shoulders...pulling her...until his lovely strong mouth brushed hers with such gentleness that she was lost in him.

CHAPTER FIVE

THE THEME SONG to "Wayward Hopes" was playing in Shannon's mind. "When friends become lovers . . . when dreams become real . . ." The melody was hauntingly familiar, an integral part of her. *So this is what it feels like.* She said the second thing that came to her mind. "I don't want to go back." She didn't feel like fighting anymore. She only wanted to soak in the things Peter's kiss made her feel . . . joy . . . belonging . . . and something this side short of safety.

"You'll do fine back there." At this moment, Peter's concern for her and her nearness were overriding the turmoil within him. "They'll be so glad to see you. You'll be lost in the script in no time. You'll win the Viewer's Choice. Your fans will mob you." Such worries she had. And here he was wanting her, holding her, as if she was a normal woman, as if she didn't belong to New York and a television network and the relentless paparazzi.

Then the turmoil was back again, crashing into him full force, like a wave. He was holding her, wanting her, as if he didn't feel the rending inside him . . . the disloyalty . . . the guilt.

Shannon saw the conflict on Peter's face. Had she done this to him? She had no right, not after all the things he had done to help her. Suddenly, she backed away.

Taylor stirred and cried inside the car. "I should get on the road," Peter told her. He watched her for a moment, waiting for her reaction, as she stood in the snow. He was alone again, as if he had been wrenched free of her. The way he had been wrenched free of Lorilee.

He stared at Shannon but he saw another woman before him now, like an angel, shimmering in the snow...a woman he had held not so long ago...one with a shaft of straight wheat-colored hair and burning opal eyes. Lorilee. His wife. The woman he loved.

At last the warring factions began to leap to attention inside him, the priorities shifted, now that Shannon had pulled away. "Oh, Shannon. This is so wrong. I shouldn't have...touched you. My wife..."

"It's all right," she said quietly, even though it wasn't. "You still love her." She could never compete with the woman who had given him his son and then had died.

"I will always love her. We both have to forget this happened." Peter was saying the words for her good as well as his own. "I have no right to drag you into this." He had effectively squelched his desire for Shannon. All that remained was the anger, the guilt, inside him. That, he wouldn't wish on his worst enemy, much less on the woman who stood before him.

"No." The starlight was only just bright enough for him to read the anguish in Shannon's eyes. He hated himself. She was frozen there, away from him, so alone. "No." Shannon clenched her fists at her side. "I'm not going to forget how it feels when you hold me. It's impossible."

"Nothing is impossible. Remember? You said so yourself. Shannon..." He had in mind to apologize to her, to tell her how sorry he was. But he didn't know what to apologize for. For helping her? He wanted more to apologize to Lorilee, for the feelings holding Shannon had evoked.

"Don't quote me back to myself." Shannon's voice was cold. "I don't like that."

He looked at Shannon, his eyes dark and sad. "Perhaps it is better that you're flying to New York City tomorrow."

Her tone was measured when she answered. She felt so empty, emptier now than she had felt before he'd touched her. "Just go."

Peter turned away from her then, at her bidding, and climbed into the car. And she stood in silence while he flipped the key in the ignition and backed the Jeep almost soundlessly up the driveway. She was still standing there, a dark silhouette against the snow, in the native grass beside the house where she had been a child, when he pulled out onto the main highway and turned toward Jackson.

THE MAKEUP LIGHTS glared with unnatural cheeriness against the violet haze of early morning that shone through the window. Shannon studied her face in the relentless light. The fatigue lines from her long flight back to civilization had softened. All that remained on her face was a hint of weariness, an incredible tan and a dullness that Edwina Cox, her closest friend on the set, had noticed immediately.

"Must have been a tough trip," she commented nonchalantly as she watched Shannon lean back in the chair so the artist could define her lips. "You look fabulous. Only a best friend could tell you were still a little ragged around the edges."

"Don't answer her." The artist brandished a sable lip liner at the same angle she would have brandished a saber. "You mustn't move your lips."

"Speak to me with your eyes," Edwina, whom Shannon fondly called Eddie, urged her friend. "I want to hear what a torture it was."

Shannon waited until the artist gave her approval before she answered. She shook her head. "You're imagining things, Eddie. I never even missed this place. It wasn't torture." Eddie always expected the worst when she went home to visit her family. She had five sisters and a mother who constantly invited friends over to get her autograph. "I'm always this way early in the morning."

"You are not. You're cheerier at 4:30 than the rest of us in the studio put together."

Eddie was right. Shannon loved mornings. And she had been waking up before dawn with her father in Wyoming to help him start the day's chores.

The third A.D., an assistant director, entered the makeup room and pitched a rose-colored script to each of them. "Here's your pinks."

"Great." Eddie rolled her eyes. "Another round of revisions. How many times am I going to have to re-learn this scene?" This was the third script they had been given for it. The colors went in order. White, blue, pink. And the prime-time shows almost always went to yellows and then green, too. "I went to such trouble to memorize these this morning in the car."

"Well," Shannon laughed. "You've got ten minutes to memorize them again."

They were both excited about the new story line. Shannon's character, Lisa Radford, was coming back from a trip today to discover her husband having an affair with Eddie's character. The evil man was going to commit her to a mental institution to keep her out of his life. Eventually, Eddie's character was going to come to the hospital and rescue Lisa. It was going to be a great conflict for her. And she was going to become a good person in the end.

Al Jensen hoped the new plot twist would secure Eddie in the hearts of viewers for a long time to come. He also hoped it would boost the show's rating. "Wayward Hopes" had been number one in its time slot for almost a year. But lately, it had been slipping. The ratings went out to the public in *U.S.A. Today* every Wednesday. But Nielson supplied the studio with "overnights," everyone came clamoring in to see them, and the show in the number two slot was giving them a battle. Jensen needed this new story line to work.

When Shannon and Eddie had first read the new plot, they had both been elated. It was a lovely testimony to the goodness of human nature. And it was a story that reflected the friendship the two of them shared off-screen.

"You should be happier," Eddie protested. "All you have to do today is walk into the house, scream when you find him kissing me and then have a mental breakdown. Gads, it's an easy day for you, Shan."

Shannon would have flipped her head at her friend's comment, but the hairdresser was arranging her hair beneath a gray beaver hat. Lisa Radford would be wearing a hat when she came home to find her husband with another woman. The hat would fall off when Shannon turned away and ran. Her hair would tumble out and would stream around her face and she would look crazy. It was all perfectly arranged.

"Will you leave me alone? If I don't get out on the set soon, they'll have to wait for me. I'll be the prima donna of the day. And it's my first day back, Eddie."

"It's a man. Gads! Some sheep-herder jilted you while you were in the wild west."

"What?" Now Shannon did move her head and the hairdresser looked discouraged. He'd have to start all over again. "Eddie, why are you asking these crazy questions? I'm fine."

"You aren't fine. You met somebody. Some wild mountain man in the boonies of Wyoming."

The hairdresser and the hat stopped her from shaking her head in quick denial. And when she looked at Eddie, Shannon's heart suddenly poured out to her friend. They were involved in a craft that communicated a great jumble of emotions and relationships, and in their real lives they were hiding from each other.

"Okay," she said. "It was rough. I made a million speeches. I traveled a million miles. I had to come back sooner than I had planned. It wasn't much of a vacation."

"So tell me about the man."

"You do not know when to give up."

"Oh, gads!" Eddie shrieked and Shannon felt as if they were both sixteen instead of sophisticated women. "Shannon. I know you too well. The world has been waiting for a Shannon Eberle romance."

"No. No romance. I'm not discussing a romance." She paused. "There was a man who helped me when I was home. He raised money for the teen program I've been working on."

"You sound like a doctor," Eddie chided her. "Don't be so clinical about it."

But she had to be clinical about it. Her heart wouldn't let her see Peter Barrett in any other way. Only Shannon kept thinking of the way his arms had made her feel and she was furious with herself. "He proved to be a friend. That's all."

"A friend," Eddie said doubtfully. "A friend who left your heart in chaos."

"*I* caused the chaos," Shannon lied. Once again, she turned away, this time to gaze at the concrete and gray glass outside that was New York. "I should have known better." Peter had only been filling a great need that must have engulfed him since his wife had died. He had touched her and then he had told her to forget the joy and the perilous womanly warmth it had elicited. And that was impossible. Impossible. Her favorite word. "It just...wasn't right."

"Oh, Shan—" Eddie bent toward her and hugged her. "—it was bad. I knew something was wrong."

"Five minutes to tape," the A.D. called.

Eddie continued the spontaneous embrace as she spoke. "I'm your friend. Remember that. I'll do anything to make you laugh again. Let's go shopping this afternoon. Nothing fancy. Just sunglasses and no makeup and the designer floor at Saks."

"That would make me laugh, all right. All those beautiful clothes..." Shannon's voice trailed off. She was thinking of her mother scrubbing the floor in the kitchen and her brother behind the counter at the five-and-dime. Just now, she couldn't face Saks Fifth Avenue. It was too soon. She hadn't come back all the way yet. The life she had left behind in Wyoming was still too much of a reality within her. And she missed her family desperately. "Why would I need new clothes? I don't know where to wear the ones I already have."

"Wear them to the grocery store," Eddie teased her. "And now that we've solved that major problem, why don't you plan to wear jeans and an old flannel shirt to the Viewer's Choice awards next month? You're only nominated for Best Actress. No need to make a big deal out of that."

"Okay. Okay." At last, the smile on Shannon's lips reached her eyes. "I get your point." But she really didn't need to shop for a Viewer's Choice dress. Lauren Taylor, the show's designer, had already agreed to create a gown for her.

"Good." Eddie was satisfied. "A nice, relaxing ride in a taxi through perilous New York traffic ought to bring you back to reality."

"Yes. It will." Shannon gazed at her reflection in the lighted mirror. She turned back to Eddie with a determined smile. "That will bring me back to reality, all right," she said firmly and, this time, not even Eddie could read the doubts she still harbored in her mind. *But what is the reality of my life? Perhaps it was the moment of myself I found when Peter Barrett touched me.*

"WE HAVE A LEAD, Barrett."

An old, familiar sense of panic welled up inside Peter. In the days shortly after Lorilee's kidnapping, Sheriff John Miller telephoned him every day. Abruptly, the frequency of his calls had fallen off. Now, each of them meant that Peter had to face something new.

"A bank president's wife was kidnapped in Texas last night. She was released unharmed after a ransom was paid. The bank was a small one. In a little town south of Dallas. The Ellis County sheriff's posse captured a pair, a man and a woman, at a Holiday Inn early this morning. I've been on the wire with the Ellis County sheriff for three hours."

Peter gripped the telephone so tightly that his knuckles were white. How long had it been? How many false leads had they followed? He forced his voice to stay even and strong. "Who are they? What do you know of them?"

"Not much yet. I need more time on the investigation. There's a possibility one of them worked with Lorilee when she was with a PBS crew in Texas two years ago. And whoever they are, they face criminal charges in Texas before they can be extradited back here. But we won't lose them, Barrett. Not if they're the ones. We're going to build a solid case."

Peter hung up the telephone and twirled the leather president's chair around to face the window. The sun was blazing against the snow. Would he never win? Would he always have to remember the time his life had been twisted and broken? Peter wanted to find Lorilee's kidnappers. He wanted justice. He wanted to testify against them and watch their calm faces and know that they were dying of fear inside. But he wasn't certain he could live through it all again—the battery of questions, the endless memory of a day when his own life had been ripped apart.

He stared at his wife's picture on his desk. "Lorilee." He said her name aloud. He felt as if he was praying to Lorilee. What an absurd thing to do. The thought of it made him almost laugh. He should be praying to something much, much bigger and more powerful. But he didn't know if he was ready for God yet. He didn't know if he had the courage he needed to let go of his own will. He didn't know if he had the faith to let some stronger, finer hand win his battles for him.

"Lorilee Barrett," he said her name again. Nothing answered him.

"Mr. Barrett?" His secretary stuck her head in his door. "Are you off the telephone now? Calvin Gleason is here to see you."

"Thanks, Barbara. Send him in."

Peter stood as Cal Gleason entered the room.

"Well, Peter—" Gleason grasped his hand and pumped it enthusiastically. "—good to see you."

"Likewise."

"I have something for you." Cal Gleason pulled a check from his suit-jacket pocket and handed it to Peter. "Made out in the amount of $180,000. I didn't know who to make it out to. You or the bank or the school district."

Peter held up one hand to stop him. "Gleason, you've arranged everything? It's all final?"

"My accountant and my lawyer both agreed that you gave me good advice. I have faith in you, Barrett. The paperwork has already been taken care of."

"The check should be made out to the Fremont County School District." Gleason's check brought him to a new place inside himself, a place where he had been victorious once. "This is wonderful." Peter took the man's hand. "These kids are so excited. I'd like you to meet them." He was talking as if he knew them, too. "I'll call you when the school district finalizes the ground breaking. Maybe we can drive down to Wind River together and attend it."

"I'd enjoy that." Gleason pointed to the check. "Will you make sure that gets to the proper party?"

"I will."

"Thanks." Gleason gave him a salute and left his office.

Peter buried his head in his hands. Here it was, his life, spread out on the desk before him. Lorilee's picture. A check for $180,000 for teens he pretended to know. And a telephone that, with one ring, had brought him news of a sheriff's investigation he didn't think he could live through.

Suddenly he longed for someone who could make him feel strong. He wanted to cry out to someone, to cling to someone the way Taylor did, to know all the pieces could be put back together again. *Why do I have to be the strong one?*

He thought of Shannon then, of the things she had said to him while they stood in the shadow of the trees on Teton Pass. In his mind, she and Lorilee became one person for a moment, blurring together in his head like two images superimposed on his life. He had thought of Shannon so often since she had left for New York. Every time he acknowledged the enemies warring within him, her face rose to defeat them all. If only he could talk to her. If only he could explain how sorry and lost he felt.

He glanced at his watch. One-forty-five p.m.

The urge to see her overtook him. Peter stood from his desk and walked downstairs to the bank's break room. Several people were there and the little television was blaring, as his employees relaxed and smoked or talked while "Wayward Hopes" played on the screen.

Her image was as crisp, as vibrant and real as if she were standing right here before him. The flow of her voice, the tone, its pleading, rang familiarly.

"Don't do this, Robert," she was pleading to the man on camera with her. She looked as frightened and angry and alone as Peter felt. *If only I hadn't gathered her into my arms.*

"Mr. Barrett." Barbara jumped up from a chair. "I'm on my break. Do you need me?"

"No...no...sit back down, please."

His secretary's eyes followed his to the screen. "See, Mr. Barrett. There she is. I told you she was wonderful."

"Yes." If only he had found the presence of mind to pull away from Shannon before he had kissed her. But it was too late now. She was back in New York City, taping television shows, forever away.

He ached to talk to her. And just now, after the telephone call from the sheriff, he needed more than ever to believe the things she'd told him. What he would give to hear that crazy "goodness of life" speech one more time. He couldn't help smiling. And suddenly, unbelievably, a plan began to form in his mind.

Last month, he had received a registration for a banker's convention in New York City. It had been on his desk all this time; he had been too busy to throw it away, and now he was grateful for that.

"Will you make sure that gets to the proper party?" Gleason had asked.

I will do it, he answered himself.

"Barbara," he said to his secretary. "There is one thing you can do for me." His gaze was still fixed on the little television as she grabbed a note pad. "When your break is over, will you come into my office upstairs? I'd like you to book a flight for me. To New York City."

TOMMY EBERLE loved his journalism class at Washakie High School. He loved the smell of rubber cement and the clackity-click sound of the old manual typewriter the town newspaper had donated to the school in his freshman year.

This was the class in which Tommy did most of his dreaming. He was always working on a story. He couldn't wait to read his own byline in a real newspaper someday.

He was always writing no matter what class he was in. He carried a spiral-bound notebook with him to the five-and-dime some evenings, for when things at the counter weren't busy and the shelves had been stocked, he knew he could write. He was working on a feature about a friend in the senior class who trained hunting dogs.

"Glad to see you working on that." Sandy Budge leaned across the lab table and read Tommy's lead sentence. They were in biology and he was supposed to be taking notes. But Sandy recognized the fat green notebook her friend had been writing in lately. She was editor of the *West Wind*, the monthly school paper, and she had already scheduled his article to run in the next issue.

"I have to finish it." Tommy's smile was shy and his voice was quiet but his eyes were dancing. "You know how editors are about deadlines. Relentless."

"They're nothing of the kind." Sandy was trying to act offended but her eyes were merry, too. Tommy was her best friend. She loved writing and reporting as much as he did. And they both wanted to study journalism when they went away to college. "You're the relentless one. You have another week to finish that story. If you don't quit writing in here, you're going to fail the test on invertebrates Friday."

Tommy looked only slightly disgruntled. "I wish Mr. Reed would just let me write a story about starfish."

"He won't. He'll make you answer the questions just the same as he'll make everybody else." She was leaning across the table and she was grinning. Her blond hair fell across her forehead in curls.

Tommy studied her. Sandy was acting differently today. She was usually reserved. Today her face was gleaming. And suddenly as he watched her and thought of how she was teasing him, he knew what it must be. "Did you hear something from Iowa, Sandy?" She had applied to the University of Iowa for acceptance and a scholarship many months before.

She was bobbing her head at him and all her curls were moving. "Do you want to see the letter?" She was already fishing in her backpack to show it to him before he could answer. She and Tommy had talked about the future often, after school, while they were arranging the galleys into a layout for the *West Wind*. They discussed how hard it was, not knowing what to plan for, but now Sandy finally knew.

Tommy walked her to her locker after biology class. "I'm really glad, Sandy," he told her again as she turned the handle on the locker and it popped open. Yet there was a hint of sadness in his voice. Sandy recognized it despite his brave words.

"You'll go, too, you know," she said. Tommy had been working and saving for college forever. He wanted to go as badly as she did.

"I'm not so certain anymore. Dad could really use my help around the ranch."

He was covering for himself and Sandy knew it. He had decided long ago to apply for one of the BEAT scholarships. But now, because of a weird technicality that hadn't been explained to them, everything had fallen through.

"Your brother is helping on the ranch. And you've already been accepted." Tommy had gotten his acceptance letter from University of Wyoming last November. She knew he had enough money saved for two semesters. "Maybe you could borrow the money from your sister and pay her back after you graduate and get a good job."

But Tommy was shaking his head. "I won't do that. It would have been different if I had gotten the scholarship through BEAT. Shannon wanted to help everyone. If the scholarship committee had decided I was worthy of one of those scholarships, too, I would have accepted it."

"Are you working tonight?" Sandy did her best to change the subject. She couldn't help but feel sorry for him, though she didn't want him to know.

He shook his head. "I'm off tonight. I've got a basketball game. They let me off work so I could play."

"I'll come cheer you on." Suddenly Sandy wanted to watch him win something, even if it was only a basketball game.

"No. Don't come." He frowned at her and then he laughed. He didn't mean to mope. "You'd see me playing and I'd lose the ball or I couldn't shoot it and you'd remember me that way a long time after you went off to Iowa."

"I'll remember you, anyway." She was grinning again.

"Fine," he told her. "Just remember the good stuff."

"I'll remember how you failed biology because you were always working on your newspaper stories in class."

"Maybe you *should* come to the basketball game," he teased her. "Maybe I *should* leave you other ways to remember me at the end of my senior year."

"Tommy." When she thought about it, Sandy could hardly fathom leaving her friends and going so far away. "I might not even make it. I might flunk out my first semester."

"You won't. Promise me you won't."

"But even if I don't fail, I'll come back to Wind River to live some day."

"My sister didn't."

"Your sister's different. She couldn't come back. She's famous."

Peter frowned again. "I don't see how that makes any difference at all."

CHAPTER SIX

THE SEQUINS on Shannon's gown sparkled even in the muted lights of the dressing room. But the little shafts of light that danced out and then disappeared could not compete with the exuberance in Shannon's eyes. She was wearing the most beautiful dress she had ever seen in her life.

Lauren Taylor, the show's designer, had insisted on creating this dress, too. At first, Shannon had been disappointed. She'd wanted her Emmy dress to be an extension of herself, not an extension of Lisa Radford. Shannon had insisted she wanted something simple and what she and Lauren had finally negotiated was perfect. The dress fell to Shannon's ankles in a shaft of crimson fire that hung flawlessly from one shoulder and one long, tight sleeve. It stopped just short enough to reveal the tips of dainty crimson satin and sequin-covered pumps.

"This is the most gorgeous thing I've ever *seen*," Shannon breathed, and when she twirled around to see every angle in the mirror, she looked like a little girl playing princess or dress-up. "Oh, Lauren. Thank you." She turned toward the woman who was standing beside her and beaming, too. "It's perfect."

She looked at herself in the mirror and twirled around once again and then she laughed. As she twirled, there were nine other Shannons twirling with her in the mirror, each an image, at a different angle, of herself.

The Viewer's Choice presentation was still weeks away. But Al Jensen had insisted everyone spend extra time on Shannon's appearance. He wanted everything perfect for her, and it was. Last week, the show's hairdresser had spent almost three hours on her hair, trimming the ends, pulling it past her chin, sweeping it up and away from her face at just the right angle to complement her features and the magical crimson dress the hairdresser had seen in Lauren Taylor's sketches. All the attention made Shannon feel like Cinderella.

Gingerly she stroked the sleeve on the dress. "Do I need to leave it here, Lauren?" she asked timidly. She was hoping she could take it home with her and just look at it waiting, hanging in her closet, but she wasn't certain if she should. The show's publicists might want to keep the dress under lock and key.

Lauren Taylor almost hugged her. Shannon was so unlike so many of the other actresses. She didn't expect a thing, while others were always waiting for what they thought was rightfully theirs, always wanting what they thought they deserved. Most of the women Lauren Taylor worked with never gave a second thought before they grabbed the $7,000 designer gowns and waltzed out the door with them. "It's yours, Miss Eberle." Then Lauren did give her a tentative hug. "Just don't wear it out to any hamburger joints before the day of the awards."

Shannon laughed. "I won't. Don't worry." Wearing this gown before the fact would be like wearing a wedding dress to a party a month before the wedding. And, in a way, Shannon felt as if that was what she was doing, getting married to her acting career. Perhaps this was the final step. The Best Actress award recognized a love and a dedication she had let guide her life for as long as she could remember.

She bundled the gown down to her hips and slipped out of it and she was still glowing when she handed it to one of Lauren's assistants to wrap it up. Then she tripped out into the unexpected sunshine, the dress draped into a plastic bag that hung across her arms. It almost felt like springtime in New York as she weaved through the crowds and found a taxi.

"You're going to win. I know it," Eddie told her that evening after Shannon had showed her the dress. The two of them were sitting on a huge braided rug at Shannon's apartment in Manhattan, cross-legged, learning lines and sipping apricot tea.

"If I win, you have to promise me you'll come to Wyoming." The jeans Shannon wore were a stark contrast to the glamorous dress. They were faded and worn, with a rip in one knee, and she sat with her hands clasped expectantly around it as she leaned forward.

"I'll come even if you don't win."

"You aren't just saying that to shut me up?" There was something about the eagerness in her friend's eyes that made Eddie want to hug her.

"I'm not. It's a good idea. I'd enjoy doing a drama workshop for those kids. Although I don't understand why they would want me if they could have you."

"They could have both of us," Shannon took a sip of her tea and almost spilled it, she was so excited. "They'll eat it up. They would die to meet you." The money for BEAT would come from other channels. But she wanted to show the teens at Washakie High School how much she still believed in their project.

"You're going to have to let me have one day off to ski," Eddie told her. "That will be my only payment. Promise me."

Shannon frowned. She was under contract to tape the show four days a week for the next twenty weeks. And Eddie's schedule wasn't much better. By the time they could both get away from the studio, it would be well past ski season. And Shannon didn't want to wait until next winter. Most of the Washakie High seniors who had helped mastermind the project would be graduated by then. "Do you have to ski?"

"What else is there?"

Shannon grinned at her. Eddie always thought she knew every angle. She was sitting on the floor against a huge quilted pillow, but even then she didn't quite seem relaxed. Eddie reminded her of a hawk. Eddie belonged in New York. She had lived this way forever, battling her way through a huge New York high school and holding her own in a fatherless family with five sisters and a nervous mother. Now she was ready to hold her own against the world.

"There's always horseback riding."

"Oh, gads!" Eddie made a horrible face and they both laughed. Shannon couldn't picture Eddie anywhere near a horse. Everything about her best friend was groomed and painted into impeccable place. Shannon hadn't seen her with a chipped fingernail in close to four months. Eddie never went anywhere unless she was completely finished. Even in faded jeans, she managed to look glamorous. Shannon envied her sometimes for that, not because she didn't feel comfortable about her own style, but because it was obvious Eddie belonged completely to the fishbowl life they were both living.

"So... I'll go, anyway." Eddie stared at one of her fuchsia-painted fingernails. "I suppose you're a good enough friend for me to waive the skiing clause." She grinned mischievously. "But you won't catch me riding a horse."

"Fine. I suppose I won't be able to talk you into trout fishing, either. But it isn't my fault you are missing out on one of the truest pleasures in the world."

Eddie stretched her long legs out on the carpet before she stood to go. She had a long drive back to her town house in Greenwich Village. It was a drive she always made alone, in a little red BMW she had bought just after she started on the show. "My greatest joy in life is the designer sportswear at Bloomingdale's. Wyoming can't be any better than that."

"You'd be surprised," Shannon said, laughing.

"I've got to get out of here," Eddie said with a sigh, "before my best friend succeeds in brainwashing me." Eddie rose and gathered her things as Shannon unfastened the three locks on the door. "I love you, you know," Eddie said, grinning, as she moved past Shannon into the hallway.

Shannon hugged Eddie. And just as she did, she glanced up and saw a man in the corridor, moving toward them, although his steps were slowing. And then she stared at him, thinking he looked familiar and handsome, not quite placing him because she had never known him in New York, as he stood there, not quite smiling at her, his expression asking a question.

"Peter," she breathed his name. "What are you doing here?" Seeing him was like being roped and twisted, pulled in a direction she was trying to run from.

"I have to talk to you."

Eddie looked from Shannon to Peter. "I was just on my way out," she said, but neither of them seemed to hear her. She was smiling as she hurried away.

After she had gone, Shannon broke the silence between them first. "I thought you had done that already."

"No." His eyes were unreadable. "I haven't."

"You did. You told me to forget. Remember?"

"And you told me it was impossible. You were right, Shannon."

"No, I wasn't," she said. "I did."

He heard the exhaustion in her voice and he realized he was asking too much of her. "I didn't, Shannon. I couldn't. No matter how I tried."

"You should have."

"No." His voice was stern and so powerful that it stopped her. Her mind was suddenly full of home, of skiing and sharing her family with him, and suddenly, there in her flat high above Manhattan, seeing him was like a renewal to her.

"You remind me of home."

"You miss it."

"No...yes..." It was the first time Shannon had admitted the truth to herself, too. It was usually so gray in New York. And it made her angry with him, because he was here, making her admit things to herself she didn't want to think about. Her question, though whispered, was charged with intensity. "What do we have to talk about?"

"I want to talk about where I want you to stand in my life."

"Last time we talked, you didn't want me in your life at all."

"Maybe I don't know where I stand in my own life."
He grabbed her shoulders for an instant and then he let
her go. "Just let me come in. Let me talk to you for a
minute, Shannon. Please."

She stepped away from the door and he followed her
inside.

"I was trying to talk my best friend into coming to
Wyoming." She shot him a sad little smile, not really
knowing what else to say. She was furious with herself
because, somewhere inside, she was happy he was here.
She studied his face. He looked good, relaxed and
stately, in a London Fog overcoat and a wool scarf
around his neck. "I think she'll come. I want her to do
a drama workshop with me for the BEAT kids."

Peter pulled Cal Gleason's check from his chest
pocket. He didn't know how long she would let him
stay. And he wanted her to have the money. "I brought
this." He handed it to her.

"This is why you came." She gazed at the amount,
wanting to jump around the room and scream with glee.
But she didn't. "This could have gone to Jim Clarkson."

"It will eventually. I wanted you to see it first."

"So you flew to New York City."

"This was one of the reasons."

"And the others?"

"I'm attending a bankers' conference at the Gra-
mercy Park Hotel. And I had to see you. I hurt you,
Shannon. I...haven't been able to live with that. I
wouldn't have booked a place at the conference if I
didn't plan to see you. It was hard to leave home...."

Camille and Taylor had come to the Jackson Hole
airport early that morning to wave him off. Peter had
almost cried when he told his son goodbye. He had

turned once on the tarmac, just before he climbed the
rickety metal steps to the plane, to see Taylor waving at
him through the glass. Peter had replayed the baby's
fluttering hand in his head all the way across the Mid-
western states until he got to the city.

"You've never left Taylor before." It was a statement, not a question. She could read the things he was
thinking in his eyes.

"Not overnight. I just feel so responsible for him."

"Daddy always told me it never gets any better."
Shannon smiled at him at last. "Just wait until he starts
going out on camping trips with friends."

"And I'm sitting at home worrying that the bears
might get him."

Shannon chuckled. "At least now all you have to
worry about is your housekeeper."

Peter smiled, too. "There are days Camille could be
classified as a bear herself." He gazed down at her.
"I've been watching a great actress on television lately,
someone with just a hint of Wyoming in her eyes. Do
you have any idea how good you are?"

"Peter, don't tell me you've been watching the
show." It still startled her, thinking of people she knew
and people she didn't know, turning on televisions in
their homes and seeing her. There were times she wanted
to run when a stranger approached her on the street and
treated her like an acquaintance. "Every day?"

"No. Just once."

"If you have time while you're here, I'll take you on
a tour of the studio." And then she threw back her head
and laughed at last, remembering Eddie's face and the
way she had scurried down the hallway while Peter
stood at the doorway looking in. "You caught my best

friend leaving. I'm sure everyone will know all about you by the time I get to the set tomorrow."

"Shannon, I just needed to apologize. I still feel married to my wife." Peter looked down at her with eyes full of the gentleness of someone growing strong. "I shouldn't have shown you...how much I need...someone."

"I'm glad you came," she said softly. She was frightened by him, by the feelings his nearness brought out in her. But she was warmed by them, too, that he cared enough to come to her, to fight against her hurting.

"I wasn't certain I should have." They were both thinking of the same thing, how fragile his emotions were, and how far, far away her life had brought her. Shannon felt so drawn to him, and she was desperate, suddenly, to pull away from him.

"So tell me what Taylor and Camille are going to do while you're here."

"He's going to stay at her house for three days and she's going to make popcorn and let him feed the ducks." Camille had great lists of wonderful things she planned to do with him. They were even going to drive to Pocatello to go to the zoo.

"It's probably good for you to get away every so often."

"I had a lot to get away from." He sounded exhausted. "Thank you, Shannon."

"For what?"

"For not saying anything. I deserve one of your speeches about the goodness of life."

Shannon searched his expression. He was so different from any man she knew in New York or any man she had known in Wyoming before she went away. The

men she had known at home were like the teenagers she
was trying to save now, afraid to dream, afraid of being
defeated. And the men she knew in New York were even
worse. They were caught up in the frantic pace, the
pulse of Wall Street or the pressures of network television. When she was around them, she felt like an or-
nament, a name with a face, that men wanted the same
way they wanted a Gucci briefcase or cuff links from
Van Cleef and Arpels. "You're right. You do deserve
one. But I don't think you need one just now." Then
she chuckled, a wonderful, homey laugh that hung in
the air between them.

"I like your place," he told her as he turned in a circle and took it all in. "It reminds me of your mother's
house."

"Shannon's quilt house," she said softly. "That's
what they all call it at the studio. They think it's the
most bizarre New York flat they've ever seen."

She had decorated her apartment entirely in multicolored calico things. The sofa was blue calico, and the
chair beside it was peach, with tiny blue flowers. The
old-fashioned wood stove in the middle of the room was
coated with speckled blue enamel.

There was a huge quilt hanging on the wall and in it
were all the colors of the rainbow. The quilt had been a
gift from a woman in Wyoming, a friend of Shannon's
grandmother's named Pearl, who had watched Shannon on "Wayward Hopes" and had wanted to send her
a personal, lovely remembrance. The quilt had been
pieced by Pearl's grandmother during the Civil War. It
was a beautiful antique, one of Shannon's prized pos-
sessions. She had searched in all the shops, from the
secondhand "trash and treasure" boutique just around
the corner from the studio to the interior design de-

partment at Bloomingdale's, for just the right items to
bring out every color in the quilt.

And she had found them. There was an ivory Pen-
dleton throw draped over the sofa and plump maroon-
and-lace pillows propped casually on the furniture and
against the hand-carved legs of the pine coffee table.
The rug on the floor had hints of all of them—the eggshell ivory that had been white but had darkened with
the years, the blues and grays and mauves.

The lamps had mauve calico shades with tiny laven-
der flowers and hand-turned pine bases Tommy had
made in woodworking class during his sophomore year
at Washakie High. The furniture was all pine. And there
was a delicate hand-painted pine heart hanging over the
hearth, with a picture of a little house, curtains blowing in the breeze, that said Home Is Where You Hang
Your Heart.

Peter didn't know what he had expected. But this
place was perfect, exactly like her, bright and lively, like
all the colors of Shannon, once more reminding him
that she was gutsy and earthy and proud of her roots.
"I like it. Shannon's quilt house. Cozy. Promising. And
honest."

They were relaxed again now, and happy, as she
moved the glimmering red dress from the sofa where she
had been showing it to Eddie. "Peter. Stay. If you have
time...."

He eyed the dress in her arms. "You don't have other
plans?"

"No." She had been too busy during the past months
with the new story line on the show. Studying her lines
and living her character and planning BEAT had taken
up all her time. She hadn't gone out with anyone in
ages. She handed him a box of matches. "Let's have a

fire. I want to hear all about the conference. And about
BEAT. Have you telephoned Jim Clarkson? Does he
know this money is finally available? Have they scheduled groundbreaking?''

He turned to her as the little fire began to blaze behind him and he told her about the day Cal Gleason had
come to his office with the check. Then he told her
about the banking conference he was attending, about
the people he had met, and as he thought about it all,
she took pleasure in the way his eyes brightened, the
way his hands drew odd patterns in the air, when he
talked about the new services he wanted his bank to
provide to the community.

"You and your bank. You love it, don't you?" she
observed after he paused. "I can tell."

"I did once." His answer was totally honest. Peter
stared into the wood stove and watched the flames rise.

"You still do." He turned back to her and her eyes
leveled on his. "You just haven't admitted it to yourself lately."

"It's the only thing in my life that has ever lasted very
long." His words were slow, his tone measured.

"Think again." The temperance in her tone matched
his. "You're forgetting someone. You have a beautiful
tiny boy with hair the color of frosted hay." Shannon
was always the optimist, so she couldn't help but see the
good things that had come from Peter's tragedy. "If not
for all the sadness you've been through, if you hadn't
loved Lorilee, you wouldn't have your son."

"I don't forget that. I couldn't." He reached for her
hand as she stood beside him. And as he touched her,
he wasn't thinking of sad things at all, but of how much
he wanted to hold her.

She smiled at him. Her expression was open, vulnerable, hers a child's face. "I spend hours each day portraying tragedies in people's lives. We sit around in a circle when we're on the set and read the next day's scripts and joke at how royally we get to mess up other people's lives. Sometimes I wonder if playing at it is fair."

"You can't take the responsibility for that. You can't become emotionally involved in the character you play. I don't know of any human who has the capacity to give that much." Peter leaned back in his chair and studied her with sad eyes. And then, out of the blue, he grinned at her. "Life isn't as horrible as all that, anyway." He was defending his own life to her and to himself now and he was surprised by it. "You have to remember the good things life offers, too."

He thought of the brilliant snow-covered mornings back home, and of the times Taylor toddled into the room, his arms outstretched, a tiny nylon Kangaroo hiking boot in each hand. It was amazing watching an infant turning into a little boy. Amazing and maybe even a little frightening. Peter sometimes felt he had very little hand in how his son was growing, for he had to work at the bank so many hours, and Taylor was always with Camille.

But the two of them had wonderful nights together, just Peter and Taylor before bedtime, when they tussled on the floor and played "dinosaur kiss." "Maybe I've been running away from the good things." He told her about Taylor then, and all their games, how they made funny pictures in the bathtub with bubbles on Taylor's tummy, and Shannon was thinking of her own father, of his strength and his friendship, of the things his love had taught her while she grew.

"You must be a good father, Peter."

He ran his hand through his hair and tousled it as he gazed into the fire. "Do you think so? Sometimes I don't know."

"He's a happy, wonderful, normal little kid." And the thing was, she was right—Taylor was normal, Peter had given him so much love, and when Lorilee had gone, Taylor was much too young to remember. Someday Peter would sit with his son on his knee and tell Taylor about his mother, how beautiful she was and how she nursed him and held him at night while he cried. But Lorilee would never be real to Taylor. He was just a tiny boy with a lifetime of growing ahead of him. And Peter felt as if he had a lifetime of growing ahead of him, too.

He gazed down at Shannon and all the gentleness he felt toward her flooded to her from his eyes. "I came here to salvage what was left of our friendship. But I find myself wanting more."

"Perhaps friendship is enough," she said quietly. But she was aching inside to touch him, to be certain of him. "Maybe it's all we can have right now." She reached up to him and traced one finger along the squarely chiseled line of his jaw. Then, without speaking again, she buried her face in the collar of his tweed jacket and clung to him. And the words she mouthed into his shoulder were almost too soft for him to hear. "I'm scared." She was afraid of the longing and the insane happiness and the warm tingle she felt now that he was near her. She was afraid of his commitment to his wife and of the guilt she knew he was wrangling with. And she was afraid of the things she would have to choose between in her own life, if she ever loved him.

She pulled away from him and he wrapped his arms around her, scarcely daring to breathe. She tried to read his expression but couldn't. She saw only a guarded darkness in his eyes, with two moving flames from the fire, reflected where his feelings should be. "Peter. Don't do this."

"I won't . . . if you don't want me to." His voice was sure and strong when he spoke to her. She looked so young, so delicate and vulnerable to him just then that the only thing in his mind was to protect her.

Anger flashed across her face. "Don't place the decision on me. You know we can't be a part of each other's life. You pushed me away because you love a woman who doesn't exist anymore."

His expression hardened. "Are you happy living the life you lead, Shannon Eberle?" He wanted her to admit she wasn't quite sure, either . . . that she questioned herself the same way he did.

"Sometimes. I know all the rules and I know how to play by them." She didn't tell him how desperately she longed for a kindred soul to share it all with. Eddie was the only person who knew how much she missed the simplicity of the life and the people she had left behind. And Eddie couldn't comprehend her feelings. Eddie was all fast lane, all New York.

"Are you terribly lonely sometimes?"

"Sometimes." She was thinking how uncanny it was that he could read her thoughts. It was her turn to stare into nothingness. Then she looked back at him, knowing full well what she would see, those deep chicory eyes, waiting to meet hers. "And you?"

He waited an interminable time, his eyes searching everything he saw in her face, and then he leaned slowly toward her, whispering the words into the rich darkness of her hair. "Maybe not as much anymore." Then he grinned. "Not since you started giving speeches about the goodness of life."

"You make it sound as if I give you a speech every day. You make it sound horrible."

"Shannon, you only gave me one speech. On Taylor's birthday. A day I let my own bitterness almost destroy my time with my son." He was learning to understand his sadness because of the things she'd said to him. Sharing her strength had begun to chisel away a sharp edge of pain in him. "You said things to me I needed to hear. You're so strong, Shannon, and I'm just learning to trust life again."

"I've spent a lot of time rescuing people," she said evenly. "I don't know if I want to rescue you, too."

Peter gripped her arms with both hands. "I'm not going to tell you I'm sorry for this, Shannon," he said, "because, this time, I'm not." His grip was so tight on her shoulders, that she couldn't have wrenched away even if she had wanted to. He pulled her toward him, desperate to fight away the doubts within him, to succumb only to the feelings of her nearness. When he kissed her, his lips were hard on hers, his desperation and frustration making him so forceful that he almost bruised her.

"Perhaps you should be." He felt her arms begin to tremble beneath his grasp. She pulled away and she waited before she added the rest of it and it seemed like an eternity to him, just waiting for her to speak. "Perhaps we both should be."

"Perhaps." She had expected him to be angry but he wasn't. His eyes were brimming with a new resolve that bored through her as he spoke. "But I don't think so."

"I will not be a substitute for your wife, Peter."

She saw the pain slice across his face. "Is that what you think?" He was furious with her for voicing the possibility. No one would replace Lorilee. He was furious with himself. And he was furious with Lorilee, too, for coming into his life and being a part of it and then ripping it away from him as though she'd ripped a rug out from under his feet. "Give me more credit than that." And suddenly, as he looked at her, he felt helpless again. "No one will replace Lorilee in my life. I did not kiss you because I need you to be a substitute for her."

"Then why?"

"Is it so hard for you to figure out, Shannon? I love the way you laugh. It makes me want to laugh, too. And that crazy lecture you gave me up on the mountain the day we were skiing. And the way you get one idea in your head and then you fight for it with every ounce of your being."

He was surprised to see her grinning. "I didn't know you knew me so well, Peter Barrett. And I didn't know the qualities you listed were quite so likable."

He swept her into a huge bear hug, one just the same as he would have given Taylor. "I do, ma'am." He winked at her. "And they are."

She reached up to him once more as his eyes took in her movement and touched one tendril of his dark hair where it curled beneath one ear. "I admire you for everything you've been able to live through." Her words were light, tentative. She wasn't certain how much she should say. Life had never defeated her the way it had defeated him.

"I had no other choice." As he looked down at her and at the great sadness in her eyes, he realized he wanted her to believe him, that he was desperate for her to understand the things he had lived through. It meant everything for both of them, being honest. It was their only hope. "I don't know if I could survive it again." He thought of his son, so many miles away, and of how much he loved him. "I'd die if anything happened to Taylor."

She sensed something in him then, a release, that told her he was relaxing. And she knew, as she sat next to Peter, exactly what he needed. He needed to talk about Lorilee's death, to relive it, to share it with someone who might care and then to let it go. "How old was Taylor when she died?"

"Four months."

Shannon stared up at him. She couldn't imagine it, having a baby like that and then dying. What could have happened? She asked the only thing that came to mind. "Was she sick?"

Peter searched her face. And then he bundled her close to him as he spoke. "You don't know how she died, do you?"

"No."

"She wasn't sick."

"Why? Why, then?"

There was silence between them before he spoke. "Someone had been watching us. They thought I'd have access to money because I was the bank president. Someone abducted her."

"Oh, God. Oh, Peter. I'm so sorry." She had heard of such things before. But they happened in big cities like New York or Chicago or Los Angeles. Never in Wyoming, where the state was filled with sheep ranchers and skiers and country people. For the first time, Shannon began to comprehend the jumble of emotions

Peter must have been feeling—the anger, the sheer helplessness.

"Peter. You musn't blame yourself for it."

"But I do." All his sorrow was there for her to see as he finished the story. "Sometimes I think...if it wasn't for me...she would still be here...alive."

"No," Shannon told him softly. "You cannot place that burden on yourself." She reached for him then and he held on to Shannon with sheer force, this time for strength.

"But what about Taylor, Shannon? And me? What about us? We're the ones left behind who have to make some sort of sense out of it."

"Cry, Peter." Shannon almost shook him. "Cry."

"I loved her so much."

"I know." Her voice was a firm whisper as she smoothed his hair beneath her hands. "But it's over now. They'll never be able to hurt you that much again."

"I've been needing someone to remind me of that." He squeezed his eyes shut and the first of his tears splattered down against his cheeks and her shirt.

"Let it come," she pleaded with him. "It's okay. I'm here. Let it come." And she was crying, too, as they sat together beside the fire, clinging to one another, and Shannon held him while he wept.

CHAPTER SEVEN

THE GOLDEN BLAZE of the fire in the wood stove burned away until all that remained were ripples of coal that glowed red through the ashes. As the fire waned, so did the tension in Peter's body. He was emotionally spent and totally drained. Still, Shannon held him without saying a word, willing herself to be calm and strong for him, wishing she could do anything for him that would take his pain away. And when he opened his eyes and saw her, he smiled. It was a tired smile, but one filled with gratitude. "So. You're still around."

"Of course I'm still around."

He reached one hand toward her and traced the curve of her lips with his index finger. He didn't kiss her again. He only gazed at her face, at the full lips he had traced and at her huge, honest eyes that reflected light from some other source besides the room where they lay. "Thank you, my friend."

"You're welcome."

"You're so beautiful, Shan. So very, very giving."

Her breath caught at his words. "Sh-h-h. You're exhausted."

He sat straight beside her. "No," he told her. "I'm not." It was true. Energy surged through his body. Just being with Shannon made him feel as if he was stretching his heart, testing it, the way he would have tested an injured limb.

Moonlight was filtering in through an open window and the rush of the traffic below seemed far, far away. Shannon's profile, with its velvet outline of soft light, was next to him, a breath away. He cupped her chin in his palm and turned her face toward him, until her features were lost in the darkness. He kissed her tentatively this time, on the nose first and then her forehead, and finally he found her mouth. And he could only think of Shannon as he gathered her hair in his hands and felt her moving closer.

When he thought of that night later, Peter remembered a thousand different emotions, the bittersweet sadness as the hours moved by in a blur while he touched her face and kissed her ears as she smiled up at him, the happiness of her laughter in the darkness when she rolled across him to tickle him.

They did not make love. Neither of them was ready to let go of the things that had once hurt him. Instead, they kissed and they laughed and they touched each other's face as the night passed by in the city below them. At 3:00 a.m., he reached for her beside him and realized they had slept. Peter's head was on a calico pillow and he was wrapped in the ivory afghan from the sofa.

She opened one eye and looked at him, and then she sighed and nestled into the crook of his arm. Peter thought he had never felt quite so fulfilled and secure as he did just now, holding her. There was something solid about her, a lifeline of strength in her that made him want to be strong, too. "Hi," he whispered to her as he barely brushed her nose with his finger.

"Hello." The next thing he knew, a light glared in the kitchen and his arms were empty. He rolled over and saw her standing at the counter, alternately humming and sipping coffee from a mug.

He raised himself on one elbow and stared at her in disbelief. It was the middle of the night. "What are you doing?"

She had changed out of her jeans into a fluffy yellow robe. Her hair was wet from her shower where it fell in curls around her shoulders. "I'm getting up." Shannon didn't tell him she had been too happy to sleep. She was due on the set of "Wayward Hopes" in less than an hour.

"Do you do this crazy thing every morning?" He was wide awake now, too, and he was amazed by her.

"Not on the weekends," she told him playfully. "On the weekends I usually sleep until six-thirty."

"You're crazy."

"I'm an actress." She took another sip of coffee and looked smug. "Besides, I have to stay in shape so I can help Dad with the sheep when I go home."

Peter reached for his watch where it lay on the floor beside him. It was 4:00 a.m. "The only thing you'll be herding at this hour is night owls, ma'am."

"Sounds good to me," Shannon chuckled, as she went into the other room. A few minutes later she came back wearing a fresh pair of jeans and an oversize white cotton shirt. Her hair was combed but still wet and she carried a huge leather bag over one shoulder.

The Lincoln Town Car the studio sent for her every morning was waiting for her at the curb downstairs. "I'll always be able to find night owls here in New York. Sheep and cows are a bit harder to come by." She grinned down at him and then she laughed again. He looked so at home on her floor, sprawled out watching her amid the quilts and the pillows.

"Maybe I can ditch out of the last workshop at the banking seminar and we can ride the Staten Island Ferry. I'd love to see Lady Liberty before the sun goes down."

"She's quite a sight," Shannon said wistfully. "New York is an incredible town."

Peter thought of spending the day without her, attending meetings in the business suits he had packed the day before yesterday in Wyoming as if nothing out of the ordinary had happened to him, and a great surge of loneliness engulfed him. "I'll miss you."

"Me too." Shannon nodded, her eyes huge, and then she showed him how to bolt the door with an extra key before she turned to go.

"CUT ON THIS SCENE," Al Jensen called from the control room. "We have to tighten it up. Come on, gang. We have to have twenty-two minutes of tape on the air this afternoon. Thirty seconds to tape. Anybody need makeup? Hair? Shannon, you okay?"

Shannon nodded from below.

"Okay!" he shouted. "Here we go. Rolling to tape. Five seconds to tape...." On his hand signal, they performed the scene again.

"That was fun." Eddie draped an arm across Shannon's shoulders after Al had called out the final cut. "We ought to play scenes together all the time." They had taped a scene involving both of them sitting on the bed talking at the PineRidge Hospital in Vermont. They had had to shoot it several times to tighten it but, in the end, it was good and Eddie was proud of it. There was something about Shannon today, some hint of yearning, that had added an extra dimension to the scene and had made it better.

"We do."

Eddie stopped and turned toward her, catching her off guard on purpose because she knew Shannon would dodge the question. "Speaking of scenes, why don't you tell me about the scene with the very handsome man on your doorstep last night?"

"What about him?"

"You were looking at him like he was an apparition."

"Yes."

"Shannon."

"Okay. He's Peter Barrett. He's my friend from Wyoming who has been helping find funding for BEAT. He stopped by to bring me a check."

"He *stopped by?* Let me guess. On his way through from Mexico to the North Pole. You just happened to be on the way."

"Something like that."

Al Jensen called for another scene before Shannon could say more. She was glad they were interrupted. Eddie knew her so well. She didn't want her to sense either how disoriented she felt or how happy. Peter was here, somewhere in the city, attending business meetings. This afternoon he would be hers again. That certainty was all Shannon could think of as she walked through another scene.

Shortly after noon she was on her way home again, with the same driver, in the back seat of the car. When she arrived at her apartment, she half expected to find Peter there. The sofa was straightened and there were logs in the wood stove ready for a fire but the flat was empty. Shannon stood at the window for a long while, just looking out and wishing for him. And just before three, she looked out again and saw him step out of a taxi at the curb. She tied a sweater around her shoulders as she ran and she met him halfway down the stairway and she was laughing when he stretched up three stairs and grabbed her. "Whatever happened to the old-fashioned sort of dates where the guy rings the doorbell and helps you on with your coat? You aren't supposed to run down the front stairs to meet me."

"I couldn't wait," she confessed as she grinned at him. "And you missed the most important meeting of the day. I can tell by the guilt I see on your face."

"I didn't."

"You did. You look like a little kid ditching school to go fishing."

"How come you always read my mind?" Peter winked at her and then scooped her up and carried her down the stairs in his arms while her leather bag swung wildly from her shoulder and knocked against his legs. When they reached bottom, they were both laughing as Peter flagged down a taxi. "To the Staten Island Ferry, please."

"Okay, mister."

"We don't know where we're going," Peter told the driver while Shannon giggled. "We're exploring. We might just ride the ferry all night long. Do you stay with us on the boat or do you leave us at the dock?"

What loonies. "That all depends on how much you want to pay me, mister."

"Stay with us, if you don't mind," Peter said, his smile widening from ear to ear. "We like you."

Great. The taxi driver glanced in the rearview mirror just as Shannon lifted her head, and he recognized her. His wife watched "Wayward Hopes" every day. "We'll ride the ferry. Fine. And maybe I could get your autograph, too, Miss Radford. My wife watches your show every day.''

He drove them onto the boat and parked the car without complaining. Shannon and Peter left the taxi so they could wander along beside the railing. They stopped halfway to the bow and Shannon leaned out over the water, with her hair blowing back around her face, and Peter decided she looked like a woman in an Andrew Wyeth painting—wistful and wise.

Peter slipped one arm around her waist just as the ferry's horn sounded. They stood in silence until the boat glided past the Statue of Liberty. "That is a beautiful sight." He was almost overcome by the magnitude of everything, that he was here in New York, in his own new world, with Shannon.

She laid her head against his shoulder as the gray waves crashed along the boat beside them. This view never failed to move her. "When I think of all the people who came across the ocean to the United States... They rode boats for months to get here.... It makes me feel like I could do anything sometimes."

Her voice faded and he hugged her closer. "Well, Miss Star of daytime television. You think you haven't done enough already?"

"I can never do enough."

"You want more than what you have now?"

"Yes." She was thinking of BEAT again. "I want to be able to help the people I love."

"That isn't as easy as you make it sound." He was sad again, and as he spoke she realized why. He had tried to help Lorilee, but his efforts had not saved her. Perhaps helping those you loved was the hardest of all.

"I'm sorry, Peter."

"I know." He stared out over the water. "It's okay."

"It isn't. I've said so many things wrong."

"You've said them right."

"To you . . . you're kind to say so. But with the kids at home, with all the things they've wanted, I've come up with glorious schemes for them. And then I've left them. Other people have had to pick up the pieces I left behind. Like you and Cal Gleason."

He glanced down at her in surprise. "You sound like you're giving up."

"Sometimes I think I am."

"You can't, Shannon."

She was gazing up at him while her hair curled around her neck from the wind and the sea spray. "You echo my own conscience."

"Listen to both of us, then." His eyes were serious. "Just because Cal Gleason appeared with funds for BEAT doesn't mean you're leaving someone else to pick up the pieces, to put together parts of a dream you started. You think if you can't give everything, then you can't give anything at all. Shan, it doesn't work that way. You're still a part of it, even when you're in New York. If it means that much to you, you've got to see it through. You've got to find another way."

"But where?"

He circled her waist with both of his arms. "I don't know. I wish I could stay with you and help you find it. It would be exciting cruising around New York City with an award-winning actress."

"I haven't won anything yet. Everyone keeps talking as if I already have the golden statue on the hearth at home. I still have to go to the Waldorf-Astoria and sit in the audience with cameras trained on my face and I have to be nervous, and just in case any of this is warranted, I have to prepare a speech. Then I'll be . . ." She wheeled around to face him, still in the circle of his arms. "Peter. That's it!" She had to fight to keep from shrieking at him. She should have seen it long before now. "The Viewer's Choice Awards." And her eyes widened even further. "But I would have to win."

"What are you thinking of?"

"The Viewer's Choice." Shannon was laughing and her logic was oddly disjointed, but just now it was the best she could do. "Everybody makes speeches when they win. Some of them thank their mothers and their third-grade teachers. Some of them get political and turn the world against them. Why couldn't I talk about BEAT? Would it work?"

"Of course it would work." Peter was beaming at her. "You could do a beautiful speech about the people in Wyoming and what they've given you during your lifetime." He was almost as excited as she was. "It would work perfectly."

"You really think so?"

"I think so."

She hugged Peter again and, this time, he picked her up and spun her around by the railing on the ferry. And as he pulled her close to him once again, she felt as if everything in the world was possible. "I'll do it, then."

The ferry docked on Staten Island and they hurried to the car. Shannon clutched his hand and danced along beside him, the sea wind trailing against them, as they walked the final block to a restaurant. They sat at a secluded table covered with newspaper advertisements from the early twentieth century, protected by shellac, ads that offered high-heeled shoes for $2.50 and an arthritis remedy for fifty cents. They shared a huge plate of fried mushrooms, dipping them into horseradish sauce as they laughed over the ads.

"Look at this one." Peter was pointing at an ad for a tonic to help bald babies grow hair. "Taylor's head was as clean as a bowling ball when he was born." It was the first time he had been able to talk about his son and his wife without sadness. "Lorilee had been talking forever about putting little clips or bows in the baby's hair if it was a girl. And then she got this hairless boy."

"Maybe someday you'll have a lot to laugh at, remembering those days," Shannon said.

"Yes." His laughter stopped. "I suppose every man does." He leaned forward and gripped her hand from across the table. "See, Shan, you *have* rescued me. I haven't laughed in so long. I'd give anything if I didn't have to fly halfway across the continent tomorrow."

"You're going back tomorrow." She hadn't realized he would be leaving so soon. She had been living each moment with him, never looking back, never looking forward.

"I have to go home." It seemed impossible to both of them. Only the night before, they had been sitting by the fire sharing their lives. Shannon hadn't thought of the endings. She'd only thought of today, of running all over New York City with him. And now there was nowhere else for either of them to go. Except back to their separate lives, so far away from each other.

"When are you coming back to Wyoming?" He hated to admit how much he was going to miss her. And he knew it would be worse when he got home, because he could turn on the television every day at his house or at the bank and see her there. He bent forward against the table, his elbows on the funny ads, and he grabbed her arms. "Why don't you come back with me for a while?"

"I can't do it." Her voice was very small. "You know that."

"Yes. I do." He had as many obligations as she had. "I can't get away from the bank much, either."

"Maybe you could." She was breathless again. "Maybe for the Viewer's Choice Awards." But he was shaking his head.

"I *will* take you to the airport tomorrow," she said.

"In the fancy studio car that was waiting for you this morning?" he asked, trying to be lighthearted.

"I could get a limo if you'd like," she said seriously.

Further conversation stopped when the waiter brought their hamburgers to the table—two baskets overflowing with curly potatoes and monstrous buns with meat. When Shannon saw their meal she tried to laugh, but she couldn't. She looked up and finally her eyes met his. "It's crazy, isn't it? I forgot this was going to be over."

They ate their hamburgers without talking much, then the waiter wrapped what was left in little foil bags for them to take home. They hailed another taxi, and this time on the ferry neither of them spoke as they glided across the harbor. Shannon stood silently, gripping the rail, and Peter held on to her wordlessly from behind.

"You've only been here one day and already I'm going to miss you," she said at last.

He hugged her closer just as the ferry bumped the wharf. Cars beside them roared to life and headlights flashed on all around them. Peter's voice was full of gentle certainty as he pulled her closer. "Tonight is going to have to last us for a long time."

"It will, Peter." She turned to him and clenched both of her fists against his chest, as if she was clutching herself, her past, against him. "We will make it so."

"I want to stay with you tonight." His words were barely a whisper, barely more of a sound than the breeze that shuffled across the water.

Shannon gazed up at him with everything she had to give to him revealed in her face. "I'd like that, too." And they held each other then, their arms entwined, as their lives had become.

Shannon clasped her hands around his waist as they walked and he moved with her, his arm draped around her shoulders, a gentle vise. *We're propping each other up,* she thought as they arrived at their waiting taxi.

They rode through Manhattan in silence. Peter watched her as the confetti of lights—reds, golds, greens—streamed past outside the car. He gave the driver a monstrous tip when they arrived at Shannon's flat, and he turned to find Shannon had already darted into the building. He chased her, laughing again, until he caught her.

"Stop it," she said, giggling, as he wrapped his arms around her waist and held her there. "You'll wake the neighbors."

"It isn't late. They're all still awake." He was grinning. "They're all peering at us through their peepholes right now."

"And you enjoy providing the show." As they moved past the security guard, she touched Peter playfully on the tip of his nose. "Perhaps you're the one who should have gone into acting."

"Maybe so." His grin was almost wicked. "'To be or not to be...'" stuck out his chest and pulled himself to his full height in a misguided imitation of a Shakespearian actor.

"But then again—" she was shaking her head "—if you had been doing that to his work, Shakespeare would have been destitute. I don't know if the entertainment industry would have survived."

"Right. And you think the banking industry fares better?"

"Yes." She kissed his nose.

They bounded up the stairs together, racing, alternately chuckling and then doing their best to silence each other. When they reached her door, Shannon handed him her keys and stood back while he found the right one.

"There you are, ma'am." The door swung open and he motioned for her to go inside before him. She plopped unceremoniously on the couch and then looked up at him, suddenly shy, her eyes the soft velvet of a doe's eyes.

"Shan." He murmured her name as he sank to his knees beside her. "Shan." She was his world now; he felt as if he was revolving around her and she was pulling him, pulling him, as he ran his palms firmly against the seams of her jeans where they folded at her thighs. He reached up to her then and lifted her down onto the floor beside him, and she stretched her arms out, push-up fashion, against the little rug in order to remain above him.

The pearl-white moonlight made a pool in the carpet beside them as her huge eyes locked on his. "Peter," she whispered. "I'm not frightened anymore."

His fingers found her skin beneath her blouse and he lifted her sweater. Her eyes, her face, disappeared for a moment as Shannon raised her arms above her head.

And he held his breath, she was so incredibly beautiful. She let her body relax and lay back on the rug, sprawled like a cat, clad only in her jeans, waiting for him. Somewhere outside the clouds moved, exposing more light, and it swept across her body as she lay there.

He gave her a smile of approval as he looked at her and then gathered her into his arms. "The spotlight again, Shan. Even the moonlight is a spotlight for you. You were meant for it."

"Hold me, Peter. Please." She was frantic for him and she didn't feel close enough, even felt as if he was drifting away even as he grasped her.

"I'm here," he told her. "I'm here." But they both knew he was leaving in only hours.

Shannon buried her head against his shoulder. His dark, cropped hair was silk against her face as she reached for his linen shirt and found the first button with her fingers.

His lips circled her ear and then he kissed her nose and then they lingered on her lips for a moment before he moved on, to her neck behind her jaw, to the hollow at her throat. Shannon pushed the shirt from his shoulders and he lay against her, feeling her heart heaving against his, as his hands tightened around her torso.

Slowly, in circular motions, he began to explore her skin with his fingers. They edged closer to her breast and she held her breath as his hands filled her with fervor. She exhaled all in one rush as Peter felt her nipples tighten beneath his touch. "Peter. Oh, Peter." Her words were only wisps of a sound. "Please. Please. Make love to me."

For a moment, Shannon did think he had heard her. He clasped her to him and rolled to his side holding her so tightly that she couldn't breathe. He loosened his hold on her and sat up beside her as he bundled her into his arms. "Shannon. Your asking makes me so happy. That's what I want, too. I thought ... tonight ... but I can't ... I just can't, Shannon."

She wanted to cry out to him, for needing her, for not wanting her. "Peter. Don't. Don't let Lorilee come into our lives again. Not now."

"She was my wife, dammit. I can't just punch a button and turn off my memories."

"And I can't punch a button and turn off my feelings."

"I shouldn't have come." He wanted Shannon as desperately as he had wanted anything else in his life. As desperately as he had wanted Lorilee, or the baby. But he thought of loving her, of his body against hers, her arms encircling him, until he came to his final release. It wouldn't work. Being with Shannon brought back a jumble of memories of his days with Lorilee, when making love had been so easy and right ... on the big couch by the fire after Taylor was sleeping ... on the massive bed downstairs, so carefully, before he had been born. She had been such a part of him. "I can't make love to you, Shannon." For a moment, he wondered if he was trying to convince her of it, or himself.

She cradled his head tentatively in her palms. "I'm sorry, Peter. I only wanted to make it easier for you to forget. I know it must be terrible."

"You don't know." No one could feel the agony of the battle inside him. He was overcome by great waves of desire, blocked by a brick wall of guilt.

"You haven't made love to a woman since she died."

"No."

It was the first time Shannon had seen the magnitude of the things the two of them were fighting against, a past that had all but destroyed his ability to love, a future that would keep them away from each other. Peter had to be awash with feelings of guilt and unfaithfulness. She wondered if she might be the one to blame for it. What was the use in wanting him? What was the use in his healing, if they were fighting for a future that would never be?

"Hold me." She was desperate again just to feel protected by his arms. "Please just hold me."

Silently, Peter rocked her in his arms on the floor, brushing her hair back from her face until it fanned out against his arm. "I want to love you," he said at last. Shannon would have known how torn he was even if his voice hadn't been ragged. "I cannot have you."

"I know." She touched his face. It was difficult but she resolved herself to peace then, just knowing he desired her, that his heart had remained steadfast while his body had been screaming at him to take the satisfaction she offered him.

Peter was angry with himself, angry at his memories. "I shouldn't have come to you.... Perhaps I was wrong...with all the memories I'm fighting...and also wanting you."

"No." A bleak desperation welled up within her now, and Shannon's anger flared too. "Don't think it wrong. Give me some credit. I'm strong enough."

"To fight my ghosts for me? I don't think so." He glared down at her, seeing her frustration, too, but softening because he still held her next to him, because he knew she was angry but she wouldn't pull away. She was right about her strength. She had been fighting for what she believed in for so long, she was doing it now, and it frightened him . . . fascinated him . . . as he pulled away. "This isn't getting us anywhere. I'm going back to the hotel, Shannon." He waited for her reaction, but she didn't give him one. He couldn't know how hard she was fighting to mask disappointment behind an impassive face.

"I'll see you tomorrow," she said evenly. And then she got up and handed him the BEAT check he had brought her only the day before. "Thank you for this. I think it would be safer if you had a courier deliver this to Jim Clarkson after you arrive home."

"I will."

"The ground breaking," she said softly. "I didn't believe it would ever happen. But it will, won't it? You'll be there?"

"I'll be there." He buttoned his shirt and stuck the paper in his pocket.

"Thank you."

"I'm sorry."

"You were fair."

"To myself. Maybe not to you."

She gave him a sad smile. "At least we both understand that."

THE NEXT DAY was no better when they met on the concourse at the airport. Shannon was still wearing her makeup from the show and a yellow wide-brimmed hat to hide her face. "Will you watch the Viewer's Choice Awards?" It was important to her that he did, but she didn't know if she should tell him so. She didn't know if it would matter to Peter at all.

"I'll watch every minute of them." He hugged her to him then as the boarding call was announced and knocked the hat away from her face. "I'll say prayers and cross my fingers and anything else I can think of."

She eyed him sadly. "The prayers would be enough."

"You'll have them, then."

"I don't know what to say about BEAT. It's like I care...too much...like I can't let go of it enough to talk about it."

"The things you should say are right where they need to be, Shan. In your heart. Find them."

"You have too much confidence in me."

"No. Not too much. Just enough. I know how much you can do."

"Get on that airplane, Peter." She stood on tiptoe and grasped his shoulders and kissed his cheek.

He felt his resolve crumble as she touched him. To Peter, Shannon was so gentle and loving, and he would have given anything if only he'd been able to give himself to her. "We'll talk soon," he said. He hadn't known if he should offer to call her. But he knew there would be many things he'd want to share with her.

"Oh...Peter." She searched his face once more, and this time, when she grasped his arms, he clung to her and the hat fell from her head and he was kissing her and he didn't ever want to let her go.

"Get on the plane," she said against his lips. "Don't do this. Just get out of here."

"Goodbye." He gripped her arms. He could feel her blood pulsing beneath his fingers.

She was holding the hat in her hands when he finally released her. And when he turned to wave to her, she was talking to a strange woman who had stopped beside her. Someone else paused beside her, too, waving a piece of paper and then he saw her put on her hat and reach for a pen.

"Lisa Radford. Shannon Eberle." He said it under his breath to no one, as a great rush of people eddied past him. He decided he wanted to remember her like that forever, surrounded by women who thought they knew her, her hat bobbing with her head like a miniature sun.

Just as he turned to walk away, she looked up and found him in the crowd. She didn't wave at him. Her eyes locked on to his for a moment, transmitting a private message of pleading and pain between them.

He couldn't move. *She's lost here,* he thought. *She won't admit it to herself. And that's the reason she needs me.*

Shannon turned away.

"Sir?" the flight attendant taking tickets asked, "Are you boarding this flight?"

"Yes." *Is that it? We both feel we have to save the other?*

Peter handed over his boarding pass. He didn't glance back at Shannon.

He walked the long carpeted corridor to the plane and found his seat. And all he could think of was Shannon as the plane roared along the runway and then soared into the sky. All New York City was beneath him for a moment, the plane seemed to hover for an instant. And then the craft banked to the south and the buildings below him grew smaller. The city was gone. Peter was alone, going home.

CHAPTER EIGHT

THE TETONS were still visible, their tips lit by the apricot sunlight fading to the west when, at last, Peter felt the jet begin its descent into Jackson. He felt a surge of anticipation when the chiseled peaks came into view. He half expected Camille to be at the airport to greet him, with Taylor in her arms, but he had told her not to come and she had taken him at his word. Only the mountains were there to welcome him as the plane pulled into the terminal.

Peter's Jeep Cherokee was parked in the long-term parking lot. Even though it was nearing springtime in other parts of the country, it had snowed in Wyoming since he'd been gone. He kept a brush and ice scraper in the Jeep and he used them now to brush off the windows before he drove home.

Taylor was waiting for him at Camille's house. When the boy saw his father, he let out a monstrous shriek for such a little child and flung his arms wide as he ran to him. Peter lifted him up and flung him in a circle while they laughed together, and Peter finally felt warm inside, and happy, as Taylor nuzzled up under his neck, and he drank in the precious powdery, sweet smell of his child.

They drove home to the big house together. Taylor rode in his car seat in the back and Peter talked to him most of the way there, about how fast the airplane had flown and how the water had lapped against the ferry in New York. But when he pulled up to park outside the dark house and turned to his son, Taylor was asleep. He probably had been since they'd left Camille's. Peter felt suddenly and overwhelmingly lonely.

The walkway was covered with an unbroken dusting of snow. His footsteps left jagged holes in it as he carried his sleeping son to the house. He carried Taylor into the nursery, tracking snow as he went, and turned on the heater, and then he stood in the middle of the little room that had once held so much promise for the three of them, and he felt as if his heart had burst.

The telephone rang in the kitchen. It was a cheerful bell, one that came from far away. Peter's body sagged with the fatigue of his trip as he moved to answer it.

"Barrett? I've been trying to locate you." John Miller's voice boomed over the receiver.

Peter didn't answer right away. His words were stuck in his throat. *I can't face it. Now now. Not ever.*

"We have them. We're certain of it."

"How?" How could they be certain of anything, when nothing was certain anymore?

"Many small details that fit, Peter. The man worked with Lorilee on a film once when she was in Texas. We found his name on the payroll to prove it. I'm having them extradited to Wyoming immediately."

"The couple doesn't face charges in Texas?"

"Yes." Miller's voice was flat. "They face kidnapping charges. They don't face homicide charges. That's why they're letting us bring them here."

From somewhere deep in his mind, Peter managed to pull out an image of Shannon. He thought of her cozy home and her quilts and her blue country wood stove. A day of laughter. And now all the pain was beginning again. Act 2. Scene 2. Peter didn't think he could bear dealing with Lorilee's death the second time.

"I need you to come down to the courthouse Monday. They're arriving with an armed escort on the 10:35 flight. I'd like you to try to identify them in a lineup. I want to know if you've seen these two before. If their voices sound familiar. Anything you might pick up that would link them to your wife's kidnapping."

"Of course."

Miller was silent a moment. "Barrett, thank you for cooperating on this. I'm sorry to make you relive this."

"Don't apologize for doing your job."

"I'm apologizing for the pain I'm putting you through."

"Thank you, John." But it has to be finished, Peter wanted to say. It isn't going to hurt anymore. But it wasn't finished. There would be a trial. Testimony. A conviction.

For so long, he had thought of it. Finding Lorilee's captors. Finally finding justice and ending his obsession. He was exhausted by his hatred for them, by the grief of finding Shannon and being unable to fulfill her. He was a widower with a child in his care. Lorilee was gone. Nothing would change that. All he could find in his heart now, as he tried to hate them, was an empty indifference. His feelings were dead, frozen.

"Something, God." He sat at the kitchen table and buried his head in his hands while the lights glared overhead and his son slept. "Please help me feel something."

He sat there for hours, long into the night, while his mind raced and his suitcase remained in the car, grasping for answers, thinking of Shannon, doing his best to feel anything, anything, but the gnawing rock-hard

numbness that had settled firmly into the depths of his
heart.

SANDY BUDGE lay sprawled on her bed, the catalog and
course booklets from the University of Iowa spread before her. There were so many classes, classes she had
never known existed, wonderful things like literature for
children and investigative reporting and business sta-
tistics.

Growing up in Wind River, Sandy had thought the
world was only sheep...sheep's wool...lanolin...
lambing time. There was an entire world she had never
seen before, and now, on the basis of her grades at
Washakie High School, she was finally going to explore it.

The front full-color glossy in the catalog was a photo
of the dormitory she had registered to live in. It looked
like a palace with students standing beside it, all of them
smiling, toting stacks of books.

She piled the catalog and the other pamphlets next to
the notebook on her desk. She couldn't wait to show
Tommy. She'd tell him about all the classes she'd registered for. He'd be so excited for her.

But he wouldn't be going.

She decided against showing him the catalog. She
wished his grades had been better. She wished he had
spent less time working at the five-and-dime and helping his father on the farm and less time writing and
more time studying in his other classes. He was smart
enough. He could have gotten a scholarship, too.

Sandy would have given anything if the dumb BEAT
scholarships hadn't fallen through. Then, at least,
Tommy would have had a chance.

She frowned. It didn't make sense. It had been a frustrating year for all the BEAT committee members. One minute, everything had been fine, planned, under way. The next minute, there'd been no funding. When she had asked the advisers to explain what had happened, Sandy sensed that they had been purposely vague.

From the other room, the telephone rang. Sandy waited for her mother to answer it. Hers was one of the few families in Wind River with a telephone. When the phone rang again, she glanced out the window. Her mother was in the yard, coming back from the clothesline, carrying sheets that had flapped dry in the early spring wind. If it had been two degrees colder, the sheets would have frozen. Sandy went to answer the phone.

"Mrs. Budge," Jim Clarkson's voice came on the line after Sandy had said "Hello." People often confused their voices. Mother and daughter sounded very much alike. Before she could correct him, Clarkson continued. "I know Herbert is probably still out at the barn. Can you tell him that the ground breaking for the BEAT teen center has been rescheduled? We've found another investor. It isn't enough money to pay for the entire program, but it's enough to get the building under way. We want to support the kids on this. It would certainly be a show of support if Herb and the other parents who signed the petition against BEAT would come out and cheer for the bulldozers." Clarkson paused, oblivious to the look of horror that transformed Sandy's features, thinking nothing of his listener's silence. "It would be a kind gesture, after all the support he mustered with those signatures."

Sandy stood mutely, staring at the wallpaper with the tiny red flowers and strawberries, trying to comprehend the things Mr. Clarkson was saying. Her father? A petition? To stop BEAT? Why?

Her mother was now climbing the back steps. "Mr. Clarkson?" she finally said. "This is Sandy. I'm sorry. My mother was outside. She's coming in now." Her mother appeared in the doorway. "Mom." She held the receiver out. "It's for you."

Sandy ran to her room and threw the catalog and course booklet onto her bed. Pages flipped open. Covers bent. Damn. Why had he done it? Her father had ruined everything.

Her mother's voice hummed on the phone in the kitchen. Sandy slammed the back door and ran down the steps, her white athletic shoes squishing into the mud and what was left of the early-spring slush. She saw her father in the distance, bent beside the corral fence, repairing it. And as she raced toward him, she was hoping he would tell her Mr. Clarkson was wrong, that he hadn't stopped BEAT, that he hadn't kept Tommy from college.

"Halloo," he called to her. And the beginning of his smile froze on his face when his daughter came closer and he saw her expression.

Sandy stopped beside him, looking down at him while he hammered a nail into the wooden railing. "What did you do?" she screamed at him. "Why are you against BEAT?" She couldn't help but blame him for the problems they had all had, all the hassle the committee had gone through, how hard Shannon Eberle had worked, and now for Tommy's not going to college. "We worked so hard, Dad. What did you do?"

"Don't you talk that way." He laid his hammer and a handful of nails on the top post of the fence. He had known his opposition to BEAT would hurt her. His decision had been a hard one to make. "Young lady, I am your father. You change your tone of voice." He hadn't wanted someone from New York City coming in and getting the kids all excited. Chasing pipe dreams.

Sandy's hands were on her hips and her face was red and she wanted to cry but she was too angry to even let the tears flow. "Now I'm one of the only ranchers' kids in this town who's going to graduate from Washakie High and go off to college next fall. But what about the others? What about my friends that are going to be *stuck* here raising sheep because you passed around some dumb petition?"

"Sandra Kay Budge." He said her full name sternly. He almost punished her for her disrespectful words. But he knew she was old enough now to fight her own battles. All the high school seniors were. It was one of the reasons he had done what he had. "Yes. I circulated a petition. I think everyone here has the strength enough to find his own way. That actress from New York. She wanted to come in here and take everything over. If she had paid for all the things she wanted to, we'd have owed her our souls for the rest of our lives. I couldn't agree to it. What I'm talking about is pride, Sandy. *Pride*."

She stood before him, her fingers clenched, her knees locked, fierce against him and against the world. "How could you *do* it?" she bellowed at him. "Damn pride. *Damn* pride." She was furious. "I'm the only one who got a scholarship, Dad. I bet you would have felt different about it if I hadn't. You're the only one in Fremont County who didn't have anything to lose."

"Wait." He reached for her then, to tell her she was wrong, but it was too late. She had already moved too far away from him. And he could only watch her as she ran away from him, across the yard, toward the house.

PETER WAS, to all appearances, casual as he strode into the Teton County Courthouse. His hands were tucked deep inside his pockets, his head slightly bent as he squinted into the sun.

No one would have guessed how disoriented he felt. He'd been here countless times before and now he had to stop and think where the receptionist's desk was. He was heading the wrong direction. He turned down a different corridor and climbed down one flight of stairs. The receptionist smiled at him as he approached.

"Hello, Mr. Barrett. Sheriff Miller is expecting you. I'll buzz him."

"Good to see you, Peter. Thank you for coming," Miller said as he came out and grasped Peter's hand in greeting. Together, the two men walked toward the end of the corridor. "We have a lineup for you. I want you to take a good look at these folks. You might have seen some of them hanging around the bank before Lorilee was abducted . . . or you might have seen them around the house, or at church, or at the table next to yours at a restaurant. I don't want you to rule out any possibilities."

"Okay."

"I need to know if their voices sound familiar."

"I have to listen to them?"

The sheriff glanced at Peter. "Eventually." He had a habit of being brusque when he was with townspeople he knew well. He often had to remind himself to be more genial. He stopped where he stood and met Peter's eyes. Instinctively, he reached out one supportive hand and laid it on Peter's shoulder. "We'll do that part later if you like. You just give us all you've got today. We won't go any further than you want to go."

"Thanks."

The two of them entered a white room that smelled of fresh paint. *The walls have no scuffs or mars,* Peter thought. *In a place where lives are scuffed and marred each day.*

Three deputies sat in a row along a table. Miller directed Peter to his seat near a window that ran the length of one wall. They talked for a few minutes, under their breath, about nothing in particular. Miller wanted to be certain that Peter was relaxed.

The sheriff signaled to the officers behind him. An array of people, a mixture of men and women, began to file by the window.

It happened the way John Miller wanted it to happen. Peter glanced up from their conversation and glanced at the stranger's features briefly, unemotionally, the same way he would look at faces in a crowd in a shopping mall. Miller waited. But there was no reaction, no sign of recognition, no look of surprise, no glimpse of hatred.

"Nobody looks familiar?"

Peter shook his head. "No. Not anyone." He was staring at the lineup through the glass.

The clock on the town hall tower began to chime in the distance.

"Which ones are the suspects?" Peter wondered who all these people were. Most of them were probably totally unconnected with what had happened to his wife.

His wife. Lorilee. He couldn't make his memory focus on her face. She was an object, something that had belonged to him a long time ago, something he had lost.

"I don't want to tell you yet. I have tapes the FBI
made while they were conducting their investigation of
the couple in Texas. There's nothing incriminating on
them yet. The public defender has issued his permission for you to listen to them."

"They haven't hired a lawyer?"

"They can't afford one. They've been spending too
much money. New boat. Several trips to Reno and season tickets with rights to Dallas Cowboy football games.
They don't have any cash left now. It's gone. And
they've left one little boy in Texas for grandma to raise
if they can't wriggle their way out of this conviction."

A wave of distaste swept over Peter. He didn't like
Miller's attitude. These people might as well pack their
belongings and move to the state penitentiary without
the benefit of a trial. Peter was struck by a sense of ur-
gency. He wanted to end this thing. He wanted to finish it now, the same way he would have closed a book
if he found himself reading a horrible story. "Let's listen to the voices now. I'm prepared."

The Teton County prosecutor joined them and they
listened to tapes for three hours. A man spoke and then
a woman spoke. They mentioned no names. They
talked about their three-year-old son. They discussed
finding a weekend baby-sitter so they could fly to Reno
and win money shooting craps.

"Interesting family." Peter smiled despite himself.
"Is that how they bought the boat?"

"That's what they say."

Miller played the tape again at a different speed. He
muffled the speaker with a towel and then with a mechanical device. Peter was thoughtful. And then he
frowned. "Nothing. I'm sorry. They just don't sound
familiar to me."

"The man worked with your wife, Barrett." Miller was growing perturbed. "Surely you can pinpoint something."

"I can't. Nothing. I never went on location with her film company."

"Maybe she said something . . . mentioned the name Jim Brown."

"No." Peter's fist crashed down on the table. "She never mentioned that name. Bringing Lorilee into this isn't going to help me identify the man. She isn't here to help me now. I have to spot something on my own. And I don't hear or see anything or anyone familiar. Don't push me, Miller."

"I'm not pushing you."

"You can smell a conviction. You want it. You want to end this thing as badly as anyone."

"And you don't?"

Peter ran his fingers through his hair, rumpling it. "I want to be fair. I want to convict Lorilee's kidnappers. I want to put this thing behind us all. But I want to do it right."

"Isn't fairness the same as justice?" the prosecutor asked.

Peter stood from the table. "I don't know."

Miller stood beside him. "Do you want to see the suspects?"

"Yes."

They walked down another hallway.

"You have them waiting for us?"

"I'm always prepared," the sheriff's voice was level. "I was hoping we would get this far."

The couple was waiting like two trapped animals in a cage. Peter found himself wishing they would talk or move. He wished they would fight. They had been on

display all day, moving from one room with a smoky
glass to another.

*They appear where they have to appear. They feel
what they have to feel.*

Just like me.

The man's and woman's jail clothes were brown and
the room was brown and their faces were brown, too,
like stones. The woman was petite, slender. Her hair
hung in a limp sheet straight to her shoulders. Her face
was empty. The man was gaunt, as if the tension he was
facing had translated itself to his skin, stretching it even
tighter across his bones.

"They know we're watching them."

"Yes."

Peter tried to feel something. He tried to hate them.
He tried to picture them with Lorilee. They would have
been the last people to see her alive. Suddenly, from the
huge chasm within him, a feeling came. Doubt. Great
waves of it washed over him. He reeled from the force
of it. He wobbled and then regained his composure as
he turned toward the sheriff. "John. What if they didn't
do it?"

It took a full three seconds for John Miller to comprehend Peter's question. When he did, his face paled
and his eyes widened. "Barrett. You can't be thinking
that. Your wife would tell you..."

"My wife isn't here," Peter snapped, cutting him off.
"She can't tell me anything. I have to go on my own instincts."

"You're a good man, Barrett, but you can't ride on
both sides of the fence on this one. My God, man. What
if they *did?*"

"Why are you so certain of that?"

"Facts match. The gold Chevrolet Lorilee was driving was registered to this woman's mother in Texas. Credit card purchases were made and signed for by this man here in Jackson the same day your wife was abducted. We dusted the items upset in your house that day and we found this man's fingerprints." Minutes before, Peter and the sheriff had been allies. Now they were on opposite sides, facing off. And maybe Peter was right to question the facts. That was how the American judicial system worked. But too many pieces of the puzzle fitted. "You're defending people the Feds brought in as prime suspects. What's this going to look like? What do you expect me to do?"

"I want you to take this doubt out of my mind, Miller," Peter said. "I want to be that certain."

"I'm willing to convince you." The sheriff offered Peter his hand.

"I'll be in touch with you, then."

"I'll call you when we schedule the preliminary hearing."

"Thank you." Peter shook John Miller's hand. Then he shoved his arms into his pockets and strolled out of the courthouse the same casual way he had come in, his head bent against the sun, his stride relaxed, his mind racing.

THE WASHAKIE HIGH SCHOOL Marching Band clanged out the notes to the school song. Several hundred students stood in the field and sang the words to the music.

"'Old Washakie, we all love you. To thy colors, we'll all be true. Wherever we go, we lift thy shield, following always your knowledge revealed . . .'"

"Ah, how I love corny high school songs," Cal Gleason said, grinning. "I wonder how many of those kids are really singing the lyrics."

"More than you might think." Peter bundled his jacket around him. It was a March day, the sky crystal blue, the temperature almost warm. He and Cal had driven almost three hours to be a part of the teen center ground-breaking ceremony. "This is a big event in the history of this little town."

Tommy Eberle appeared at Cal Gleason's side. "Mr. Gleason?" This was supposed to be Sandy's job but she hadn't come. "We're ready to begin. Will you turn the first shovel of dirt?" Tommy didn't know why Sandy wasn't here. Her father had come, along with a group of other parents, who were gathered together in a little group alongside one of the huge bulldozers.

"Surely there must be someone more qualified to break ground for you. I came to dig, but there must be someone else to turn the first sod."

Peter winked at his associate. "Go ahead, Gleason. You sent a big check for this project. You get to dig in the dirt before the rest of us. You paid for the privilege."

"If you put it that way, I will do it."

Tommy handed him a new shovel embellished with a huge gold and blue bow. "If you'll come with me."

The band began playing the national anthem while Peter watched the two of them walking toward a platform, side by side. Shannon should have been the one walking forward beside Tommy, the shovel in her hand. She had paid for the privilege, too, with her heart.

Peter had tried to coax her to come. "You should be there," he had urged her when he called her the week the ground breaking had finally been scheduled. "It's happening. And it's really all your fault."

"No. I won't come." Only Peter knew how desperately she wanted to.

"I'd like you to be there so I can see you."

"What for? So we can hurt each other one more time? I don't think so. That's all the more reason for me to stay in New York."

"I'd like to see you come and finish what you started."

"You and Cal Gleason can finish it."

"Shannon, please. Come be a part of this. You can work out a way to be here."

Shannon would have given anything to have been with Peter and the BEAT kids. But she couldn't face Peter. She was angry and happy every time she talked to him on the telephone. But she could control her voice. Standing beside him without wanting to touch him was impossible. She couldn't do it. And she cared too much about him to let him see the discord he caused inside her. He would blame himself for her conflict. And the last thing Peter needed now was something more to feel guilty for, so she hadn't gone.

Peter stood shading his eyes with one hand while Cal Gleason stomped against the shovel with his shoe. Grass and roots ripped apart beneath the blade. Gleason pushed against the tool with both hands as the rending sound continued. The ground sliced open at last and Cal Gleason raised a shovelful of soil over his head. The teachers applauded and the Washakie High School students cheered as the yellow bulldozers stood by, waiting to turn the bare ground into a building. And all Peter could think of was Shannon and her dreams.

"YOU NEVER HEARD Lorilee mention anyone named Jim Brown?" Peter was questioning Sylvia Saunders, Lorilee's mother, over the phone.

"Never, son. He must have been someone she hired on location. She did that often, you know."

"I know. He has to be the man they say he is or they wouldn't be holding him for a preliminary hearing. I wish I was more certain of everything."

Sylvia's voice was warm over the miles. She loved Peter. He would always be her son, the father of her grandchild, even though her daughter was gone. The two of them had made a promise to continue on as family at Lorilee's funeral. Sylvia had her own pain to work through, but she had been desperately sorry for her son-in-law. "Maybe you don't have to be so certain anymore."

"The Browns have a child. Another little boy just like Taylor, one who will live without his parents if the jury comes back with a conviction."

"Are you feeling your doubts on account of the child?"

"If this thing goes far enough, he won't have a mother, either."

"Yes. But his mother made a choice," Sylvia said firmly. "She may have decided that money was more important than being around for her son's future."

"Lorilee had no choices." Peter's voice was grim.

"Peter. She did."

"How can you say that? What were they?"

"You don't know?" she asked sadly. "My daughter could have done several things differently that afternoon. She could have fought them harder. She could have talked to them and asked them to release her. She could have stayed where she was and waited for you to get the money to the kidnappers. She knew you had access to your father's funds. She knew you loved her enough to pay for her. But she didn't wait for you. She made a choice to escape. You did not make it for her." It was the first time Sylvia realized the depth of Peter's guilt.

Peter's voice was monotone as he listed other possibilities. "She could have walked and hidden in the trees instead of taking the car. She could have driven more carefully."

"Yes. Peter, yes."

"You don't hold me responsible for the death of your daughter?"

"I don't. Neither does Carl. We love you, Peter. You are a member of our family. And we know how much you loved Lorilee."

"But how can my wife be responsible for a choice when she didn't consider the outcome?" So often he had pictured Lorilee buffeted by other people and outside events that day. He hadn't stopped to think she had made decisions of her own.

"That's the way life is, Peter. The large decisions we wrangle over for days often don't change a thing. The small choices that are made in an instant are the ones that shape our futures."

"I could have done something. I could have hired bodyguards for her. I could have stayed at the house with her. I could have told Dad I didn't want to be president of the bank." Peter had been running the list of coulds and shoulds through his head constantly lately. He should have been stronger. He should have been smarter. He should have reacted faster.

"Tell me," his mother-in-law demanded, "if you could have done anything differently that day. Tell me what it would have been."

From somewhere deep inside him, a tide was beginning to rise, a buoyancy within him that was easing away portions of his grief and his guilt. "Sylvia. I honestly don't know," Peter said, his words whispered, and Sylvia had to strain to hear him over the miles.

CHAPTER NINE

"YOU WERE RIGHT, Peter! It came so easily." Shannon had been awake all night, sitting at a little antique desk beside the wood stove writing her Viewer's Choice acceptance speech. "All the things I wanted to say." Her voice was breathless with an edge of anticipation in it that was infectious, like a child's voice on Christmas Eve. Peter smiled and tried to picture what she must have looked like, standing at the telephone, rumpled and without sleep, with the traffic streaming past below her window. "Now if I can just say it the right way. If I get the chance to say it at all."

It was so much like her, he decided. The Viewer's Choice Awards ceremony was only hours away. And Shannon wasn't thinking in terms of victory or defeat. She was thinking past that, to a shining moment when she might be standing on stage to tell all of America what was in her heart.

"Have you talked to your family this morning?" It was just past seven a.m. in Wyoming, just past nine in New York. The studio was closed for the day. Mark Troy wanted the "Wayward Hopes" cast at the Waldorf-Astoria to cheer Shannon on. Al was escorting her to the event. It would have been crazy to try to tape the show around them all.

"Dad called first thing this morning. He woke me up at six-thirty." Shannon was so excited that she was giggling and she sounded like a happy bird. "He said he wanted to talk to somebody who had more talent than his ewes."

"What a compliment." Peter was laughing, too. "I'll be watching this afternoon," he promised. His tone was even but in truth he was almost as excited as she was. He had planned his entire day around Shannon's victory. He was going in to the office this morning. He was coming home shortly after lunch. Taylor would be sleeping then. He'd told Camille she could have the afternoon off.

Peter had a desperate need to be alone when he watched her. He had watched Shannon on "Wayward Hopes" several times since he had come home from New York. He always came away from the show with a haunting discontent. He hadn't been watching Shannon. He had been watching a character, someone he didn't know, saying things Shannon wouldn't say. It unnerved him, watching her, thinking of how much he missed her and not quite knowing who she was.

Today would be different. Today the person on the screen would be Shannon Eberle, with no costumes other than the one she had selected, with no lines other than her own.

"Peter, I'm so scared." It seemed to Shannon as if he was the only person in the world who knew what she was fighting for and why. He was the only person in the world who knew what standing behind that podium with the award in her hand would mean to her. She hadn't told anyone at home what she planned to do. And she hadn't told anyone at the studio, either. She didn't want anyone dissuading her from saying the things she had to say.

"Don't be. Taylor and I are rooting for you with pom-poms."

"Let's hope the voters were on my side, too."

"I should hang up," he said at last. "I know you have lots to do."

"Not really." Shannon sounded forlorn. Peter could guess how lonely she was. She would have probably given anything to have been surrounded by her family. The day stretched before her like a wedding day. Everything was prepared. Nothing was left for Shannon to do except slip the dress over her shoulders and hold on to the people she loved. Only the people she loved were thousands of miles away.

He held his breath for a moment before he spoke to her. He didn't know if he should tell her what he was thinking. And when he did, he didn't know if he was saying it for her benefit or for his own. "If you win, you ought to come home and have a party."

Shannon laughed, a sad little tinkling sound that might have been glass shattering. "There will be enough parties here, thank you. And none I really want to attend."

"WE WELCOME YOU to this special broadcast," an announcer's voice informed viewers as the network's logo spun into view. "Live from the beautiful Waldorf-Astoria Hotel in the heart of New York City... The Viewer's Choice Awards." The music swelled as the screen filled with glitter... a ballroom... multitiered crystal chandeliers and golden gowns. Peter felt as if he was watching a modern-day version of Cinderella.

Where was she? Without the camera focusing on her, he'd never find Shannon in the crowd. Adrenaline was shooting through his body. He had to remind himself to breathe.

"Here are scenes from moments ago," the announcer said. "Fans have been waiting outside all morning, hoping for a glimpse of their favorite daytime stars." The picture switched from the blazing ballroom to an outdoor canopied walkway lined with people. A limousine swept to the curb in a ripple of chrome and polish that sent shards of light into the camera lens. A man and woman emerged from the back seat as people around them applauded. Another limousine arrived. Three more actresses alighted.

A chant rose from the crowd. "We love 'Wayward Hopes'... We love 'Wayward Hopes'...*Li*-sa...*Li*-sa..."

Peter's heart stopped when he realized what they were saying. They were calling for Shannon. A third limo waited at the curb and Shannon was in it. They were screaming for her, wanting her.

The chauffeur got out of the car and moved around to open the back door. Al Jensen stepped out first. Peter saw Shannon's hand flutter against his sleeve and then she appeared, her dress a pillar of crimson. The crowd was calling her name as she turned to the spectators and waved, the lights and reflected flashbulbs dancing against her dress. She leaned toward Al Jensen and whispered something. Her director nodded as he led her toward the door.

Only when Peter felt actual discomfort did he realize he was gripping the sofa's arm. His knuckles were white. Shannon grew more of a treasure to him every time he saw another facet of her. Knowing her was like peering through a kaleidoscope, the colors proudly displayed in ever-changing patterns. Today she was sparkling and stunning and strong. She was mentally prepared for disappointment or for elation. Peter wondered if he was the only one who understood how much BEAT still meant to her. The bulldozers were in Wind River on the lot digging a basement that very moment, while she sat helplessly in the ballroom beside her director...waiting...wishing...praying for something more than a miracle.

Shannon disappeared into the doorway then and Peter caught one more glimpse of her before the picture faded, her dark hair a sable mantle against her neck, the skin of her shoulders the translucent color of coffee with cream.

Peter turned away from the television screen. A month ago, he had held her in his arms and touched her and felt her come alive beneath his hands. Now he felt as if she belonged to everyone else in the world except him. "Dammit." He slammed his fist against the coffee table and sent what was left of Taylor's blocks flying. He had no right to want Shannon Eberle. No right.

Peter sat crouched on the sofa, hating the announcer who talked as if he knew Shannon well. He sat through the best writing awards, the best game show awards, the best ingenue awards and, during breaks in the show, five different laundry detergent commercials. Apprehension grew within him. What if it didn't happen for her? What if she never got the chance to make her speech? He was suddenly desperate to be there for her, to hold her when everything fell through, to tell her...to tell her what? That he cared about her? That she would always have a home in Wyoming no matter how many high school kids went to hell in a hand basket?

His life was changing. The thought came to him as if a mental cue card had been jammed in front of his face. He was willing to fight for her. He was willing to fight for a great many things.

The camera panned the crowd. Peter glimpsed the familiar crimson of her dress. She and Al were sitting near the center of the stage five rows back. As he watched, the cameras focused on her and zoomed in on her face. She didn't know she was on camera. She was clapping for one of her colleagues, her presence captured poised and perfect on the screen. Peter thought of the day they had skied together. Shannon and her speeches. *The goodness of life.* He thought of her red nose and her hair tangled beneath the Ragg wool cap.

God, he wanted to watch her win.

"Ladies and Gentlemen—" A game-show host stood at the podium and gave the camera a wide smile. "The nominees for Best Actress in a Daytime Drama are—"

The man read several names Peter didn't recognize as the camera focused on unfamiliar faces. Then, with great flourish he pronounced, "From 'Wayward Hopes,' Miss Shannon Eberle."

The cameras caught Shannon's expression as the other contenders applauded. She nodded at the man on the podium. She knew the camera was on her. She stared straight ahead, her head cocked, her lips in a tight smile of anticipation, her hand with her crimson-glossed nails clutching Al Jensen's sleeve.

"And the winner is . . ." The host tore open an envelope. Shannon didn't move. The screen divided into four boxes, one box for each nominee. The cameramen wanted to catch every nuance . . . the rush of reality . . . the winner . . . the downward nod of disappointment and obligatory clapping of the losers.

Please. Peter was praying. *Do it for her, God. Please.*

The announcer pulled a slip of paper from the envelope. He paused as he read it. Peter felt every one of his muscles tense. On camera, Shannon lifted her chin slightly.

"From 'Wayward Hopes,' Shannon Eberle."

The orchestra broke into a fast-paced rendition of the "Wayward Hopes" theme song. There were hands from all directions pushing Shannon, grabbing at her, holding her. She was rising now, the dress falling in a shaft of red light around her, the one sleeved arm reaching for Eddie who waited to hug her in the aisle. Then she was moving toward the stage, gracefully, her hair gleaming, her head erect, her smile much wider now. She bounded up the stairway onto the stage and reached out both arms for the gold statue that belonged to her now. She held it at arm's length while she pivoted toward the cameras and the lights and the microphone.

"Thank you so much," she said, her voice husky. She hesitated. "To my producer, Al Jensen...to the writers...to my family in Wyoming...to our incredible cast of actors and actresses on the show..." Peter could see her trembling as her eyes scanned the rows of people sitting below her. "I wish my brother was here. Tommy." Peter could tell how disoriented she was. The reality of the win hadn't hit her yet. She was right where she had wanted to be. The Viewer's Choice Award was shining in her hands. "There have been a number of people in my lifetime who have loved me enough to guide me." Her voice was low. The applause died down and the room was silent except for Shannon's words, words that rose over the crowd of people, her voice suddenly soaring, clear and strong. "There are kids all across America who have the right to wish for this, the right to dream, just as I did...."

Peter saw her eyes focus and knew she was seeing more than the faces before her. She was imagining a childhood come alive again. She was tasting old defeats even in the face of this one brilliant victory. She was envisioning a white clapboard house circled by waves of native grasses. She was seeing the people who loved her.

Quickly, she defined the BEAT program.

"The ground has been broken for the new BEAT Teen Center. What BEAT needs now is money for scholarships, awards like this one—" she raised the Viewer's Choice award higher "—to help the outstanding performers.

"BEAT fights to replace low self-esteem with the power of vision. It needs volunteers like Edwina Cox—" she pointed to her best friend in the audience "—who has volunteered to fly to Wyoming and teach an acting workshop to teens who might never have had that opportunity otherwise. BEAT could become a national network, governed by teens, built by teens. We need funds from you to make this happen—" she toasted the audience with the Best Actress award she held in her hand "—for all of them."

There was silence in the great hall.

"Thank you."

Shannon walked off stage. For a moment, the camera didn't follow her. The cameraman was still, the same as the stars and producers, the writers and the advertisers who had heard her speak.

Shannon's speech had taken four minutes.

The camera found her again, halfway up the aisle. People all around her were standing, giving her an ovation for the things she had said.

She had done it. What a victory she had won. What a grand power she possessed. Peter knew he had witnessed perhaps her greatest act of leadership. She had given away her own glory. She had used it to motivate her peers.

"Shannon Eberle for president," he whispered to himself. And then he buried his head in his hands and drew a long, ragged breath as the television blared before him.

"MOMMA? I can't hear you."

"It's okay," Agatha Eberle shouted into the receiver. "Go back to your party. It was wonderful of you to call. We're so proud of you." Shannon's entire family had driven to the pay phone at the gas station as soon as the show was over. She had promised to telephone them there if she won.

"What did Tommy do?"

"What do you think? He shouted and danced around the room."

"Good."

"The basement in the teen center is almost finished. Your father is going to help with the bricks tomorrow."

"I'm sorry. I can't hear you. I love you, Mom. Give everybody a hug."

"I will!" Agatha shouted as a huge truck barreled past. "I always do!"

Shannon waited a moment before dialing Peter's number, listening to the crackle in the receiver after her mother had broken their connection. She was homesick. But when Peter answered his telephone on the first ring, she forgot about feeling alone.

"Shan. You *did* it."

"Did you watch?"

"All of it. You were wonderful."

Shannon giggled. "I'm still wonderful. I'm still here."

"Not on my TV set you're not."

"Was it really okay?"

"It was perfect."

"I can hardly hear you. We're having a celebration."

Eddie gripped Shannon's arm. "Get off the phone, you crazy. The Dom Perignon is flowing. Everyone is asking for you."

"It sounds like a great party," Peter said, overhearing.

"I have to go."

"I know." She had to go back to her life. "Give yourself a big hug for us. From me and Taylor."

"I will."

Eddie was at Shannon's side, handing her a goblet of champagne. "Get off the *phone*. Why didn't you tell anybody you were going to do that?"

Shannon hung up the receiver gently. She was longing for them all again, her parents and Peter, and a place where lives were quiet and simple.

"I thought I was going to *die* when you started talking. You and your causes."

Shannon stared at the glittering liquid in her glass. She imagined facets of her own life there, Peter's face, home. She gave Eddie the steadiest smile she could muster. "You're my best friend, Eddie. You know where my priorities are."

"You used *my name*." She was teasing Shannon now, doing her best to bait her out of the pensive mood she didn't understand. "You told millions of Americans I volunteered for the job. Anyone present during that conversation would tell you I was hog-tied."

Shannon grinned. "You said you wanted to go fishing. Remember?"

"Right. I volunteered to pull slimy fish out of a stream in Wyoming. It must have slipped my mind."

"Eddie? Did I make a fool of myself?"

"No." Eddie smiled then, her admiration for her friend evident. "You were wonderful. You're one of the bravest people I know."

"I'm not brave," Shannon said quietly. Eddie could barely hear her over the roar of the voices in the room.

"Well, I love you no matter what." Eddie squeezed Shannon in an emphatic hug.

Al Jensen joined them. "Well, Miss Eberle," he said, giving Shannon a little salute. "It was an honor to escort you this evening. It's an honor to have you starring in my show." He kissed her hand.

"Cut out the dramatics." She gave him a light punch in the stomach. Al had always been a second father to her and she knew she owed much of her success to him.

Several men walked toward them through the crowd. "Everybody behave," Eddie said, her voice low. "Here come all the network execs."

Shannon snapped to attention. Mark Troy was "Wayward Hopes'" executive producer. He was the one who had made the final decision about hiring her. "Hello," he said to them. Then he turned to introduce Shannon to the network's president of daytime programming. "Congratulations," the man said. "You've done a fine job for us."

"Thank you."

A woman appeared beside Troy. "Ah," the executive producer smiled smoothly. "Here's someone else you need to meet. Gabrielle Cohen. She's another director, Jensen." He gestured toward Al.

Eddie winced and whispered to Shannon, "Gabrielle Cohen. They call her 'Gabby the Saber-Tooth' when she works."

Al extended his hand to the petite brunette. "What are you up to these days, Gabby?"

Gabrielle eyed him coolly. "I'm in a period of transition."

Al nodded. "I hope you find what you're looking for." She had just finished a dramatic series for teenagers for a pay-television network. He had read about it in a trade publication.

"Accept my congratulations again, Miss Eberle," Mark Troy said and nodded briskly as Al and Eddie looked on. "Your award and your speech are both victories for 'Wayward Hopes.'"

"Thank you."

"I don't believe you have any idea what you've just done for us."

Shannon looked at the executive producer blankly. "No. I don't."

"You've thrown open a market we've been trying to penetrate for months."

"I don't understand."

"Your Q Rating is already high, Miss Eberle." The subject was something they didn't talk about openly often, but the "personality quotient" that Nielson gave each of them after randomly surveying viewers constantly hung over the actors' heads. Their "Q Rating" was a horrible, scary, personal thing.... It affected their pay…their contract negotiations…how they slept at night, everything. It was something Shannon did her best to ignore. "Any teenage girl in America who does not adore you after that little speech today is going to be way out of step. Any one of them who does not videotape 'Wayward Hopes' so she can watch it when she arrives home from school is going to be a social outcast. In four minutes, you've become the spokeswoman for them all. It's what we've wanted for months, something to grab teen viewers, something to keep them, something to make them want us. And you've done it." Mark Troy gave her a slow smile. "You have flung the door wide open. A teen following on a daytime drama opens up marketing and advertising possibilities network advertising execs dream of."

Shannon's voice was soft but strong. "That was not what I intended to do, Mr. Troy. Advertisements foster teen conformity, and BEAT dares teens not to conform."

"Go with it." Al Jensen laughed and nudged her in the ribs, doing his best to make light of the discussion, to placate Mark Troy. The man could fire them all on the spot if he wanted to. "It's great. Just go with it."

"Don't you see?" Troy's voice was smooth and he made Shannon want to back away. "There is a certain conformity…even in nonconformity." He turned, his movements almost military, synchronized with the other executives and Gabrielle Cohen, who was still at his side, and silently they all walked away.

"I think I'm fighting against people like that," Shannon whispered to Eddie after they had gone. She didn't know whether to laugh or cry.

"Advertising dollars," Al sang, doing a little dance step around them all, "I love advertising dollars."

"I'm in the wrong business," Shannon said wryly.

"No." A dainty hand touched her bare shoulder. "You aren't." The woman at Shannon's side wore a fluffy cloud of a dress that seemed to revolve around her tiny frame when she moved. Everything about her matched her delicate voice. "I'm Daphne Roberts."

Shannon knew the young woman's reputation well. "I like your work, Daphne." The actress had started out as a day player, a walk-on, and now she had a recurring minimum guarantee the same as Shannon. She was a twenty-four-year-old who played an ingenue. There was something ethereal about her that made the men who watched her and the men in the cast all want to take care of her.

"Congratulations on your award. Someday I want to win that one." She pointed to the statue Al Jensen clutched in his hand. "I wanted to sneak through the crowd and give you this." Daphne pressed an envelope into Shannon's palm. "It's for BEAT. I grew up in Cincinatti. When my friends at school found out I wanted to come to New York to be a dancer, they laughed at me. I never did make the dance company. I started doing this instead. I'm happy now. But I'd like to do something for some kid whose parents can't afford ballet lessons."

"Daphne Roberts!" Shannon felt her heart wrenching free of a weight that had bound it inside of her. Her eyes brimmed with tears. "Are you certain?"

"Never more certain in my life. Please, Miss Eberle. Take it."

Shannon ripped open the envelope. The check fluttered out at her, as if it was a bird or something else that had taken on a life for her and had sprouted wings. The check was in the amount of $30,000.

Daphne extended her arms, a dainty circle that encompassed them both.

The hug gave Shannon just enough strength to smile again, to stand proud and poised surrounded by groups of admirers and writers and production staff. People milled around her all evening as if they were milling around a prize exhibit at a museum.

Shannon imagined they were the sea's waves lapping against her, wearing her away, pulling her in, as they moved toward her, at the edge of a magic circle, and exclaimed over her golden award.

CHAPTER TEN

THE TELEPHONE woke Shannon. It was six-fifteen a.m. She reached for the receiver beside the bed. It rang three more times before she could find it. When she picked it up, the person on the other end did not give her a chance to say anything.

"Shannon Eberle." The voice was angry. It took her a full minute to identify its owner. Joe Mistral, the president of the Actors' Guild. "I can't believe you pulled a stunt like this. I thought you were one of the most ethical people we had in our membership. Apparently not." He had always respected Shannon. He thought she was honest and beautiful and wonderful in her role. But this morning's *New York Globe* had changed his opinion. That and the telephone calls he had been receiving since five this morning when the paper first hit the newsstands. He hadn't been awake at first and he had felt so outraged that he had wanted to throttle the callers and tell them all they were wrong about her. But he couldn't argue with the *New York Globe*, even though the story's sources were anonymous.

Shannon sat straight up in bed, not fully awake and not knowing what was wrong. She didn't understand why Joe Mistral sounded so furious. As he continued talking, the color drained from her face.

"Joe." She tried to interrupt his tirade. "Joe. You know me. I wouldn't do anything unethical." Shannon was pleading with him now and she wasn't even certain what for. She couldn't say anything intelligent now, not when she had awakened from a dead sleep and she hadn't even seen the newspaper. "Joe. I can't explain anything to you. I have to see the story first, to see what you're talking about."

Shannon hung up after promising to call later and pulled on a pair of jeans and a sweater. She knew she could find a copy of the *Globe* at the newsstand just outside. She purchased the morning's issue and carried it back upstairs. Then she plopped on the bed and unfolded it. And when she saw the story, she didn't want to touch the paper as it lay there, in her house, on her bed, taunting her. She sat against the pillows, silent tears of anger coursing down her face.

"Viewer's Choice award-winning actress takes kickbacks for speech, advertising hype," the headline read. It was on the first page of the entertainment section, where everyone would read it.

Shannon Eberle, female star of the popular daytime drama "Wayward Hopes" and recipient of the Best Actress Award at yesterday's Viewer's Choice Awards, made a speech touting teens in return for advertising contracts for the show, industry insiders say.

Sources who asked not to be identified say Whitney and Williams, the show's major sponsor, agreed to triple advertising revenues for "Wayward Hopes" only minutes after Eberle completed her presentation. Whitney and Williams has been "Wayward Hopes'" primary advertising sponsor

since 1978, and the company is actively trying to
enlarge its teenage market share.
    Eberle, 28, made her remarks while accept-
ing...''

Shannon couldn't read any further. She couldn't believe anyone would take something so obviously positive and turn it into this. No one from her own cast and
crew had even known she was going to make the speech.
Most of the facts in the article were technically correct.
But someone had lined up the facts and had reordered
them to create a story that was fiction. Several people
at the party last night had agreed to donate funds for
BEAT. Now this story could kill everything she had
been working for.
    She reached for the telephone and dialed her agent,
Larry Wills. ''Shannon? It isn't even seven yet. What's
wrong?''
    ''Has your paper boy delivered the *Globe*?''
    ''Yes.... Just a minute....''
    ''Read it. The first page of the entertainment sec-
tion. Explain to me what this is going to do to my career.''
    Larry was silent while he scanned the article. ''Shan-
non, who would have done this?''
    ''Nice little fairy tale, isn't it?''
    ''Someone is after your career.''
    ''Larry. I care about my career. I also care about
what this is going to do to BEAT. Help me.'' Her voice
was tiny and she was frightened and Larry wanted to
ball up his fist and slug the whole world for her.
    ''You've got to get to the paper and have them re-
tract that article.''
    ''How?''

"You can start by telling your side of the story. And you can finish by threatening to sue them. And somewhere in the middle, maybe we can find a lawyer who will make them reveal their sources." But Larry knew resolving the matter wasn't as easy as he made it sound. Reporters sometimes went to jail to keep from revealing sources. And if Shannon sued the *Globe*, she would have to prove not only that the story was false but that it had been published with malicious intent. "How does that sound?"

"Horrible."

"It might be your only option."

"What do I do now?"

"I'll telephone Max Phillips. He's the best libel lawyer in this country."

Shannon was crying again, but she didn't want him to know it. "I haven't even eaten breakfast yet," she told him. "Boy, the cereal sure is going to taste good this morning."

"Do you want me to send somebody over to field your phone calls?"

"No. I'll answer them." She would face this the same way she faced everything else. Head-on. The people who had agreed to donate BEAT money would call. Or they would have their lawyers call. She needed to telephone the network's legal advisers. And maybe a reporter from the *Globe* would call, too.

The phone rang again the moment the line was free. It was Al Jenson. "Shannon? Are you okay?"

"No. I'm not. I'm just sitting here enjoying my new outlaw image."

"Somebody's after the show, Shannon. It isn't your job that's in trouble. It's mine. Someone was sharp

enough to step in last night and use the stage you set.
I'm sorry. I know how much BEAT means to you.

"Joe Mistral from the guild called first thing to
complain about my ethics."

"I've consulted our legal adviser. He expects this to
heat up into a national news story. A major network
sues a major newspaper. The media goes after itself.
This one has definite public appeal."

"Larry is talking to a lawyer on my behalf, too."

"When you talk to him, have him call the network.
The adviser on this end wants to make certain everybody's story is the same. At this point, he's hoping we
can threaten a suit and force the newspaper to print a
retraction."

Shannon didn't want to go through this. The dam-
age to BEAT had already been done. And when Max
Phillips called from Washington, D.C., he made her feel
even worse. "You know you can walk away from this
thing with more money in your pockets than you've ever
dreamed of."

"I've lost a great deal," she said slowly. "I have no
desire to lose my integrity as well. I want you to threaten
the *Globe* with a lawsuit, Mr. Phillips. Just threaten.
I'm guessing they'll print a retraction. And don't do a
thing until you've talked to the network's legal advisers."

Four hours later, the story of the complaints against
Shannon and the threat of a media lawsuit filtered out
over the national newswires. Reporters from two
national television news programs telephoned her and
requested interviews. She agreed to both of them. One
was scheduled to air that evening. The other would air
the following morning.

One by one, Shannon telephoned the actors and other people in the industry who had agreed to donate money to BEAT. "I'm sorry," she told each of them in a stoic voice after she explained the news story. "I will not accept what someone has done to me. But I can't jeopardize the teen program by taking money for it now." She thought it only fair to give each of them an opportunity to cancel their commitment. And after the fourth person told her he would withhold his donation until his lawyer did more research into BEAT's background, she slammed her fist on the table so hard that she toppled the vase of "good luck" flowers Eddie had brought to her the day before.

The last person on her list was Daphne Roberts. Shannon telephoned her at the studio, but she was taping the show and they couldn't interrupt her. There was nothing more Shannon could do. Despairing, she sat at the kitchen table.

The next time her telephone rang, Shannon almost didn't a answer it. She picked up the line after twelve rings. It was her father. "I just heard about it on the noon news. I love you. Everyone here knows you did the right thing."

"Thank you, Dad."

"Your brother wants to talk to you."

Tommy came on the line next, and Shannon was so glad to hear his voice that she almost laughed with pleasure. "You were wonderful yesterday, Shan," he told her. "We all watched and Mom made gallons of popcorn and when you won I jumped around and so did Dad and the popcorn was flying everywhere. And then we all walked to the gas station because you told Mom you'd call there."

Shannon smiled. "Mom told me you jumped around. She didn't tell me you had a popcorn fight."

"It was mostly Dad. He had a big bowl in his lap when you won. He forgot it was there and he jumped up—"

"Your mother promised not to tell her that story!" Shannon heard Daniel Eberle bellow in the background. "I should have known somebody in this family would let it slip."

"Wiley had a great time, though," Tommy said, chuckling. "The old dog got to eat all the popcorn off the floor."

Suddenly, a great, hollow sadness filled her as her brother laughed. They were so far away living a life that didn't belong to her any longer. She had lost that part of herself, too.

"Shannon," Tommy was saying, "thank you for everything you've given me. You just won the greatest award you'll ever win in your life and you stood up and talked about us. Thanks."

Was I really giving you something? Or was I just trying to hang on to you? Shannon felt her insides crumpling like paper. The last bit of her strength ebbed away. She fought to keep her voice steady despite the angry tears welling in her eyes. *No,* she protested silently after the line had gone dead between them, *someone had no right to take that part of myself away from me.*

PETER GLARED at the nightly news. A handsome anchorman with a perfect voice was telling Shannon's life story. Peter felt isolated and helpless. The camera switched and Shannon's face filled the screen as she sat on the set, a microphone attached to the collar of her blouse. He clenched his fists at his sides. It was all he could do to keep from smashing his knuckles through the television set in a demented attempt to reach for her. She looked so frightened, and she was as pale as ivory china under the lights.

"What have they done to her?" he asked aloud. He stared at her, transfixed, feeling empty and unprotected, as if life was dashing against both of them, a huge wave, as they flailed against it.

He closed his eyes and gritted his teeth, as if the sheer effort might communicate his thoughts to her. Shannon today was a different person from the composed, beautiful woman he had seen accept the Best Actress award only yesterday. She had been glowing then, embracing the life she believed in. But now it was gone. In its place was nothing, that same horrible numbness Peter had lived with for so long. He knew the look of it. He could see it in the flatness of her eyes and he could hear it in the dull sound of her voice, and he felt a new desperation to help her rising within him.

Peter's hands were shaking as they opened the phone directories and struggled to find a pen that worked. He scribbled with three of them before he found one that would write. There were two commercial flights leaving Jackson this evening, he recalled. Peter was certain both would arrive in Denver or Salt Lake City too late to make a connection to New York. He pulled out a leather-bound business-card file. He flipped through it until he found the card he needed. Sparky Hansen. Chartered flights.

He dialed the number. "Hello, Sparky. Peter Barrett here. How fast can you get me to New York City?"

"You want to go *tonight?*"

"I want to go immediately."

"I'll meet you at the airport. It will take an hour to file a flight plan and fuel the plane. I could have you off the ground by 6:45. The flight takes a little over five hours. That puts us into LaGuardia in the wee hours of the morning."

"We'll do it." It wasn't soon enough but it would have to do. Then Peter frowned, thinking of something else. "I plan to bring a woman back with me. Is that a problem?" If he could just get Shannon away from a life where she was on constant display, a city where strangers thought they knew her and a career that was tearing her apart as a vulture might pull apart its prey.

It was only after he made final arrangements with the pilot that Peter thought about his son, the little boy he loved so much, who was sitting in the high chair eating the noodles and meat that Peter had prepared for him. He had called Camille early in the afternoon and told her not to cook supper for them, that he wanted to do it himself. It was unusual for him to be brave enough to fool around in the kitchen. But he was determined to show his love for his son, to reach out and begin to nurture him the way Lorilee would have done if they had still been a family.

For a moment Peter toyed with the idea of transporting Taylor to New York with him. But, in the end, he decided against it. There was no telling what Shannon's schedule might be in the next days. And he wanted to be there for her, whenever she needed him, instead of caring for his son.

He telephoned Camille, explained the situation, and asked her if Taylor could stay with her. When she consented merrily, he rushed together his things and the baby's, the diapers and the fuzzy pajamas with little ~~p trucks all over then, the blanket and a bottle. He delivered Taylor to Camille's house and he was at the airport by six-thirty. He felt afraid for a moment, just waiting there, while mechanics filled the little jet with fuel and Sparky Hansen walked around the craft with a clipboard, knowing he was soon going to see Shannon, and now knowing what she would say.

By six-fifty they were in the air and Peter felt suddenly unencumbered as the little craft climbed into the sky, as if the plane had taken off and he had taken off, too, for a new world, a new place, where he no longer felt buffeted by his own guilt, where his old ties weren't painful any longer, instead only memories that made him strong.

HERBERT BUDGE sat at the kitchen table paying his bills. His wife, Nancy, stood at the stove beside him, stirring round steak and a thick mixture of tomato paste and green peppers.

Herb sighed and slapped one more windowed envelope down onto the pile. "We're going to have to sell some of the ewes before Sandy leaves for college. I don't see any way else to do it." Sandy had gotten a complete scholarship. But there were so many expenses they would have to meet when the time for school came, things he hadn't thought of before—moving expenses, her supplies and books, and she would need a new coat, too.

"Won't that make us short next lambing season?" his wife asked from over the sizzling pan.

"We will have to rebuild a bit. Yes."

"Perhaps we could ask my father for help." Sandy's grandfather had a fund he was keeping to help Sandy through college.

But Herbert Budge shook his head. "No. I don't want to ask for help right away. I want to wait on that until…" He was going to say, until we really need it, but he stopped when he saw Sandy standing in the doorway. "Did you finish your work in the barn?"

"Yes, I did." His daughter still held a bucket in one hand. She had been out cleaning stalls, pulling out the musty straw and replacing it with fresh hay from the bales they had cut last August. She didn't smile at him. Recently, she made a practice of not smiling at him. She had stayed angry at him for weeks. She had missed the BEAT ground breaking, too, because she didn't want to stand with him, and with all the other parents who had been so against their own sons and daughters.

Her friendship with Tommy had suffered. She hadn't told anyone what the group of parents had done. Sandy didn't know how she would tell any of her friends. But mostly Tommy was the one person she didn't want to know the truth. And when she held herself back from him because she didn't feel she was being honest with him, a little portion of their friendship slipped away.

"Are you hungry?" her mother asked, trying to break the difficult silence. Anyone who spent two minutes in a room with Sandy and her father was aware of the tension between them.

"No. Not really," Sandy said. But she was. Supper smelled delicious. But she wasn't going to say so in front of *him*.

Herbert Budge's brows knitted together. This was not the evening to cross him. He couldn't decide whether to keep enough money in the bank account for groceries or if he should pay the overdue gasoline bill. They had gone over budget on gas this month, because Sandy had so many activities in town, because it was her senior year, and because she was on the committee for BEAT. "You should be thankful for everything this family provides you, Sandy. Since you aren't, you may go to your room and skip supper."

"Herbert. Don't." Nancy made an attempt to keep peace between them. But it was too late. A full-blown battle had been building for weeks.

"Oh, yeah!" Sandy shrieked at him, the bucket she held clattering to the floor. "I'm really thankful. You've done a lot to help, Dad. I've got friends at school who aren't going to college because of you."

"You can't blame it all on me. Over a hundred residents of Fremont County signed that petition."

"But you started it."

"The people of Fremont County don't want handouts."

"Yeah." Her face was flushed with anger. "But I know a lot of people who *earned* those scholarships."

Nancy had left the room. And secretly while Sandy's father watched his daughter's eyes blazing, he was proud of her for standing up for what she believed in, for having her own pride and for loving her friends. The two of them were very much alike. "I am your father. You have to respect my decisions." For a moment, he felt sorry for her. It was hard being a teenager, especially in Wind River. And it was hard standing up for what you believed, when you didn't quite know how, because you weren't quite grown up.

"I won't respect your decisions when I don't agree with you."

"The two are not the same things. You can respect me even while you disagree. When you grow up—"

"I *am* grown up!" Sandy shouted at him. "I've been grown up forever!" With those words, she suddenly realized who she was really fighting for. She was fighting for Tommy. Her coat was hanging on a peg in the kitchen and she yanked it down. She was going out.

"What do you think you're doing?"

Sandy started to tell her father she was going for a walk. And then she decided to be more dramatic. "I might just run away."

"You will not." He stood up from the table and grabbed her arm but she wrenched free. "It's suppertime."

"I'm not eating supper, remember," she said coldly. Fighting tears, she continued, "I'm going for a walk. I just have to think. I'm scared, Dad. I'm scared everybody at school will hate me."

When he made no further movement, Sandy left, banging the door behind her. Herbert Budge watched her figure fade in the porch light, aching, because he knew he had to let her go. In six months, she wouldn't even live with them anymore. He had to let her find her own way.

Sandy walked across the front pasture for a mile, listening to the far-off bleating of hundreds of sheep. And as the wind kicked up across the field, she began to decide on a plan. She wanted to talk to Tommy. She wanted to tell him the truth.

By now Sandy was almost to the highway, where she knew, if she hitched, she could find somebody from Wind River who would give her a ride. And, after that it would be only fifteen minutes before she'd be knocking on the Eberles' door. Only moments passed until a blue pickup she recognized came to a halt. The driver, one of the local ranchers, dropped her in front of Tommy's house. "I have to talk to Tommy," she said when Agatha answered the door.

"Come in," Aggie insisted and then she called for her son. Sandy looked terrible. Her hair was disheveled because of the wind and the little mascara she wore was smudged beneath her eyes. Her nose was bright red from the cold.

"Sandy? What is it?" Immediately Tommy knew something was wrong, too, just by looking at her. He had known something was wrong since the ground breaking, when she hadn't come.

"You're going to hate me," Sandy said, sighing. "I've got some stuff to tell you."

"Come on in," he said as he reached for her coat. "We were just watching my sister on TV."

"I don't want to go in the family room." Sandy tugged his sleeve, pulling him in the opposite direction. "This is about your sister. I just ... don't want anybody to know." Despite what she was doing now, coming here and being honest, the facts hadn't changed. Tommy wasn't going away to journalism school and she was.

"Sandy? What is it?"

"Your sister. Did you know she had trouble when she came here? Everything was all planned and set and that's why she was here?"

"That's right." Tommy was nodding. For some reason, he sensed he needed to support his friend. "But something about the funding fell through."

"Your sister wanted to pay for everything with her own money. Which was really neat. But my Dad thought, as an outsider, she was trying to do too much by herself. So he started up this petition."

"I don't understand."

"My Dad wrote this petition and passed it around the community. Your Mom and Dad didn't know about it.

But a lot of other parents did. And they signed it, too.
They gave it to the school board. And then the school
board had to call off BEAT and tell your sister they
couldn't take her money. So that's why BEAT didn't
work. That's why I'm going to college and nobody else
is."

"Sandy."

"Oh, Tommy, I'm so sorry. I know you hate me."

"Why should I hate you? Why should I even be *mad?*
It isn't your fault."

"But I'm going to *college.*"

"And I'm not. Do you blame your dad for that?"

"Yes."

"Well, I don't. I could have applied for another
scholarship. But I didn't. I wanted to wait for the BEAT
money just because my sister believed in it so much.
And—" he winked at her "—I could have studied
harder in my classes. I could have studied for the biology test that I just made a C on. But I didn't."

"But it seems so unfair to me. And I don't understand why Dad did it."

"Sit down, Sandy." Tommy touched her arm and
waited for her to find a place on the couch in the living
room before he sat down beside her. "I think I understand why."

"Tell me."

"If lots of people have their hand in something, it
makes it stronger somehow. By giving little donations
and helping dig the ground and laying the sheet rock,
it's like we all did part of it ourselves. And I think we'll
take better care of it. It belongs to us more that way."
He glanced into the other room, where his parents were
watching the news on television. "I think Shan's learned
a lot from it, too. It wasn't as easy as she wanted it to

be." He didn't tell Sandy about the trouble Shannon was having now. "She's having to fight right alongside us, you know."

Someone knocked on the front door and Tommy's mother went to answer it. And this time it was Jim Clarkson, his arms full of notes and a grin on his mouth that stretched the width of his face.

"Come in, Jim, come in," Agatha said warmly. Mentally she was already adding two more plates to the table and hoping the pot roast in the oven would feed her family and Sandy and Jim Clarkson, too.

"I came to see if you had heard from your daughter. I've been trying to reach her all day and her line is tied up. Understandably." He glanced toward the next room, where the anchorman was summing up the day's top stories.

He dropped the pile of notes right in the center of the kitchen table. "If you talk to her, will you please tell her to call me? Look at this. Just *look* at this. This is a list of three hundred names and addresses, people from Wyoming and all over, who heard Shannon's story today on the news. They're calling and offering money for BEAT. Look. I've got enough dollars pledged on this first page alone to go ahead with the BEAT scholarships."

"Oh, Tommy!" Sandy was jumping up and down now, and shouting. "Oh, Tommy!"

"See?" he asked as he stuck his hands in his pockets. "Sometimes things just work out."

Someone else knocked on the door. Agatha laughed. "Well," she said. "I was going to invite you all to stay for supper. But if the person on the porch now is very hungry, I'm going to have to serve my pot roast as a shish-ka-bob."

She swung the door open and saw Herbert Budge standing with his hat in his hand. "I'm here for Sandy."

"Dad?" She was the first one to reach him. "How did you know to come here?"

He hugged her to him. "I knew you'd come here eventually," he said softly. "I knew it was what you needed to do."

"Thanks." Sandy laid her head against his chest. And then she told him the news that BEAT had money enough for scholarships, just before she told him that she loved him.

SHANNON DIDN'T ANSWER the buzzer when it rang. She was certain it was yet another reporter wanting another angle on the same story. She was already dressed for the morning news show she was scheduled for. The network limousine would arrive for her in ten minutes.

The buzzer rang again, then again. Thinking it might be the limo driver early, Shannon finally answered.

"I hope I'm not too late," Peter said with a chuckle. It was not yet five a.m. But he knew her schedule. Just seeing her standing there filled him with relief. And then his composure broke and his emotions rushed out. "I was so angry when I heard the story. And worried. I came to see if I could do something to help you." Peter was guessing her life had been ghastly during the past twenty-four hours. He knew how hard she must have been fighting just to stay sane, dealing with the lawyers and the reporters and the network. She was dressed in the same suit and the same columbine-blue blouse she had worn for the interview on the news the night before. Larry had told her it would be good to wear the same clothes. It would make her look consistent and credible to the American public. She hadn't yet donned makeup. She was waiting for the artist at the studio to do it. Every line of fatigue on her face was there for Peter to decipher.

"Oh, Shan..." He reached out to her and she moved into his arms, feeling surrounded by the steel presence of him. "I saw you last night. I couldn't stand hearing about the things they were doing to you."

Shannon's entire body was trembling as she leaned against him, and it felt so good, just knowing he was there. She tilted her head to face him.

"It's good to see you." He was thinking of how she had looked that day, on the Viewer's Choice Awards, and of the awe and the loneliness that had engulfed him when he saw her.

A spark of hope was rising up in her and she was suddenly angry. So much was happening around them now, and she didn't know if it was right to need him. "Peter," she said finally, quietly, knowing she was forcing a fragile issue but desperate for an answer. "Why are you really here?"

He took her face in his hands so that she couldn't turn away. Something deep inside him was driving him, some part of his soul that demanded a second chance, something that wouldn't let him shy away from the renewal he was feeling. "I came here hoping you needed me."

Shannon didn't know what to say to him then, she reached up and touched his face, too, and drank in the tender certainty in his eyes. "I *do* need you." And she added the rest so softly he almost couldn't hear her. "I have needed you before."

He clutched her to him as if he never wanted to let her go. It had been such a long time since he had been strong enough to buoy someone else. He had been right

to come. He bent to brush her lips lightly with his own.
"Are you okay, Shan? Really okay?"

"Don't ask me that question today." She couldn't
help the bleak smile that touched her lips. "Yes, I suppose I am." And when she told him so, she knew it was
true. She was fine, and stronger now that he stood beside her.

"I'm proud of you for fighting."

"I always fight. It isn't anything new."

"I should know that," he said, chuckling.

"I'm doing another news program this morning... with my director. It would make it easier for me
if you would come."

"I will." He took her hand.

"Thank you."

She leaned against him, knowing her life was
changing in a myriad of ways, because of the Viewer's
Choice Awards and the lawsuit and the things she had
been brave enough to say. He gripped her arms as they
started down the stairs. Shannon felt as if a burden had
finally been lifted, freer than she had in such a long
time, and happy, because Peter had appeared and now
she didn't have to fight alone.

The car was waiting for them at the curb. When they
arrived at the studio, a staff assistant led her toward the
dressing room, and she saw Daphne Roberts walking
down the corridor toward her. "Daphne!" Shannon
shouted and ran to the actress, hugging her. Then they
were both talking excitedly at the same time. Shannon
was trying to explain about the news story, but Daphne
wouldn't let her finish.

"Yeah. I heard the stories," Daphne told her. "But
anybody with ears and eyes knows why you made that

speech. Anyone who heard you speak at the ceremony knows how much that teen project means to you."

"I'll give you your check back. I have it here...." Shannon was fumbling in her briefcase.

"Are you crazy? Don't you dare give that check back. I want that money in Wyoming to help those kids before another day goes by."

If Daphne believed her, Shannon reasoned, then others probably did, as well. Shannon cherished that hope as the A.D. pointed her in the direction of make-up.

The show would be taped. It ran live in New York but it would air three hours later on the West Coast. The makeup artist was panicking. Shannon had arrived late. They didn't have long before the show went on the air. And suddenly Shannon didn't care what the makeup artist did to her face, whether she smeared purple across her cheeks or painted orange around her eyes. Yesterday everything had seemed so bleak, but today things were different—Daphne's trust...Peter's presence when she needed it most. And when she walked onto the set, as the stand-ins were waiting for the gigantic lights to be adjusted, Shannon saw Eddie arrive, too.

Eddie sat in a vacant seat in the audience three rows behind Peter, and Shannon waved at her from the curtained entrance where she stood. Eddie made an Okay sign with her fingers while Shannon shook her head at her best friend. Surrounded by people who cared for her, Shannon couldn't keep from smiling.

That morning, as Shannon talked, she remembered the sight of a hundred hopeful faces looking at her from the bleachers at Washakie High School. She told the interviewer about her time in Wyoming, about searching for funds and doing what she could to avert the failure of the BEAT program, about students who even now were waiting in Wind River for well-deserved financial help.

Al Jensen made a presentation, too, about "Wayward Hopes" and the future he had planned for the show. And while the director talked, Shannon didn't have to glance at Peter to know he was there. She could feel his confidence. He was sitting on the edge of his seat, his eyes riveted on her face, rooting for her.

Toward what she thought was the end of the interview, his was the first face she sought. And as he nodded at her and grinned, the cameras followed her gaze. Shannon found herself telling the news reporter how she'd gone to Peter's bank in Wyoming for BEAT funding.

Someone called him onto the set and he was suddenly sitting beside her, an extra microphone in his hand, telling the nation about their meeting in his office. He talked about BEAT and how it would aid the teenagers in Wyoming. He explained how his hands had been tied when she'd contacted him in Jackson, how he hadn't been able to help her. And then, on the air, he told her he had mailed a personal check to BEAT himself this week.

The show completed taping and then, from somewhere in the studio, the applause began and it continued, while she thanked Peter and he held her arm and helped her away. Eddie ran to her and threw both arms around her neck and the two of them rocked back and forth together while Peter shielded them from more reporters.

"Mr. Barrett." One of the attendant newspapermen flipped out a press card. "I'm Harold Rasmussen. Investigative reporter for the *Globe*. We'd like to do another story about the 'Be Aware of a Teen's Dream' program. This time we'd like to do some investigation of the group firsthand. If it works out, we'd like to run it as a double-page spread in Sunday's feature section."

"Seems to me you might want to run it on tomorrow's front page," Peter growled at him, "after all the trouble you've put Shannon through."

The reporter ignored his comment. "We're going to need photos. Can you give me a contact at Washakie High School? We'd like to send somebody over there to get photos and to interview some of the kids."

Peter gave the man Jim Clarkson's telephone number. And when he told Shannon about the reporter's request, she decided to call the school board president so he would expect the interview from *Globe* reporters.

Clarkson's line was busy. Shannon dialed his secretary and asked if the woman could cut in for them. When Jim Clarkson came on the line and she began to tell him, he just laughed. "I *know* what's happening," he told her in a merry, booming voice. "The phones have been going crazy in this office for three days. The show you were on this morning doesn't air here for another hour. And it just started in the Central Time Zone. But people from all over the East Coast are calling in to support BEAT. They're pledging money, Shannon. For scholarships. And we've had money come in from Wyoming, too, since you appeared on the Viewer's Choice show. None of the pledges are large. But there are so many of them. We've got money for scholarships. We've got enough support now to make BEAT a national nonprofit corporation if we want to. We can certainly implement the program at any high school in this state."

Stunned, Shannon bade him goodbye, hung up the pay phone and turned to Peter. She didn't say anything for a moment. She couldn't say anything.

"Shannon?" Peter was trying to define the expression on her face. "What is it?"

"It's BEAT," she told him slowly. "People are sending money. Lots of people. Lots of money."

"You did it, didn't you?" he asked her gently.

"No. I haven't done any of this. I think God's taken it over for me. I couldn't have done this. Not like it is."

"It has been spectacular."

Peter pulled Shannon toward him, his palms resting securely against the small of her back, supporting her, as they stood by the pay phone in the hallway while producers and actresses and assistants carrying steaming coffeepots or pieces of somebody's wardrobe rushed past them.

"I'm taking you home," he whispered against her hair. "I have a plane waiting at the airport. I'm not leaving you in New York."

Shannon gave him one swift, searching look. "I don't think I can, Peter.... The show..."

"Mark Troy and Al Jensen will let you come with me." Peter stood before her, letting her hold his hands in her own and consider what he was proposing. "Shannon," he whispered, and when she turned her eyes toward him, he read all her bewilderment there. "Don't you think you've already given them enough?"

"I don't know."

"What do you want from this? Your life in New York?" He knew they were both talking about much more than her career.

"I wanted to prove to everyone at home that it could be done."

Peter sized up the raw dedication he saw on her face as something new welled up within him, a swirling possibility that had not entered his mind before, one that encompassed all the feelings he had for Shannon, the new protectiveness and the need. *God has done this, too,* he thought. *I'm falling in love with her.*

The realization came from the very core of him. It was so precise that the truth of it cut him, like a knife. It was a welcome wounding, for now he was finally free of the familiar numbness. "You've got your own life, Shan. You're so busy winning battles for people that you don't have time for the things that were once important in your own life."

"My life is fine the way it is."

"It isn't."

"What am I missing?" She was stalling for time and he knew it.

"Fishing...and laughing...and sitting on a rock feeling the sun oozing into your bones."

"What can I do? I can't go back in time, Peter."

"You can't be Lisa Radford for seven hours every day and then fight your own battles, too. I saw the defeat on your face last night. It came across on camera just as clearly as if you were standing before me the way you are now. You can't lose yourself, Shan." Peter knew what he was saying because he had once lost himself, too. And he was standing beside the woman who had brought him back to his life. "You're no good to anyone if you do that. Least of all yourself."

This time, when Shannon spoke, it was the first time he realized how much she had come to trust him. "Have I done that, Peter? Have I come so far that I've lost sight of my own life?" When she turned her face toward his once again, her features were ravaged with defeat. "I haven't been any good to anyone, have I?"

"No. Oh, Shannon, *no*." Seeing the look on her face made him want to die. "The things you have given other people...their own possibilities and hopes..." He hadn't known she could be so fragile. He wondered now that he hadn't seen it long before. "Come here, little one." He stroked her hair and held her, and he willed himself and his strength into her. "It's you I'm worried about. I want you to be happy. And sometimes I wonder if you are."

Peter's arms around her felt comfortable and right, like the feel of an old shirt or a pair of jeans that had belonged to her long enough to mold themselves to her shape. Despite his long flight and the hours at the studio, he smelled the way she would always remember him: like home, the faint tang of spicy pine, the cutting freshness of the high country. Shannon leaned her forehead against his chest and let him support her. "No," she told him. "I'm not often happy." She felt safe, and for a brief instant she forgot to guard against her physical attraction to him. He was like a brother to her and a helper and a friend, but he was more than that, too. Shannon was suddenly very aware of the firmly carved muscles beneath his linen shirt, aware of what she had needed from him once, the lovemaking he'd been unable to share.

"Let's find Al Jensen." Peter guided her up the hallway. "You can ask for a day or two off." *You can ask for a life off.* He didn't know if he could fly her to Wyoming and then ever let her go again. He knew he was doing the right thing for her now, no matter what the emotional cost to himself. He had to get her away from this place with its monumental victories and defeats. New York City was eating her alive.

"If I go to Wyoming, I have to face all the people there, too. I'd have to tell them all the same stories I've been telling here."

"Maybe not. Suppose you hide out in Jackson Hole for a while? You could rest. You won't have to see anyone until you're ready."

It was a beautiful season in the mountains, and Peter found himself longing to share springtime with her. The native grasses were verdant, the ground black with moisture from the newly melted snow. The snow that remained in seams high atop the Tetons was still fresh and white, a crisp contrast with the azure blue of the sky. This was what Peter knew she needed now—the brilliant silences, the splashes of color her life had lacked since she went away. "You could stay with Taylor and me. Camille comes in every day but she wouldn't bother you. You could just . . . breathe easily for a while."

It was the idea of running away and hiding that appealed to Shannon the most. She relished spending the time with Peter, who was becoming such a solid, strong part of her life. She gave him an impish grin. "Okay. So maybe it's a good plan. I'd like to come to Jackson. Particularly if you'll take me fishing." She hadn't been out to capture Native Cutthroat trout for years. It would be better than coming home. It would be like quietly, solidly, coming back to herself.

"That," he said as he grinned back at her, "could be arranged." It was everything he could do to keep from shouting, Peter was so happy. "Have I ever told you

how cute you look when you're about to do something
you're not quite certain you should do?''

Shannon covered her face with her hands but, behind them, she was laughing. All of a sudden the aching sense of defeat had left her.

CHAPTER ELEVEN

THE CALL for a senior assembly at Washakie High School came over the loudspeaker at one-thirty p.m. Obediently, students made their way to the gymnasium, where they filled up the bleachers.

"Quiet, please," Jim Clarkson said into the microphone. He gave them several seconds to calm down before he continued. "The reasons for this assembly are twofold," he said. "Most of you know about the national attention our BEAT program has attracted. We have a reporter here from *The New York Globe*. He brought a photographer with him. Release forms have gone home to your parents telling them that the newspaper will be doing a feature about the BEAT program. If the reporter asks you questions, and your parents have given their permission for you to be interviewed, please answer questions to the best of your ability. The photographer will take pictures during this assembly. He will also take photographs at the teen center site. Any questions?"

The room was silent.

"There is another reason your school board decided to call you to assembly today. We are proud of you. You are an outstanding group of young adults. These are things we would usually tell you at graduation or during the annual senior float trip. But we wanted you to know now.

"During the past two days, many people have donated or pledged money to go toward the BEAT scholarships. Long ago, a BEAT scholarship committee made a list of deserving students. During the year, many of you have applied for the scholarships. The BEAT scholarship committee met this morning for three hours. I am proud to announce that BEAT, 'Be Aware of a Teen's Dream,' is able to grant these scholarships now. Melanie..." He handed the microphone to Melanie Bybee, the president of the Washakie Student Council. The photographer from the *Globe* circled the podium snapping pictures.

Tommy gripped Sandy's arm. They were sitting together eleven rows above the podium. "I didn't know about this. I'm on that committee. They didn't call me to a meeting."

"They couldn't. You're up for a scholarship. It's called conflict of interest," she whispered back.

"Each year, BEAT will award five full college scholarships to the students who need them and who earn them," Melanie was saying. "They will go to seniors who prove themselves and who believe in themselves. This year, the five seniors selected are as follows..."

"I'm not ready for this," Tommy whispered frantically to Sandy. He had waited so long. And now it was happening so fast. What if she didn't call his name?

"Stacey Gardner..."

The students applauded as the recipient came forward and the photographer snapped her picture.

"Georgia Henning..."

"They'll call your name," Sandy said as she squeezed his hand. "They have to. I'll drop out of school if they don't."

"Cut it out," he whispered back. "Don't joke about that."

"John Hicks..."

The students continued to applaud. *They're calling them in alphabetical order. My name would have been first.*

"Mary Jane Jackson..."

This one will be the last one, Tommy thought. *It isn't going to be me.*

"And Dan Talmadge."

Tommy turned to Sandy. He tried to look nonchalant. He didn't want her to know how badly he had wanted it. "Oh, well. Back to the five-and-dime."

"Tommy—" Sandy was shaking her head. "—I can't believe it."

But Melanie was still talking. "We're giving one more award this year. It is a special scholarship, one for a full four years at the university of the recipient's choice. We award it in honor of a woman who graduated from this school over ten years ago. She continues to return to support us, to encourage us, to love us. I am proud to announce that the recipient of the Shannon Eberle Honorary Scholarship is someone we all admire in our senior class." Tommy stopped talking. He hadn't been listening. What was Melanie saying? "Here's hoping you become an award-winning journalist someday, Tommy. The Shannon Eberle Honorary Scholarship goes to Shannon's brother, Tommy Eberle."

Sandy shrieked and stood up on the bleachers and the other students around them followed suit, while Tommy sat stock-still, in total disbelief.

"Get down there, bud." Someone pushed him from behind and then he hugged Sandy and started down the bleachers and the photographer took his picture, too.

"Congratulations, Tommy." The reporter was jotting down notes. "So you're the baby brother of Wonder Woman Shannon. I heard her speak this morning in New York. I know how much she believes in you. You've done her proud."

"Thank you, sir." And then Tommy couldn't resist asking, "What's it like working for a big-city paper?"

"Well, if you want money and prestige, don't do it. Be a lawyer or go into marketing. But if you like challenge and excitement, it's the only way to go."

Tommy grinned. "It sounds perfect. Do you need someone to give you a tour of the building site? They've got the beams up and they're going to start sheetrocking next week. Maybe I could take you through the rooms and tell you what they're going to be."

"That would be good. Let me get a few more notes here." The man stopped beside Georgia Henning. "Common spelling of Georgia? Henning? H-e-n-n-i-n-g? Thank you."

The assembly adjourned, and Tommy led the reporter out to the lot next to the high school. The site had been vacant for years, but now it was bustling with activity. Paid workers hammered beams in the company of people who had volunteered their time. A donated city dump truck from nearby Lander stood ready to haul trash away. "It's going up fast," Tommy said. "All these will be the studios. Someday we'll have a piano. After that, they're going to put in electric typewriters or maybe even computers with a word processor. Do you use a word processor when you write your stories?"

"I do," he said. "Now, I have a question for you. I'm going to call this story in to my editor tonight. I have another day before I have to go back to the city. Is there anybody here who would benefit from a journalism workshop? I'm not organized but I could tell you a lot about meeting deadlines and covering features."

"Would you? It'd be great. Lots of people would come."

"Who should I talk to to set it up?"

"The journalism teacher. Miss Marshall. Do you want to talk to her now?"

"Sure. No point in wasting time."

"Great." Tommy did a little skip step through the last studio room. "I want to learn everything."

"In our newsroom, we use VDTs," he explained. "They are all part of a word-processing system hooked up to a giant file in a central computer. It's very advanced."

"I'm getting great shots," said the photographer, who'd joined them. "This scenery coupled with the determination on those faces will get me two full pages, probably."

"Feel like telling some kids what you know about taking snapshots, John? I'm going to volunteer to do a workshop before we go back tomorrow."

"Why not?" the photographer agreed.

Tommy grinned from ear to ear, knowing all his dreams were finally coming true.

"THE TETONS are not like any other mountains in the world," Shannon observed, sighing as the little jet touched down at Jackson Airport. "They look like somebody cut them out of paper and pasted them against the sky."

"They are lovely," Peter agreed. "I miss looking at them when I'm gone."

Shannon touched his hand as the plane pulled up to park at the tiny two-gate terminal. She felt drawn to him and grateful for his concern.

They drove the thirty-five minutes to Peter's in silence, and when Shannon saw his home, it was so magnificent that it made her gasp. The house stood alone in a meadow amass with dandelion blooms. The cedar and moss-rock structure seemed to spread out forever across the waving grass. She could already guess at the rustic elegance she would find inside.

"Oh, Peter." Shannon breathed deeply, one long breath that filled her lungs with the crystalline, delicious air. "Thank you." She turned to him and laid her fingers against the nubby woolen threads of the sweater he had donned at the airport.

"Come in." He wrapped one arm around her waist and led her into the foyer while she leaned on him, her head resting against the rigid warmth of his chest.

"This is some place to recuperate." She turned to him and her eyes were sparkling, she was so entirely happy, to be in this place, to be with him. And then he caught the trace of mischief in her voice. "How close is the nearest fishing hole?"

"Pretty close." He pulled back a curtain and pointed to the east. "That's the Snake River. It's a bit early in the season to be fly fishing. A day or two of this cool weather ought to slow down the snow melt enough to make river fishing interesting, though. There are some nice lunker trout lurking in that river."

"How soon can I outfish you?"

He waggled a finger at her. "Not before you take a long, hot bath and a nap." It had been an endless, emotional day for her. And Peter didn't tell her it had been even longer for him. "Not before I pick up my child."

He carried her suitcase downstairs to a lovely little room with ivory lace curtains and a lace bedspread on a bed made of pine logs. "The bathroom's here." He flipped on the light for her. "Make yourself comfortable. Oh—" he walked down the hallway and she followed him, and when he stopped, Shannon caught a glimpse of the master bedroom. Inside there was a moss-rock fireplace and adobe window seats and a massive king-size bed. *The bed Peter and his wife had shared.* "Use this bathroom if you want to really relax. This is a Jacuzzi tub. You turn it on here."

Peter left her alone to explore the house while he drove to Camille's to pick up Taylor. Shannon slipped off her shoes and walked around, thinking how intrigued she was by the place. It told her so much about Peter, with its rustic profile and its soft colors. *His home is very much like him,* she thought.

Shannon went back downstairs to the tiny bathroom adjoining her own room and soaked in the tub. She was finished, her face scrubbed clean of makeup, her old, soft jeans outlining her long legs, her hair pulled away from her face with a ribbon, when Peter came racing in the front door with his son.

"Shannon Eberle, come see Taylor Barrett," he called out to her and she had to smile at him because she could tell how happy he was to be home, with his child, in the place that was their own.

She bounded up the stairs, still barefoot, and when Peter saw her looking so relaxed and happy, as if she belonged in his house, in his life, forever, his heart wrenched as he handed her his son. "Remember the kid? Taylor Levi Barrett. Toddler Extraordinaire."

"Hi, Taylor," Shannon said gently. "Remember me? You came to *my* house once." But he hadn't come to her house. He had come to her parents' house. The house where she had once been a child. She grinned and the little boy grinned back, displaying a nice set of teeth and a smile that did not look anything like his father's. Shannon's eyes noted the opal eyes and the hair the color of hay. Then she turned to Peter and waited for his eyes to lock on hers before she spoke. "He's so beautiful. I had forgotten, Peter." She whispered her next words. "He must look like Lorilee."

During the past several hours they had been together, Peter had not mentioned Lorilee once. Shannon was desperate to get Lorilee into the open, to say her name, to let him know she understood the shadow that still fell over them, the invisible tie that bound him. Until she walked into the master bedroom, Shannon had not realized how hard it was going to be for her to be near him in the place he had shared with his wife.

"Yes." Peter's gaze remained riveted to hers. "He doesn't look much like me at all." Shannon was surprised by the calm reassurance on his face. "Luckily for him."

She laughed, a light wafting melodic sound. "Don't be mean about yourself. Taylor's a cute kid. But you could have babies tumbling all over you, fat ones and skinny ones, and they'd be beautiful if they looked like you, too...." Her words trailed off. She met his eyes. Her smile faded when she realized his had, too. She was thinking of what she'd just said, how much Lorilee's death must still have hurt him. For a moment, Shannon couldn't breathe, thinking what it would be like to have a child with him and then almost hating Lorilee because she had been the one who had given him his son.

Their faces were both still, measuring neither pain nor defeat; they were silent except for the sound of Shannon's breathing through parted lips as she waited for an angry response. "Peter. I'm sorry."

"No." Taylor was still in her arms, but Peter reached out for her, anyway, and his hands were like claws against her shoulders. He would have given anything to hold her tightly against his body. "Don't be sorry. Please. I've had enough pity."

When Shannon had mentioned babies, it was the first time in so long he had allowed himself to hope again. He wanted a life that might mean something, after having thought everything was lost. Peter had seen the longing in Shannon eyes. For one instant he had watched her defenses go down, the defenses he knew she had thrown up weeks ago when he had gone to her in New York City, when she had wanted him and he had been unable to give. "Here." He reached out for the baby and took Taylor from her. "Play with Daddy's keys." He set Taylor on the carpet while she stood before him, hating herself because she was starting to cry, because there was so much between them, yet nothing, and she wanted him to hold her so desperately that she thought her body might shatter.

"Don't you see?" He stood frozen before her while she ached for him. "You're the one who has helped me come alive. Do you think I didn't anticipate this? Bringing you here...feeling the things I feel for you...to stay in the house that was once hers?"

"I don't want to stay here." It was a bleak little cry, a last-ditch attempt to keep her head above the things her heart was telling her.

Peter grabbed her and crushed her against him with a force Shannon needed as much as he did. His arms formed a vise around her shoulders, holding her soul together when it wanted to fragment. "Look at me, Shannon."

When she didn't, Peter let go with one arm, while Taylor played at their feet, and twisted her chin until her eyes met his. "Look at me, dammit." He loved her. And he had to tell her. For his own sanity as well as hers. "I love you, Shan. I knew it this morning when you were so hell-bent on giving yourself to the multitudes that you almost wouldn't come home with me. Can't you see it? Don't you know?" He paused. "I love you." He said the words again, this time savoring the sound of them, caressing them with his tongue the way he wanted to touch her. "I love you, Shannon."

"Oh, God, Peter." She pulled back from him while her eyes flew across his face, back and forth, trying to find something, some fatal flaw, in the things he was telling her. "How can you?" She was waiting for him to say Lorilee's name again, waiting for him to tell her how costly his loving had been before.

"Easily. Too easily." He fingered the heavy clump of hair that had fallen over her shoulder. "Look at you. You care so much and you believe in the good in people and you remain dedicated to the parts of life that have been good to you."

"I don't know how to feel, Peter," she whispered. "I've tried so hard not to need anything from you...not to want you...because of your wife."

"Don't say it. Don't explain." He couldn't hear her excuses now, not today, when he had brought her here and had found the strength to be so perfectly honest.

"My memories are happy ones. But I'm not married anymore."

Shannon released one tormented breath and closed her eyes. She was standing before him the way she might stand before a television camera, fragile and vulnerable, ready for him. And she felt him, rather than saw him, when he moved toward her and brushed his lips across hers. She reached for his neck and clung to him, the curve of her body moved closer against him and, at last, she gave way to the hunger she had been frightened to feel. His lips were warm, demanding, upon her own, as his tongue traced the ridge of her teeth and then circled deeper.

When he pulled away and gazed at her, she could barely see him searching her face, so great was the circus of emotions within her. "Thank you," she whispered recklessly. She was doing her best to focus on him. "I think you're saving my life." There was so much more between them now than there once had been. Peter's lips and his gaze seemed to sear her, leaving every part of her exposed to him.

"Perhaps I should save your life all the time. This is fun."

"Perhaps," she said, laughing.

He bundled her to him once more with a wry grin, and they both laughed as their breath intermingled. It was suddenly a game to them and it seemed like a miracle as her lips found Peter's this time and she grasped his neck and stood on tiptoe, while he ran his palms in huge, firm circles down the small of her back.

Shannon felt a tug on her jeans. She looked down to see Taylor standing beside her knee. "Hey, kid," she said, giggling, breathless from kissing. "You're missing all the action down there." She bent to Taylor and hoisted him up onto her shoulder. "The fun stuff's up here." She bent forward and gave Peter another playful kiss full on the lips.

"Dinosaur kiss." The little boy pointed at Peter and laughed.

"No," Shannon told him, grinning. "Not dinosaur kiss. Daddy kiss. I just kissed your daddy."

"Come here, kid." Peter stretched out his arms for his son. Taylor leaned out and tumbled forward into Peter's arms, while Shannon laughed at both of them.

"You two make quite a pair."

Peter eyed her over his son's head. "We'll finish this after he goes to bed."

"Ah," she teased him. "Finish what?"

"You'll find out."

She followed them to the family room and watched as father and son plopped on the couch. "I am not a dinosaur." Peter tousled the little blond head. "Dinosaurs are big and fat and funny looking."

"And green." Shannon couldn't resist bending over and kissing Taylor, too. "Dinosaurs are green."

"Or gray," Peter added. "Or orange."

"Oh, don't make it so complicated," she said and laughed at both of them. Then, abruptly, she sobered. *Don't make it so complicated.*

Everything was happening at a breakneck pace. This time yesterday, she had been in New York fighting the press. Today she was in Peter's arms. She felt very far away from herself. There was something uniquely frightening about how far she had come so fast and how frantically she felt herself needing him.

"I'd like some hot tea." Suddenly Shannon wanted to physically draw away. She flipped on the light in the kitchen. "Do I have permission to explore?"

"Go ahead," he called back.

She found the kettle, filled it with water and put it on the stove to heat. She waited, watching the steam rise from the spout. Peter's business calendar was lying open beside the telephone. She couldn't seem to help but glance at it and then read the notes Peter had jotted down while talking to Sheriff John Miller. "Jim and Gloria Brown. Texas. Gold car traced to grandmother. Preliminary hearing and arraignment. Worked with Lorilee on bobcat documentary."

"Peter?" She hurried to the family room. "You didn't tell me they found Lorilee's kidnappers."

He gazed up at her in silence before he answered. He wondered why he wasn't angry that she'd been snooping, but he wasn't. "The right moment never came."

"Have you seen them?"

"Yes."

"Peter, you should have told me. I could have helped."

He rose beside her. "Maybe I didn't need help on this one."

"How are you feeling?" she asked him somberly. "Happy? Relieved? Disappointed?"

"Add *confused* to that list and you've got them all," he said as he stood and gripped her shoulders.

"Oh, Peter, I'm sorry." She hugged him. "I knew it would come. I just . . . didn't want you to have to face it again."

"I'm not dreading it as much as I thought I would," he said softly. "I feel compassion for the people in jail. They have a little child. I want to be fair. And I want to be finished with it."

She leaned her head against him as he stroked her hair. Shannon felt buoyed by his new courage but saddened, too, because she knew now without a doubt what he needed, what she could never be—a woman to fill his house and his life and to stand beside him at the trial. She was a New York actress. She couldn't give Peter those simple, basic things.

Peter disappeared behind the couch again. He was on the floor holding Taylor in the air above him, and it was everything Shannon could do to keep from crying out. She felt like a sad intruder to their tumbling. And she felt strangely cut off from the rest of the world, too, as if she didn't belong anywhere at all.

"What are you doing just standing there?" Peter asked as he sat up from behind the sofa. "Come join in on the tickle fight."

"I'm going to make some more tea." Shannon did her best to sound nonchalant. But the look he saw on her face was a familiar one. It echoed the expression she had worn on-camera just the night before. Peter saw numbness. And a great battle for reserve. "Shannon?" He cradled Taylor in his lap. "What is it?" She looked emotionally exhausted again. Lost. And sad.

She didn't say anything to him, just shook her head, and he put the baby in the playpen and moved toward her. He cradled her in his arms while the water hissed in the kettle on the stove. "Tell me what it is, Shan."

Her words, when they came, were released as tiny sobs, each one a disjointed, separate cry to him. "You deserve so much," she said to him. "You deserve someone who will stand beside you during everything that is coming. The trial..." She knew it was going to be terrifically hard on him. Lorilee was going to become very real to him again. Shannon almost choked on the words she had to say to him. "And I'll be going back to New York...."

He held her for a long time while she sobbed, and he wanted to weep for her, too. "Shan—" Stroking her hair, he asked, "Why have you decided to take on the entire world in one day?" She was wearing a white angora sweater that buttoned to her neck with tiny pearls, and she felt fuzzy and soft and fragile in his arms.

"I'm not taking on the entire world," she said softly. "I only take on the little parts I care about." She buried her head in his sweater without looking up at him. She couldn't bear to see the gentleness in his eyes. And she couldn't bear to tell him how defenseless she was against her own longing for him.

"It doesn't matter," he told her, even though he knew it did. "I love you, Shannon. I know you have to go back." He felt his heart rending. "I'm not asking you to commit your life to me." Peter knew he had no right to keep her from the dreams she had followed and fought for ever since she had been in school. He knew he had no right to ask her to give up her own life so he could salvage what was left of his own. He knew, but it didn't stop either of them from hurting.

CHAPTER TWELVE

"I CAN'T BELIEVE Peter didn't tell me about you." Camille was chattering a mile a minute and moving even faster than that around the kitchen. "He tells me he has a houseguest. I suppose he wanted me to have a heart attack when this big star walks into the kitchen. Lisa Radford here! Imagine it. Eating Cheerios out of a bowl in this very kitchen. Aren't you supposed to be on TV today? Aren't you supposed to be in an insane asylum somewhere?"

Shannon chuckled. Peter had probably not realized Camille would recognize her from the show. "Yes. Lisa Radford is somewhere in Vermont in a mental institution. But that's make believe." *This is make believe. I shouldn't be here pretending to fit into Peter's life.*

"How do you know Peter?" Camille had never been one to mince words. "He came home once while I was watching 'Wayward Hopes' on TV. Now I know why he was staring at the screen and stomping around. I thought he meant to ban soap operas from the house for the rest of my life. But he knows you. Lisa Radford. In this kitchen. Eating Cheerios out of a bowl."

"My name is Shannon." Taylor waddled across the floor and handed her a wooden block. She lifted him into her lap. "And yes, I *do* eat Cheerios. Sometimes out of a bowl. Sometimes with my fingers." She was doing her best not to laugh outright. She tried to pic-

ture Peter stomping around the family room while
Camille innocently watched "Wayward Hopes." "I'm
glad to meet you, Camille. Peter has told me all about
you."

"Well, he certainly didn't tell me about *you*. I think
he's trying to get rid of me. What a story it would make.
'My housekeeper died of a heart attack the other day.
Lisa Radford came upstairs and sat down in the kitchen
and started eating Cheerios.'"

"Shannon," she reminded Camille once again. "My
real name is Shannon."

"It's time for Taylor's snack." Camille broke a banana off the bunch and reached for a knife to cut it into
pieces.

"Can I do that?" Shannon asked. "I sort of like this
little guy. I'll feed him."

"Fine with me," Camille said. She handed her the
knife and a banana as Shannon hugged Taylor to her.
Shannon couldn't decide whether or not Camille welcomed her presence. But then she decided the woman
didn't know how to treat her because she had watched
her on television every day, because she was Lisa or
Shannon, and a star. And after she poured Taylor a
glass of apple juice from the refrigerator, she volunteered to knead the bread Camille was working on.

"I didn't know city people had much use for knead-
ing bread. It's easier to grab a wrapped loaf off the shelf
at the store."

"True. But I'm not a city person. I grew up in Wyoming." Funny. Now she was defending herself to Camille by clinging to a life she had tried to run away from.

"Good." Camille turned toward her from across the
kitchen. Full-breasted and erect, she reminded Shannon of an army sergeant or a rooster determined to

protect the flock. "You seem like a down-to-earth girl to me. Probably just what he needs."

Shannon kneaded the bread dough with the heels of both hands. Peter's needs. She had been thinking of them ever since she had found out about the Browns' arrests. Peter had not reached out to her again, not since they had talked of her returning to the city, and Shannon was almost glad of it. He'd proved he was not as nonchalant about her committing herself to him as he claimed to be.

Peter hadn't even touched her again after Taylor had gone to sleep for the night. Instead, Shannon had tossed and turned alone in the little log bed, covered by lace she knew Lorilee had put out for guests. She could hear Peter in the other room, his breathing labored, the massive king-size bed groaning every time he turned in it. And she had almost gone to him. Almost. But it would have been too painful for both of them and she knew it, as frantically as they wanted one another, with Peter talking of his love for her, when they both knew she couldn't stay.

"He's been hurt worse than most people ever ought to be," Camille was saying softly, her face a tender network of tiny wrinkles. "He's still so young...and they were all so happy once."

"Yes. I know they must have been." Shannon felt like a traitor. She was only hurting Peter more because she had agreed to come to Wyoming with him, because she needed him now, because she responded to his kisses and to the searing touch of his hands.

She was pushing the bread dough against itself with all the force she could muster when she heard the front door swing open. She knew it was Peter even before Camille greeted him. "You could have told me about her, you know. She just walks into the kitchen this morning like a normal person. Lisa Radford. Sitting right here eating Cheerios."

"I thought it would be fun to let you discover her yourself."

Peter was in the kitchen now, with Camille by his side, and he froze when he saw Shannon. He had wanted her beside him last night, and when he had slept at all, he had dreamed of her fingers against his skin. But wanting her hadn't been the reason he had brought her to his home. He had brought her here to heal. He was furious with himself today for the pressure he had put on her by being honest about his love. He had told her the truth mainly for himself, he had decided sometime during the long night. In fact, his confession hadn't been for her at all, but he forgot that now as he saw her in his kitchen, her hair pulled back into a sleek French braid that hung halfway down her back, one of her cheeks streaked with flour, holding bread dough in her hands.

His eyes were expressionless. He was looking at her as if he hadn't remembered she would be there. "I should have told you the Browns' preliminary hearing is at the court house this afternoon. They will be bound over to district court for trial.

"Do you have to be there?"

"No. But I'm going."

Peter was going to the court house to face his crumpled life yet again. And, in a way, the revelation made Shannon feel as if she was a part of it once more. Now she remembered there were other menaces against him, not just their love or her caring, but a justice of the peace and attorneys and two people who might be the ones who had seen fit to spirit a part of his soul away.

Camille sidled up beside Shannon. "That bread was ready to bake a long time ago. Your hands give you away. I don't know why you're pushing so hard on that dough, but the bread's going to be all the better for it."

Shannon didn't take her eyes from Peter's face. "I want to go with you to the hearing, Peter. I don't know what I can do but I'd like . . . just to be there."

Peter reached for her hand. "I'd like that, too. We haven't long."

"I'll dress quickly." Shannon dusted her hands on a tea towel and raced down the stairs. She was standing in the little bathroom in a blue silk slip applying a coat of mascara to her lashes when she heard him come downstairs, too. He tapped lightly on her door. "Just a minute," she called out, "I'm not . . ."

But he hadn't understood her answer. He opened the door, and she faced him. She was almost glad when she saw the devastated look on his face as his gaze swept over the blue satin and the lace.

"We have to talk, Shannon."

"I know."

"Perhaps we should talk in the car." He tried to back away from her then, to turn around or leave so she could dress. He couldn't tear his eyes from her. "You look beautiful with flour on your face, Shan." He was waiting for her to slip on a robe or her blouse but she didn't. She stood before him, her breasts heaving with determination, daring him to come nearer, daring him to prove she was wrong about him, that he didn't need her commitment, only her love.

He took one step closer and then, gingerly, he stretched one hand toward her bare shoulder. "Do you know," he asked her with a tremor in his voice, "how good it is for me just to *feel* something again?"

She stood motionless, a statue, before him. "You can't do it, can you, Peter? You can't love me when you know I'm not giving you everything I have to give."

He moved then, like lightning, toward her. He reached for her hips, his fingers slipping against the silky fabric until they met her skin. "You're putting a price tag on everything we've done for one another. Is that it?" He was growling at her, suddenly furious, still wanting her.

"I have to know the truth." Her words were a whisper against his neck. "I have to know how much I'm going to hurt you when I leave."

"What does it matter? Kiss me. Stop talking and just kiss me." Peter's hands were lifting the satin from her thighs and she was frantic for him as she gripped the back of his head and pulled it down until his lips met her mouth. She kissed him, his nose, his eyelids and then his mouth, time and time again, trembling because of the futility of it, as his hands roved against her bare back and her shoulders.

"This isn't enough, Peter. You know that." She felt wetness against his cheeks as she kissed them, too, and she realized she was crying again. "Peter. Don't do this." She was frantic to tell him now, frantic to stop the aching in her body, frantic to be honest with him, too. "You're making me feel things I shouldn't feel."

He pulled away from her and gave her a sad little grin. "Well..." he said slowly, his fingers trailing over her throat, the tingle of sensation they left against her skin not quite outweighing the desperation she felt. "Isn't that what makes this enough? For both of us? For now?"

"You know it doesn't."

"Are you that afraid of hurting me?" It was amazing how strong he felt now, as he touched her, "Haven't you heard the old story about hurt? That if something doesn't kill you, it makes you stronger? Give me some credit, Shannon. I'm not going to go reeling every time I get another hard knock."

"Maybe I'm the one who can't handle the hard knocks," she said to him. "Maybe I just don't want you to have to face them again."

"Do you care about me that much?"

"Yes."

"Then that is all I need," he said. "That knowledge. And you."

THE HEARING ROOM at the Teton County Courthouse was deserted except for reporters from the two local weekly newspapers. Peter and Shannon sat alone on an oak bench.

At precisely twelve-thirty p.m., Fred Kelton, the Teton County prosecutor, entered the room. Five minutes later, public defender Gary Rankin entered. He accompanied his two clients, Jim and Gloria Brown.

For a trial, the couple would have been allowed to don street clothes. For the hearing, they had been brought directly from the room where they were being held, in jail clothing, dull brown jumpsuits and handcuffs that rattled as they sat down. Two armed guards stood behind them.

Peter rubbed Shannon's arm. "It will be over soon."

The district attorney entered the hearing room and chatted easily with Fred Kelton. The Justice of the Peace approached the bench and they all stood, even Jim and Gloria Brown, and the handcuffs rattled again, while Peter clutched her hand.

"Be seated." Justice of the Peace Richard Baker nodded toward them. His eyes lingered a moment on Peter. And then the district attorney began to speak as the county prosecutor handed documents to Judge Baker. "Lorilee Barrett was at home the morning of February..."

It was as if a light had flared beside Shannon, illuminating Lorilee, draping Shannon in shadow. Shannon wanted to run out of the room. She had been wrong to think she could help Peter just by being at his side. Nothing could help him now. Nothing. He was going to have to rely on the inner strength he had told her about only an hour before. And she prayed, as she sat beside him and squeezed his hand, that he had been right, that the parts of his heart that had been welded together during his past months of loneliness had only been made more resilient and solid.

"I love you," he leaned over and whispered to her.

"Thanks." She gave him a sad smile.

During their drive to the courthouse, Peter had told her that, ninety-nine times out of a hundred, the defense attorney does not present any evidence on behalf of his clients at the preliminary hearing. The defendants generally attend the hearing to hear what the DA has to say against them.

"He won't say anything?" Shannon asked him under her breath.

Peter shook his head. "Probably not. He'll only reconfirm the bail that was set at an initial appearance. It's all very routine."

Shannon turned her attention to the Browns. They both looked so colorless and tragic. She tried to imagine them sitting somewhere, at a kitchen table or on a couch, or an outdoor café somewhere amassed with flowers, plotting to kidnap a man's wife. She couldn't.

The DA was still talking. "Although the victim's husband did not recognize the suspects in a police lineup, the state has evidence that Mr. Brown worked for Mrs. Barrett on location in Texas. Company records show a weekly payment of $350 was made to the defendant for his help in searching for and locating animals. The payments were made for nine consecutive weeks."

Fred Kelton presented two witnesses. Each of them told about money the Browns had spent during the previous year.

The public defender jumped from his chair, surprising both Peter and Shannon. "Your Honor, the people who kidnapped Mrs. Barrett never received money. According to the sheriff's reports, the woman escaped before her husband could ransom her. I fail to see why testimony about money and how it was spent affects this trial. You will not convict my clients for this kidnapping by trying to connect them with other ones."

"I agree, Mr. Rankin."

"Your Honor," Fred Kelton said, "I am simply trying to show you that Jim and Gloria Brown have an unusual life-style. They spend lots of money."

"It isn't necessary to discuss that now. Thank you, Mr. Kelton. Will the defendants approach the bench, please?"

Jim and Gloria Brown stood and took two steps forward.

Kelton stood silently and the reporters sat poised with their notepads, waiting to write down the date and the time of the upcoming arraignment in district court.

Judge Baker frowned down at all of them. Then his eyes found the Browns. "I bind you over to district court in the Ninth Judicial District. Arraignment is set for next Monday, May 27, at two-thirty." He slammed his gavel against the bench. It was over. At least for a while.

THE FIRELIGHT played against the adobe walls and the pine furniture. Shannon lay stretched on the couch, mesmerized by the fire, her mind racing, as Peter and Taylor sat together in a chair beside her. They were discussing pictures in a huge book spread out across Peter's lap.

"Eat," Taylor said, pointing to a page.

"That's right. The sea otter is eating. What's this? What is he eating?"

"Cake," Taylor said. "Birthday cake."

"No." Peter couldn't keep from chuckling. "That isn't a cake. That's a fish. Can you say *fish*?"

"No."

They had been sitting together all evening, Peter and his son, talking about things, not playing, and Shannon had watched them, all the while knowing Peter was clinging to his child for a reason.

Shannon swung her legs off the sofa and went to him. She traced his dark hairline where it scooped across the back of his neck and when Peter turned his face toward hers, she could read the thankfulness there.

"Feel good?"

He nodded.

"Why are you so lonely tonight?"

He looked up at her. "Why do you ask that?"

"Because you're clinging to Taylor as if he were a life preserver."

Peter closed the book and stared into the fire. Shannon bent forward and kissed his head.

"She's here, you know," he said finally. "I always think I'm getting away from her. I always think she's finally gone."

"Lorilee?" She took Taylor from his arms and hugged him.

"The Browns' little boy is named Toby."

"Peter—" she sat on the chair's arm beside him "—Toby's parents made a choice for him."

"I know that. Choices. It comes back to that, doesn't it?"

"What do you mean, Peter?"

He grasped her hand and looked up over his shoulder at her. "Lorilee doesn't chastise me anymore, Shannon. Or maybe I don't chastise myself. I made the right choices the day she died. I did everything I knew to do and I still lost her. But I don't think it was my fault anymore. I did my best, Shan. Just like I'm doing my best now...to get along."

"Trust is a powerful thing, Peter. Especially when you're learning to trust yourself again." He was gripping her hand the way he would have gripped the end of a knotted rope. She was talking as much about herself as she was talking about him, about BEAT and the things she had fought for and had won.

"Maybe it's just that I don't feel life is running away from me anymore. I felt it today as I sat beside you in that hearing room. I felt it first when I spoke up for you in New York City."

"I needed you so desperately that day, Peter. Thank you."

"Do you still need me?" he asked her.

"Yes," she told him gently. "I always will."

Taylor's head slumped against Shannon's shoulder. "Your kid's gone to sleep," she whispered. "He feels so wonderful. Like a floppy teddy bear."

"I'll take him." Peter rose from his chair, his arms reaching out to cradle the bundle of blankets that held his son. "Let's get this little wump to bed."

Shannon padded into the nursery behind him and watched in the muted light while he gently placed his son in the crib. Taylor's cheek pressed against the printed sheet. There was a zoo of stuffed animals along the railing, and Peter took one, a fuzzy yellow cow with a bell tied around its neck, to lay beside the baby. A bittersweet happiness surged up in Shannon. How she needed this man and this boy. Knowing them both had added such levels of joy to her life. Peter made her feel so many things—contentment, safety, a physical desire for him that overwhelmed her, a sense of belonging, things she had been searching for, things she had needed even before she left for New York. *Dear heaven,* she thought. *I love him so much.*

She laid her head against the back of his shoulder. *I can't do this. I cannot fall in love with him. I cannot let myself need him.*

He turned and took her hand. "Come here, Shannon." He reached around behind her and unfastened the black clasp that held her braid in place. Then he combed through her hair with his fingers, starting with the ends, working his way up to the back of her head, until her mahogany hair fell in disarrayed ripples around her face. He cupped her hair in his hands and lifted it toward him until it lay forward against her shoulders. "You're like silk," he whispered to her. "All of you. Your hair. Your body."

Shannon moved toward him and clasped her arms around his neck in the semidarkness of the nursery. *I can't fight my feelings any longer.* She was helpless when he was beside her, touching her. She drew one long, tortured breath as Peter scooped her easily into his arms and carried her from his son's room.

He put her down on the hand-woven rug before the fire and she could feel the heat from the flames leaping against her skin. *It isn't enough,* her mind protested. *It isn't enough.* But it was enough for them—it had to be; it was all they would ever have. "Peter." She could see only his eyes and the flames were reflected there, too. "Make love to me. Please."

His expression didn't change. "That was what I had in mind."

Peter was sitting above her and unbuttoning his finely woven shirt, and when he peeled it back Shannon gasped when she saw him, the tanned curves of his torso entranced her so. His chest was lightly covered with fine tendrils of hair the same color as the hair that fell across his forehead. She gripped his shoulders and pulled herself up to him. "I want to touch you," she said and then her tongue began to trace curves as graceful as the curves she had watched him make while skiing. "All of you."

"Oh, Shan." He gently pushed her back against the floor. "Me too."

It had been so long for him, so many aching months alone in the monstrous bed downstairs, listening sleeplessly in case his son should wake during the desolate hours of the night. For weeks, he had dreamed Lorilee was alive, that it had all been some horrible mistake, a funny secret between the two of them that she was really still here, and then he would awaken and the emptiness would hit him like a wall, his body still aroused from the dream of her lying beside him.

Now it was Shannon he held in his arms, her body all fluid and fire beneath him, and he realized as he lifted her blouse up beneath her shoulders and she lifted her arms up to help him that he needed them all—Lorilee's soul and Taylor's life and Shannon's love. His emotions were in a fever pitch as he tossed Shannon's shirt onto the sofa.

She was easing her own jeans down off and over her hips, and he touched the tips of her fingers with his own as he watched her. He bent to her, his body burning. He was frantic for her. "I can't..."

For a moment, Shannon thought he was going to tell her he couldn't fulfill his intentions yet again. But when she saw the raging desperation in his eyes, she understood. "Don't hold back for me, Peter." Her own hands slid down her thighs once again, this time taking with them the last lovely layer of lace.

Wordlessly he tugged off the remainder of his clothing and then he reached for her and she clung to him. His entire body was stiff and shaking with his physical need for her. He called out her name over and over again as his very soul seemed to gyrate within her.

"I'm here, Peter," she told him every time he called out her name. "I'm here."

"I'm so glad...so glad...so happy," he whispered. And then, at last, he arched cleanly against her, three, four, five times, before he lay spent. He lay beside her silently for a long while and then he rolled over, his chin propped against his palms, and looked at her. "You, ma'am," he teased her weakly, "are a he-man's dream."

"Oh, I know," Shannon shot back at him as she touched his cheek and her heart overflowed with joy at the satisfaction she saw on his face. "I saw He-Man at the studio last week and he told me that."

"Great," Peter laughed. "A real comedian on my floor." He sat up beside her on the hand-woven rug, and she lay there watching him, not quite satisfied, still wanting him, but bathing in the lingering pleasure she had given him.

He felt her eyes on his body and he turned to measure them, still dark and smoldering. "Oh, Shan..." He bent toward her again, gripping her ankles with his hands and then trailing his palms firmly up the length of her body, touching all of her in a rush, her thighs, her waist, her breasts with his thumbs, until his fingers met her own. "How I love you."

She was stretched out before him, her translucent skin seeming to soak in the golden glow from the fire and then reradiate it. Peter felt his blood surging once more, for he wanted her again, he wanted her always. And this time, he knew she needed him to satisfy her, just the way she had so graciously satisfied him.

"Again," Shannon whispered as she smiled up at him, lost to everything except his body and the things he made her feel. "Again and again and again."

"Whatever you say," Peter agreed and gave her a slow smile. He bent toward her then and heard her sigh as his tongue began to dance against her skin like the flames.

CHAPTER THIRTEEN

IT WAS well past midnight when Peter bundled Shannon into his arms and carried her downstairs to the massive log bed in his bedroom. "Get some sleep," he whispered to her as she stretched languidly beneath the down comforter and then reached for him. "I know how tired you still are."

Shannon felt wonderful, more at peace than she had ever felt before, like a flower whose petals had finally unfurled to catch the sun. "I want to stay awake with you all night." She spoke with the slow easiness of someone just on the brink of sleep.

Peter kissed her again. "I'll be back." He walked back upstairs to make certain the glass doors were closed on the fireplace and to lock the front door. They were routine tasks, but his thoughts were filled with their lovemaking of the hours before. They had loved each other, each giving and, just as they did in their friendship, in turn, taking. They had seemed to slip into one another that night, to meld together, forming a unified sturdiness. His body was sated and his mind was at peace. No ghost of his former wife would lie beside him tonight. Lorilee's ghost was gone. And in its place was a beautiful, vital woman, a woman who had proved her feelings for him over and over again as the fire dwindled to coals. For a moment, Peter stood at the bay window and peered out at everything that suddenly belonged to him again, the silvery mountains and the sky peppered with stars and the moon and the flawless night.

When he tiptoed back downstairs, he found Shannon asleep. She was exhausted, although she wouldn't have admitted that to herself. He was filled with concern for her as he watched her. When he pulled back the comforter and lay beside her, she moved ever so slightly toward him. Her body curved against his own, secure against him, and he held her there as the hours passed, drinking in the feel of her, and the night was no longer desolate around him. It was soft, as her breathing, and cozy and warm.

He awoke the next morning to the routine sounds of his home, Taylor waking, dishes clattering, as Camille, who had her own key because she always arrived early, took pots and plates and glasses out of the dishwasher. Shannon was still sleeping next to him and he reached for her, knowing his touch would waken her, knowing he should let her sleep.

"Mmm-m-m-m," she moaned as she rolled toward him, her eyes only half open. All she could think of was how warm and safe it felt to be enveloped in his arms first thing in the morning.

"Good morning, miracle," he whispered.

"Hi." Shannon opened her eyes a bit and smiled at him. The sun was already streaming in the east window, falling across the pine floor and the bed in long, golden strips. "Is it late?" She wanted him again. His palm ran the length of her bare arm and he bent to brush her shoulder with his lips. "Do you have to go to the bank?"

"Actually—" he gave her a boyish grin that reminded her of how he'd looked the day she had first skied with him. "—there *are* benefits to owning and operating your own bank."

"Like taking the day off to go skiing—" she buried her face in his chest "—or just to stay at home in bed."

Peter wrapped his arms tighter around her, wanting her, wishing they could stay in his bed forever. "Or to go fishing," he said simply.

Shannon propped herself up on both elbows as her dark hair made a curtain around both of them. "Surely you aren't that brave? To compete with me at a fishing stream? You're either crazy or else you're a glutton for punishment."

Peter grabbed both of her arms and flipped her down while they both rolled and she giggled. He was on top of her then and he swept her hair back from her face. "You have a high opinion of your own fishing abilities."

"Yes, I do. I'm very good."

"I ought to challenge you to a contest. We could seal this business with a fried trout dinner. I'm one of the best, as well."

"You'd never outfish me." There was something new in Shannon's eyes, not a challenge, just happiness, carefree memories she carried with her from her childhood. Peter had never seen her look so joyous and relaxed. "You think you can outfish me just because I'm a girl. Well, you can't. I've been fishing forever." Her father had taken Shannon out into the back pasture when she was seven years old and had taught her how to cast a fly into a paper cup. She had been fishing Wyoming's rivers for almost as long as she could remember. She had captured every sort of trout imaginable, German Browns and Brookies, Native Cutthroats and Rainbows.

When she was in junior high school, she had learned to tie her own flies. She still had them, stuck by the barb into the rolled brim of a lopsided straw hat she had long since stopped wearing. Her fishing prowess was a part of the life she had lived a long, long time before. It was another part of herself that Peter had brought her back to.

"Actually," he said, grinning at her, "I have been considering the risks of putting a fly rod in your hands for a long time. And I would much rather stay here." He was silent for a moment and they both heard the dishes clattering upstairs and a rhythmic clanging that had to be Taylor banging against his high-chair tray with a spoon.

"But you don't think it would be such a good plan to stay in bed with your baby and your housekeeper banging around in the kitchen upstairs," she finished his thought for him.

He kissed her full on the lips. "Exactly." He said, chuckling. "And I was listening to the Jack Dennis Fishing Report on the radio yesterday and the trout are taking flies up in the park."

"Well, get off me and let's go." Shannon laughed as she tried unsuccessfully to roll away from his arms.

His expression sobered. "I love you, you know."

She reached up and tousled his hair. "I know. You told me that in a thousand different ways last night." *And I am pretending, for now, it's that simple.*

Peter released her and he hurried to dress while she sat on the bed, her arms wrapped around her knees, watching him. She had seen him so many times in tailored suits and an expensive tie, and she almost laughed aloud when she saw him now, in khaki jeans and a navy blue chamois shirt and an old pair of canvas shoes that had turned green from what looked like years of stomping through wet grass. "Nice outfit," she commented as he plopped a fishing hat on his head.

"Thank you, ma'am. Next year I expect you to nominate me for the best dressed list. You have seen me now—" his grin was so wide that it stretched all the way across his face "—in top form."

"Was that before or after you put on those pants?"

He jumped back on the bed again, stained sneakers and all, and he tickled her as she writhed and laughed against him. "Take that back, young lady."

"Never." Shannon was giggling so hard that she almost screamed,and she was so happy, her heart felt as if it might swirl up out of her body. "You *were* in top form. I mean it. You should be taking it as a compliment instead of attacking me."

"I enjoy attacking you."

"I noticed."

He pulled away from her. "I'm going upstairs now. I don't think it would look good if we both went up together. I'll tell Camille I think you're still sleeping."

"You're sneaking around—" she touched his nose "—just like a little kid."

"I feel like a kid this morning." He kissed her once more. "Thanks." He left her then and Shannon could hear him whistling as he bounded up the stairs and she laughed at herself, for she was humming, too, as she spread up the comforter and went to her own room to dress. She pulled on a pair of maroon sweat pants and a matching rugby shirt. She brushed her hair until it gleamed and tied it back with a twisted blue bandana before she hurried upstairs to join Peter.

"Good morning," she said and smiled at all three of them in the kitchen as Camille poured her a cup of steaming coffee.

"Did you sleep well?" Peter asked nonchalantly. The mischievous little-boy expression was all over his face again.

"Oh, yes." She suppressed a giggle and lifted her chin. "And you?"

"Yes." He sipped his coffee, his eyes sparkling at her over the rim of his cup, and she wanted to hug him. "Very well."

Camille pulled a plate of hot apple turnovers from the oven and Taylor climbed into Shannon's lap, as they all lapsed into silence. Shannon's and Peter's eyes kept locking over their coffee cups, and finally Peter couldn't stand it any longer. he reached for her beneath the table and grabbed her thigh, and Shannon choked on the coffee she was sipping.

"Are you okay?" he asked her innocently as tears came to her eyes and she coughed.

"Oh, fine." She was laughing now, too, as she jumped from the table. "I just didn't want to spill my coffee on the baby." Camille couldn't help seeing the look that passed between them as Peter reached for her and hugged her, the baby wedged between them, and Shannon kissed him.

"I'll load the car. Most of the fishing stuff is in the garage," he said.

"I have to stop somewhere and get a license."

Shannon helped clear the table and Camille kept watching her. The housekeeper was happy for them both, and for Taylor, too. Peter went outside and dismantled several fishing rods in the garage and piled them into the back of his Jeep Cherokee. It wasn't until he had loaded his hip waders that he realized Shannon didn't have any of her own. He lumbered in through the front door. "Shan? You don't have any waders, do you?"

She was running around the house, stooped at the waist with Taylor on her back, giving him a bumpy jaunt around the family room. "No, I don't." Taylor was still on her back. "I'm giving him a Shannon ride. Sort of the same thing as a horsey ride, only I'm not a horsey. I'm a Shannon." Taylor was grinning from ear to ear, but she couldn't see his face from her position. "Think he likes it?"

Peter had his mind on fishing. "I've got an extra pair." They had been Lorilee's. But this morning it didn't matter if they might have once belonged to the Queen of England. He wanted Shannon to use them.

They drove north of Jackson into Grand Teton National Park to a beautiful place named Oxbow Bend. And the only thing Shannon could think of as they drove farther into the forest and into the mountains was that she was moving ahead, too. She wanted to be part of Peter's life so much that she ached inside, but she could never belong to it for more than a month or two at a time. She knew she could never pursue her career in New York City and maintain a life in Wyoming, too. She would be acting in both places, playing two different roles and hiding a soul that magically switched loyalties every time she boarded an airplane and flew across the continent.

So many elements in Peter's life represented the things Shannon had longed to run away from. In many ways, his life had run parallel to her own father's. Daniel Eberle had stayed in the place he'd loved for a lifetime, raising children and sheep in a state where there were more pickup trucks than there were people. If Peter had elected to pursue his banking career in New York City instead of at his father's bank in Wyoming, he could have built a worldwide reputation for himself. He had ultimately settled for much, much less.

And much, much more. Taylor Barrett would grow up much as she had, fishing with his father, climbing rocks, skiing in an old pair of jeans while the tourists from the East Coast skied in color-coordinated bibs and jackets that would have cost the same price as one of her father's ewes. And, as she studied the scenery while Peter parked the Jeep beside the river, for the first time in her life, it almost seemed like a fair trade.

Peter handed her a rod. "Do you have a fly preference," he asked without meeting her gaze, "or do you need advice?"

Shannon covered her eyes with one hand to shade them from the sun. She looked at the movement of the water. "Oh, not really. But considering the time of year, why don't you let me try a Kiwi streamer?"

Peter's head jerked up and he eyed her with open admiration. "Okay. So maybe you *do* know what you're doing."

"Every so often," Shannon said as she took the rod from him, "I do." Then her voice dropped a bit and she touched his shirt sleeve. "I think...last night...I didn't know..."

"What?" Peter stared at her, standing beside his car with the fly rod in her hand, and all he could think of was how much she had brought into his life, how beautiful and happy she was and how she had felt beneath him and how she had almost laughed aloud when he had asked her how she'd slept, in front of Camille. "Are you trying to tell me you think you made a mistake last night? It's too late for mistakes, Shannon. You can't take away the things you gave me." And as he watched her face change expressions from confusion to anger, he saw something clearly in his own mind for the first time. There were two warring camps in her. "How long do you think you are going to be able to separate your mind from your heart, Shannon?"

"I have no idea what you're talking about."

"How long is it going to take you to get away from what you feel for me and get back to the studio in New York City? You can't call that a life, Shannon. What you have in the city is a huge stage and a huge piece of playacting."

"You have no right to say that, Peter. You are the one who brought me here. You are the one who knows how very much my success in New York means to me."

"Yes," he said slowly, precisely, "but the woman I brought back with me did something very, very right last night. There are parts of you that belong to both worlds, Shannon. Don't kill off portions of yourself just because you want to prove a point to people." Now Peter's fists were clenched at his sides. He wanted to grab her, to shake her, but he didn't dare.

Shannon turned away from him without speaking, and she gathered Lorilee's things, the waders and the vest and the little hat Peter had said she could wear, too. He watched her tug the waders up past her knees and then walk away from him, her back rigid, knowing full well she was fighting herself, warring against something in her life that had taken root long before he'd met her.

She reminded him of the geodes he had seen in the rock shop near the town square, as hard as stone, but if you could break them open, you found crystals and hollows and colors inside. And he wanted the hidden beauty she could bring into his life. He wanted it more than anything.

Peter started after her and then he stopped. Once again, he had done his best. He had made choices. He had done everything he knew to do. He had brought her to his home. He had shown her how desperately he needed her. And she had discovered that she needed him. He knew it. He could do nothing more. He could only love her. Peter watched as Shannon threw her first perfectly formed loop cast onto the water.

CHAPTER FOURTEEN

"You're cheating, you know," Peter called out as Shannon released her fifth catch of the morning. "You keep catching that same fish and turning it loose again. You can't expect me to believe you've caught five different ones."

"Yes, I can," she called back to him and he listened as her voice echoed across the water. They had been this far apart all morning, a current separating them, but Peter had almost relaxed now. He hadn't caught any fish, and he was almost ready to start laughing at himself. Shannon was a much better sports fisherman than he was. He had figured that out as soon as she had come back to shore and had taken pliers to the flies he had given her, pushing down the barbs on the hooks so that the fish stood less chance of being injured.

He hadn't been able to keep from smiling at her. "So you're a conservationist, as well."

"Yes."

She had reeled them in all morning and he had seen her massaging the fish in the water to ease their shock before she let them swim away. And as she trudged upstream past him, in the fishing gear that had once belonged to his wife, he had to compare the two women.

Lorilee's technique was to beat the water constantly with the fly, always on the offensive, her movements effusive and strong. And she didn't stay on the stream very long. She had always given up if she didn't get a strike during her first half hour of fishing.

Shannon's casting was slower, more rhythmic, like watching a waltz, and she was patient beyond belief as she played a fish, casting the fly at just the right angle into a quiet pool, moving it through the current as if it were alive.

"I could learn from you," Peter told her, his voice soft, when she finally made her way toward him. Something had changed about her when she had been on the stream, some extra hint of confidence had guided her, and despite the words they had exchanged earlier, Shannon seemed content. It was as if she had forgotten about the outside world as she flipped each fly on the water and waited for a response. It was as if she was baiting and casting for an old part of herself, bringing something to the surface in her that she had pushed away when she had left home.

"I had a good morning."

"Are you ready to go back? We could drive to Wind River this afternoon if you'd like. Do you want to see how the teen center is progressing?"

Shannon raised her eyes to scan the silhouette of the mountains. "Peter, I didn't know I could still do this."

"Fish? You were grand." He touched her arm tentatively. He didn't want to startle her from her reverie. "You should never have left these trout streams behind."

"They have trout streams in New York."

"Yeah. Right down West 57th Street. I noticed that as I was weaving through traffic in a taxi the other day."

He had thought she would be angry but Shannon was silent as she dismantled her rod. As they drove through the trees, a cow moose and her calf crossed the road in front of them and Shannon cried out. "Look. Oh, Peter . . . they're beautiful."

Peter nodded somberly. "It's a beautiful place. You should think about living here someday."

"Don't do this," she begged and they lapsed into silence.

Later, Peter parked the car on the square in town and they ate lunch at a Mexican sidewalk café called Merry Piglets. They both laughed as they tried to eat the huge tostadas with their hands while hot salsa dribbled down Peter's shirt sleeve and Shannon spilled cheese in her lap. Then they strolled along the boardwalk together, walking side by side, never quite touching, counting out-of-state license plates and weaving in and out through the tourists coming out of the little shops.

They drove to Wind River next and she gasped when she saw the building site. There was a skeleton of a building standing where once there had been only bare earth.

"Do you want to see anyone while you're here?" he asked. "Your family? Jim Clarkson?" He had already glanced around the lot to see if anyone there would recognize her.

"No," she told him. "It would be hard to explain why I'm here. I just wanted to see everything, to know it's really happening."

"It is."

They got out of the Jeep and Peter walked her through the partial building. They made a game of guessing what each room would be. Shannon remembered enough from the blueprints to recognize the studios. "I can't believe they've gotten this much done." She wheeled to face Peter. "Now BEAT has a life of its own, doesn't it? It's come about and it's a good thing and it's unstoppable." Her eyes were huge and bright and then she realized this was no longer her home, and she stood feeling empty and hollow, her face a mirror of the vacuum that the emotion had left in its wake.

Peter saw her eyes go dark. "They have done a lot since I was here last," he said. "Somebody had done the sheet-rocking in the basement. Your father volunteered to put up the corner beads around the windows and doorways. Soon they'll be ready to spread mud compound on the walls."

"All this," she said softly. "They've done all this."

"Did you expect to come back and find just a bare piece of ground after everything you've done?"

"I don't know what I expected."

"Shannon." Peter knew he had to ask her an important question. "Shan, why don't you stay here? Don't go back." Her eyes were huge, hollow, darting back and forth across his face. His heart went out to her as he gripped her shoulders. "There are so many people here who love you. Your family. And me." He didn't say what he was thinking: *You're lost in New York. You've told me that in so many different ways.*

"Peter? Do you have any idea what you're asking?" His question was one she'd been asking herself for hours now, ever since she had made love with him, and felt so totally absorbed and at home and at peace in his arms.

Shannon had spent hours in the car realizing the implications of her jumbled emotions. What good could she be to BEAT if she turned away from the dream of acting, a dream she had nutured ever since high school? It was strange but she didn't think of the acting, of what it would feel like never to stand beneath the lights again with the director calling for silence, or never to have people approach her because they recognized her from the show. She thought only of the implications for the teenagers she had fought so hard for. "You're asking me to give up."

"No. I'm not. I love you too much for that. Giving up is not the same thing as changing direction." He was still holding her by the shoulders, silently begging her to stay. "I know it's a loaded question. Twenty-four hours ago, I would have thought it selfish of me to ask it. But not anymore. You've shown me too much of yourself, Shannon. Last night I got to know the woman who's behind the celebrity."

She wrenched free of him while a huge yellow crane swung lumber to workers waiting to hammer it down. "Last night, we made love, Peter. Can't we both just be satisfied with that?"

"Can you?" He stared at her, his empty hands dangling at his sides, daring her to prove him wrong.

"No." She had to be honest. "I can't."

"I was right about you, then." Peter's anger and frustration bored into her.

Shannon closed her eyes then, to escape the horrible pain she saw on his face. "This will never get us anywhere." She glanced at her watch. "There must be a plane leaving Jackson this evening, Peter. I think it would be best for both of us if I was on it."

She saw a muscle tighten in his jaw. It was Peter's only reaction. "Fine. We'll drive back to Jackson. I'll take you...to my house to gather your things." He had almost said "I'll take you *home*." But it wasn't her home, it was only his, a hollow excuse for a place where their life together might have been. "I'll stay at the bank while you pack. I'll pick you up in time for the flight."

"I can take a cab."

"No. I'll take you." He wasn't going to let her leave him without seeing his face, for it was going to be the hardest thing he had done since Lorilee had died, letting Shannon go. He wanted her to know it.

The last of her composure crumbled. "Wyoming isn't supposed to be my life anymore, Peter. Why are you making me want it?"

"'WHEN FRIENDS BECOME LOVERS...when dreams become real...'" The theme song to "Wayward Hopes" swelled louder as Shannon stared at the television screen. Taylor was in his room sleeping and Camille was propped up on the sofa watching the show, a half-knitted afghan spread across her legs.

"It's an odd feeling to have you walk in the door—" Camille's knitting needles clacked together like the wheels of a toy train "—when I'm waiting to watch you on TV."

"I won't be on today," she said. "The episode you see today was only taped this morning."

"Oh, you should watch it, too, then." Camille patted the sofa beside her.

"I seldom watch the show," she said stiffly. "It's just such a part of my life, I...don't need to live it twice."

A familiar set flashed on the screen. Lisa Radford's living room. And then Eddie strolled in, wearing a red Lauren Taylor knit dress with a Gucci purse slung over one shoulder. "Roger?" she called out in a voice that Shannon loved. "Has the hospital in Vermont telephoned you? I need to know the status of your wife."

"Darling." Bud Masterson entered from the left. He was the actor who played Dr. Roger Radford. "It's you." The two of them exchanged a perfectly choreographed kiss. In her mind, Shannon could hear Al Jensen directing them. "Turn your head to the right. Just barely. There you go. Now raise your chin. Fine. Bud, come right down on top of her. Lightly. I don't want our viewers to think you two know how to slobber."

The camera switched to a different set. It was an electronic lifetime, where all the action took place through the camera's eye, where all the cuts and switches and editing were done in a control room. It was so real, yet not real at all. The room whirled around Shannon. Dizzily she gripped the back of Peter's arm-chair.

Camille saw her wobble. "Shannon. Don't fall. Are you okay?"

"Yes," Shannon said sharply. She was angry at her-self. She shouldn't have watched the show. She should have gone downstairs immediately to pack. "I'm fine. I have come to gather my things, Camille. They need me back in New York."

"But you only just arrived. Don't they give you any time to yourself?"

"No," Shannon said quietly, "They don't."

Shannon gripped the railing and ran downstairs as Camille looked after her, frowning. The housekeeper knew something was terribly wrong.

As Shannon pitched items haphazardly into her suit-case, she allowed herself to be honest. She was Shan-non Eberle, soap opera star. The longer she stayed in Peter's home, the more she would hurt him. "They won't be able to hurt you this much again," she'd told Peter once, while she'd held him and he'd cried. And now she was the one who was hurting him, after she had promised that no one would. "It will be better," she said aloud to him, to no one, "for you to stop trusting me. Then you can stop loving me."

She had not stayed in Peter's house long enough for her things to mingle with his. Her packing was uncomplicated. A sweatshirt. Mascara. The eyelet cotton nightgown she hadn't worn last night.

She couldn't find her jeans. She remembered removing them, Peter's hands on hers, as the glow from the fire played against their bodies and the warmth of his loving coursed through her veins. *Stop it,* she ordered herself. *Don't think of the things you give to one another.*

Her jeans had not been on the floor this morning when she had gone up for breakfast. Peter must have put them away, Shannon decided. She walked down the hallway and opened his closet and found them neatly folded on the shelf. She stood in the closet for a moment, drinking in the smell of him, surrounded by his clothing, the rich tweed coats and the leather jacket and the starched shirts. And then she saw something else hanging in his closet, a white satin dress she couldn't turn away from, covered with tiny seed pearls and a trace of lace on a mandarin collar. Lorilee's wedding dress.

It hung in his closet like new, as if it had never been worn, and she stared at it, hating it. "You ask me to let go of so many things, Peter," she said aloud. "How can I? It isn't any easier for me than it is for you." She stood motionless, her body rigid, an unyielding shadow, alone.

She heard footsteps upstairs. She hurried back to her own room, packed her jeans and carried her suitcase up the stairway.

"Taylor's awake," Camille informed her.

"Did Peter come in?"

"No. You must have heard me go into the nursery."

"Can I play with Taylor before I go?" It had been such a short time, but Shannon had grown to love the baby so much, too.

"Here he is."

She cuddled the little boy close to her. He was still warm from his sleep. "Taylor Barrett," she whispered. "I hope you grow up fine and happy and strong."

She gave him a ride to the sofa on her back and then she dumped him onto a cushion and kissed him while he giggled. "How's that? A dinosaur kiss." Shannon felt as if her heart was wrenching free of her body, binding itself here, to this tiny boy and the man that she loved. "Only," she echoed Peter's words, slowing only slightly when she realized she was doing so, "I'm not big and fat and funny looking."

Taylor giggled.

"Or green," Peter said, only he wasn't smiling, as he stood in the doorway watching them.

"Hello, Peter."

"Are you packed?"

"Yes."

He was grim. He didn't even attempt to be jovial for Camille's sake. "I'll load your things into the Jeep."

It will be so much better for you. To drive me out of your life.

She rose to hug Camille. "Thank you so much." Shannon was still holding Taylor and the housekeeper encircled the two of them with her arms. "For everything." She had to say the rest of it, too, although the way Camille twisted her lips in sudden anger made Shannon want to cry out. "For taking care of him."

"You had better let me have the baby," Camille said as she wrapped her fingers around Taylor's stomach and pried him loose from Shannon. Camille finally

understood what was happening, the reason Shannon
was shaking and sad, the reason Peter was furious. The
actress didn't have to go back. She was going back because she wanted to get away from him. And Camille
could tell by the anguished look in her eyes that Shannon thought she loved Peter, and that it was killing her.

Taylor flailed out against Camille and began to cry.
"Please," Shannon stroked his silken hair with one
hand. "Don't cry. Not now."

"You had better go," Camille said firmly, but Shannon saw tears in the housekeeper's eyes, too. "You're
going to miss your plane."

"I'm sorry," Shannon whispered, then she turned
and mutely followed Peter to the car.

PETER SAID NOTHING to Shannon as he drove her to the
airport. He was frightened of what he might say. He
was furious with her and furious with himself, and
helplessness surrounded him like humidity, clinging to
him, soaking into his bones, draining him.

He spoke at last after he had parked the Cherokee in
the airport loading zone. "Are you going to stop and
see your parents on the way through?"

"No." A travel agent had confirmed a nonstop flight
to Denver for her only an hour before. And Shannon
didn't want to say so, but she was as frightened of seeing
her parents as she was of staying with him.

The porter had already come to the car to take her
suitcase. Peter gripped the steering wheel with two fists.
"Take care of yourself, Shannon."

"I will." Her voice was quavering again, small and
uncertain. "Peter..." She paused for a moment, waiting for him to look at her, but he didn't. "Thank you."

"For letting you go?"

"For a great many things."

"All of them mistakes." He faced her at last. The resignation in his eyes made her want to comfort him. But she couldn't. Not now.

"I . . . have to go. I'll miss my plane. Don't . . ." She reached for his arm to stop him as he opened his door. Just touching him, feeling the cool smoothness of his sleeve beneath her fingers, made sadness lurch inside her. Another flight to New York. She didn't think she could bear it. She felt a rending in her heart, as if an invisible seamstress was ripping out stitches, and she was falling apart piece by piece. She pulled her hand away from his arm and stepped down from the Jeep before she turned back to face him. "Goodbye, Peter."

"Goodbye, Shannon."

How could I ever share my life with him? I don't know what I want my life to be. She touched his face without saying anything more. Then she turned and walked away.

Peter wanted to call after her, to tell her to telephone him when she arrived in New York City. But he had no right. He had no claim to her. Now, even their friendship was gone.

He laid his arms on the steering wheel and rested his head. He couldn't bring himself to drive away. Shannon was still there, a hundred yards away inside the terminal. He could still run to her and tell her not to go if he wanted. But she was gone from him. She'd left him hours ago.

This was the second time in his life he had been powerless, unprotected, because he had allowed himself to love someone. Peter despised himself for the devastation he felt. He would not make the same mistake again.

He heard a plane picking up speed on the ground, but
he turned away from it, not looking, not wanting to see
it rise gracefully above the mountains into the sky. But
the roar the plane made as it echoed against the Tetons
seemed to gather itself inside his body and shake him.
Peter felt he would rather face a firing squad than this,
and he buried his head in his arms again, while the plane
disappeared into the clouds and the skin on his hands
shone wet from his tears.

CHAPTER FIFTEEN

"IT'S ALL HERE—" Eddie held out a round basket lined with a blue-and-white checked cloth "—all the makings for a welcome-home midnight feast. We've got Brie cheese and baby Swiss, hot mustard and Canadian bacon, French bread." She threw her head back and laughed. "Do I sound like I'm calling roll for the United Nations? Well, the wine's domestic. From V. Sattui. My favorite winery in the Napa Valley."

"Thanks, Eddie." Shannon hugged her friend, basket and all, as she came inside the door.

"For the wine? I got a whole case of it yesterday."

"For coming over at eleven o'clock at night when you have to be at the studio at four-thirty in the morning."

"You'll be there, too, won't you? They've shot around you for two days. Al Jensen is going to be turning somersaults of joy to have you back. The star kid. The winner of—" She glanced around the room. "Gads, girl! Where is it? I can't find your Viewer's Choice award. You should have it hanging from the ceiling in the middle of the room."

"I haven't decided where to put it yet."

"Where to *put* it? Wear it on your head. Right in the center of—"

"—my life." Shannon's soft words cut into Eddie's sentence. "I don't know where to put it in my life."

Eddie reached down and flipped on a blue ceramic lamp. "It's gloomy in here, you know." It was as if Shannon craved the darkness. And it wasn't until the light shone on Shannon's face that Eddie knew something was very wrong. Shannon's hair fell in tangles against parchment-pale cheeks. There were purple circles beneath her eyes. She had been ravaged by the raw, cutting pain that leaving Peter had inflicted on her. There was a heaviness to the way she moved, as if her hands and her feet were made of something unwieldy and hard. "Shannon, my God, what's wrong?"

Shannon took the basket and furiously began to unload it. "Cheese. Meat. Bread."

"Tell me. Now." Eddie pulled the basket's handle from her friend. "The makeup artist is going to die when she sees you tomorrow. She won't have to use any makeup at all to make you look like you belong in a mental institution. This will be the first time she hasn't had to work for an hour to make you look haggard. She gets upset every time you come back from Wyoming. You always look so sad."

Shannon froze, the loaf of French bread in one hand and a wineglass in the other. "Every time I come back? Eddie? Am I sad every time?"

"You're always a little bit melancholy. We all know it. But tonight you're in mourning. Who died?" A thought occurred to Eddie, one that had been flickering in her head since Peter Barrett had testified in Shannon's behalf on the "Good Day" show. "Why did you come back so soon?"

"I just...missed New York."

"You never miss this place when you go home. You told me so yourself. You come back talking about your father's sheep wagon and that dog named Wiley and your mother's cooking."

"I wasn't with my family. I was with..." Shannon couldn't go on. She couldn't bring herself to say Peter's name. She could only think of his stricken face, of the sadness in his eyes when she had told him goodbye.

"Shannon, oh, honey..." Eddie hugged her.

Shannon pulled away from Eddie, her confusion and loss obvious on her face. "Spend the night tonight. Let's have a slumber party. I feel so alone. You can borrow a pair of my pajamas. We can ride in to the studio together tomorrow morning."

"Like a new girl in scouts who has to go with her best friend to the meeting? Shannon, what are you afraid of? That studio is your territory. With that award, you ought to feel like you own the place."

Shannon was still, staring at an empty spot on the mantel she had cleared for the Viewer's Choice statue. "I don't know what's important anymore, Eddie. I'm trying to forget the things he makes me feel. He makes me satisfied and happy and cozy and he makes me want the simple things I haven't wanted since I was a child. Like quiet talks and tickle sessions and fishing and sliding down a snowy hill on an inner tube."

"So you love him. I thought so. And does this Wyoming mountain man love you, too? Let's see. He flies to New York City in a chartered plane in the middle of the night to make certain you're okay. He drums up funding for BEAT. He testifies on your behalf in front of millions of television viewers. And when you thought you had to leave him and come back here, he didn't stop you. He let you follow your own dream. I'd say the feeling is mutual."

"Yes—" Shannon gave her best friend a gentle, watery smile and then laid her head on her shoulder "—it is. Mutual. And wonderful. And scary."

"Where is that award?" Eddie pulled away abruptly and pranced into the bedroom. "Do you have it hidden under the bed?"

"It's right here. In the closet. You're so worried about the dumb thing, why don't *you* take it home and sleep with it tonight?"

"No, Shannon. I'm spending the night here. You invited me. You promised me I could wear your pajamas. I want that old pair with I Climb Mountains written down one leg. But I want you to get out your Viewer's Choice statue first. I want you to look at it."

Shannon stood on tiptoe and pulled the little box down from the closet shelf.

"I'm putting it in here where all your guests can see it. On the mantel. In that empty space you made for it."

"Can a little gold statue and a career really fill the empty spaces?"

Eddie turned, the award still in her hand. "No. You need your people, too. Shannon Eberle, you won this thing because you gave your heart to it. Every time the cameras focused on you, you gave your guts to them. We all learned from watching you work."

"I'm destined to be the shining example for everyone." The heaviness was still there, in her voice, when she spoke.

"But you don't want to be."

"I don't know what I want. I don't know which parts of myself I want to give away. Maybe I want the freedom to be wrong once in a while, to get mad, to give up."

Eddie shook the statue at her. "Forget about this thing, then. You're a beautiful actress. But do you think it will be the same now? If your heart is in a different place?"

"Peter doesn't know I'm in love with him," she said quietly. "I couldn't tell him. It would have made everything even harder. I didn't want to leave. I wanted to stay with him forever."

"Shan . . ." Eddie stretched her arms toward her best friend and Shannon moved into them. "I hate to see you so unhappy. Do you think if you leave this behind that the things you've accomplished in New York will go away? Whatever you've done here is a part of you. It's a part of Al Jensen and me and a hundred different other people who have known you. A dream doesn't go away."

"Oh, Eddie." Shannon lowered herself onto the calico sofa and fingered the rich, golden patina of the statue. "If only I could believe that was true."

THE JURY SELECTION for Jim Brown's trial took three days. The attorneys questioned a stream of prospective jurors in order to find a few who didn't know Peter Barrett and who hadn't known his wife.

The public defender called in the judge, and the two of them discussed a change of venue. But in the end he decided against it. All parties involved, including Jim Brown, wanted to proceed with the trial. Gloria Brown would be tried after her husband, as an accomplice.

Peter did not attend the first days of the trial. He had dreamed of it for so long, wondering what it would be like to sit in a courtroom, hating someone who finally had a face. But now, he could only see a child's face, a little boy named Toby, someone very much like Taylor, who waited in Texas for his parents to return.

Toby and Taylor drew together in his mind like ghostly images on a screen. Two children who both needed others. And the only person he could hate was himself. He had lost Lorilee and he had lost Shannon. The two women who had come to mean everything to him.

Lorilee was gone through no fault of his own. He had done everything to save her. He had loved her with his entire being.

It was Shannon who haunted him now. Her words came back to him like wisps of clouds, floating into his mind at unexpected times. *I believe in human will*. He tried to banish her from his thoughts. But it never worked. *I can't understand people who sit back and let events tumble over them*.

Events had tumbled over both of them during their months together. Shannon had learned she did not have perfect control over her own life. And Peter had learned that, in reality, he had done his best to fight for Lorilee. But now, in his thoughts, it was Shannon who seemed to be crying out to him to rescue her, begging him to fight for her.

Both attorneys had questioned him extensively during the weeks before the trial. Six times, he'd told them everything he remembered. He'd helped them sift through every mug shot the same way they would have sifted through objects in a drawer.

Peter had been subpoenaed to testify during the fourth day of the trial. He had nothing much to tell the jury. He could identify the ransom note. He would tell the jurors he was unable to identify Jim Brown in a lineup. John Miller's testimony was similarly brief.

Peter would not be present for the coroner's report. The last day of testimony would center on the Browns' financial statements and the days Jim Brown worked for Lorilee. But both attorneys wanted Peter's testimony to be the last. He was the only person who could give the jurors a firsthand account of the events that had occurred.

John Miller telephoned him every evening with reports of the trial. The testimony was unemotional, the evidence specific. The defense was basing its case on an alibi. The public defender produced witnesses who told the jury Jim Brown had been in Lake Tahoe playing craps on the day in question. But a cashier from Fred's Market testified she had sold him groceries in Jackson Hole the same day. And a security officer from the airport thought he looked familiar even though there was no record of a Jim Brown flying in to Jackson from Lake Tahoe. As Daniel Kelton noted later, it would have been easy for Jim Brown to board an airplane and fly into Jackson under an assumed name.

On the fourth morning of the trial, Peter left the bank shortly before eleven and walked to the courthouse. His jacket flew open in the wind, and people who knew him called out greetings to him as he walked beside the little shops. Even so, he felt as if he was embarking into a different world. Nothing around him seemed real. Peter arrived at the courthouse ten minutes past the hour. He stood in the hallway gathering the courage to walk into the courtroom for another ten before he entered.

The public defender asked him if Lorilee had ever mentioned a man named Jim Brown. It was strange. In telling the truth, Peter was admitting the fact to the jury and to himself that there had been times in their relationship when he and Lorilee had been very far apart.

She was often too tired to tell him about her filming sessions when she arrived home after a trip. And she had been gone for weeks at a time before Taylor was born. There had been times Peter had missed her desperately. And yet he hadn't been able to get away from the bank long enough to join her on location.

It was Shannon he thought of now as his hands gripped the sides of his chair. *I'm fighting for fairness,* he reminded himself. *I will not condemn the man, but I will not release him.* He wondered, for a moment, if he was thinking of Jim Brown or of himself.

Peter strolled back to the bank shortly after two. He sorted through the stacks of mail Barbara had placed on his desk. At three, he met with a man he had decided to hire as an assistant. He wanted someone directly below him who could take over decision making when he went away. The candidate was in his fifties. The man had been vice president of a large corporate bank in Denver for ten years. He was anxious to move away from the city now that his children had graduated from college.

The meeting went well, and the man agreed to join Peter's staff. At four-forty-five, Sheriff John Miller called to say that the jury had gone out. Jurors would be sequestered at the Antler Motel until they reached a verdict.

Peter drove home and ate the dinner Camille had left in the oven for him. Taylor was restless and silly, as though he sensed something important was happening in the household. He threw blocks across the room and hit his head against the coffee table and turned the train over on himself on the kitchen floor. "Okay, wump," Peter said as he held the child close. Taylor began to cry and Peter realized he was exhausted from the effort of controlling his own emotions. But he was getting better at it. Since Shannon had flown back to New York City, it was getting easier and easier for him to retreat back into numbness. "If you don't kill yourself tonight, it will be a miracle. I think you should climb into a bed with nice bumper pads on the side so you won't smash your head on anything else."

Peter went to bed, too, and he slept in snatches, alternately resting and tossing, halfway conscious at times, waiting for the telephone beside his bed to ring. But it didn't. The alarm woke him at six forty-five as always, and Camille arrived twenty minutes later. He dressed in silence and sipped coffee at the breakfast bar while Camille chattered to him about her grandson's visit to Yellowstone National Park.

"These big city schools. They don't teach anything important like they used to. He's in the fifth grade in Chicago, and he doesn't know anything about the people who traveled the Oregon Trail. But they taught him animal calls. Animal calls! We were driving through Yellowstone and we saw a coyote and a cow moose within three miles of one another. He kept rolling down the window of the car and screaming these horrible calls. I thought we were going to come home with a cow moose in the back seat of the car."

"Sounds exciting." Peter laughed politely, but Camille knew he wasn't concentrating on her story. And when he walked toward the door to go, she followed him.

"I'm saying extra prayers for you today, son," she told him. "I'm proud of you and your boy. I feel like the two of you have become my own. And you've grown so strong."

"Is that what I've done?" His question was a sincere one. "Or have I just learned how to hide from myself?"

"Lisa Radford loves you, you know," she said softly.

"You didn't answer my question."

"I think I did."

"Her name is Shannon."

"Lisa Radford...Shannon Eberle...they're both the same girl."

"No." Peter shook his head. "They aren't."

"I always forget which one was here and which one I see on TV. The one who was here loves you. I could see it in her eyes when she left. I was mad at her then. But I keep remembering those eyes. As if she thought she had to sacrifice herself to keep from hurting you."

Peter leaned against the wall. "Did you see that in her? I wish to God that I had. I want to fight for her, Camille," he said, and the gentle longing in his voice made his housekeeper want to cry for him. "I want to ball up my fists and take a swing at all the things that are hurting her. But I don't know where to start. I don't know what to fight against. And I have this horrible feeling I can't rescue her again. She's the one who has to rescue herself.

"Maybe," Camille suggested gently, "the best way you can fight for her is to be here when she needs you."

"Maybe so," Peter said just as softly. "I'm learning that time can take care of so many things. But is waiting a form of fighting? Or is it an easy way out?"

"Sometimes I think waiting is the hardest thing of all," Camille told him.

The telephone on the breakfast bar rang. Camille answered it while Peter stood in the foyer. "It's him," she called to Peter. "The sheriff."

Peter took the receiver from her hand. "Barrett here."

"It was a good trial, Peter," John Miller told him. "A fair trial. The jury came in at seven-forty-five this morning. They deliberated fifteen hours."

"What did they decide?"

"It's over, Peter," the sheriff told him. "They found Jim Brown guilty."

"THIRTY SECONDS to tape," Al called out. "Makeup. I need you on the set. Fix Miss Cox's nose. Move a little to your left, Shannon. Fifteen seconds. Okay. Here we go. Rolling to tape. Five seconds to tape. Five. Four. Three." He held up two fingers and then one. He started them silently, with a hand signal.

"Help me, please," Shannon said to the nurse who walked onto the set. "I shouldn't be here."

"Camera two, get ready," Al called from the control box. "We're gonna come to you on your left."

Shannon was dressed in a wrinkled hospital gown, white with tiny blue designs that looked like little eggs. The makeup artist had smudged purple under her eyes to make her look ill.

An assistant director slipped onto the set beside the nurse. "Back up. We're going to come to you." He slipped away.

The nurse pulled out a hypodermic syringe to give Lisa Radford another tranquilizer. The needle moved toward her arm. She sat there, waiting.

"Okay," Al said from the box. "That's a cut on that scene."

"This is not my favorite outfit," Shannon told the director later. Everybody had been teasing her while she lounged around the studio in her gown and a fuzzy white robe someone in wardrobe had found for her. "It isn't very glamorous."

"I'll talk to wardrobe and see what I can do." Al gave her a fatherly kiss on the cheek. "Maybe we can get you one that's been ironed."

Al had to go back to the control room. Next he would direct Eddie and Bud Masterson in another perfectly orchestrated love scene. "Another segment of those delicious kisses," Eddie had said with a laugh earlier, while they were together in the dressing room. "My favorite thing to do is kiss Bud Masterson all day." But the two of them looked perfect under the lights together, their hands roaming in the right places, their mouths meeting and then drawing back. *Did we look like that? Were Peter and I that perfect together when we touched?*

"Miss Eberle. Hello." An impeccably groomed man's hand rested on her shoulder.

"Hello, Mr. Troy." She hadn't seen him since the Viewer's Choice Awards reception. "We don't usually see you on the set," Shannon commented lightly.

"You don't. But today is an unusual day." Troy turned to Al, who had walked up beside her. "I'm calling a meeting. I've been conducting some of my own...investigations. We have several problems. The lawsuit is just one of them."

Al Jenson's face turned to stone. "What do you mean *problems?* You agreed to that lawsuit, too. The legal advisers recommended it."

"Yes—" The executive smiled wanly "—but our image has been injured. Teenagers don't like to think they've been duped, Jensen. And statistically it takes ten positive statements to overcome one negative one. I want everyone included...makeup designers, boom operators, even the janitor who sweeps the floors. I want to make certain everyone understands what's happening. I want them in my office at noon, immediately after you finish taping."

Al narrowed his eyes. "I didn't expect this."

"It isn't as sudden as you might think," Troy told him. "I suggest you be first in line at the door. The future of this production is at stake."

Al stared after him as he walked away. "What's Troy doing on the set today?" He asked no one in particular. And then he saw Gabrielle Cohen, standing just outside the great pools of light, watching them all through the darkness, like a cat. Gabrielle Cohen, the director who specialized in programming for teenagers.

"Troy has brought in a new director." He said it aloud, to himself, but Shannon heard him, too. "They're maneuvering this thing into a major shake-up. Troy is ousting me."

CHAPTER SIXTEEN

SHANNON WANTED to scream one word for all to hear. *Why?* If this had been brought about by her speech, why hadn't the network dumped her instead of Al? Mark Troy held a one-way option on her contract. She couldn't get out of it. He could. He could tell her to walk anytime he got the urge.

"The idea has been in the works longer than you might think," Troy informed them smoothly. "We've known a change was needed for quite some time. Of course, we had to wait for the foundations to be jostled a bit." He was smiling now, like a practised politician.

Gabrielle Cohen would be their new director, he announced. Gabrielle was bringing in new writers. Al Jensen was history.

Shannon felt as if the floor had dropped out from beneath her. Everything she believed in had turned topsy-turvy, like the carnival ride where the sides are whirling and the bottom collapses. She was stuck there, suspended between the reality of what these people had done and the career she had put so much faith in. *"We've known a change was needed for quite some time."*

It was all she could do to keep from shouting out at them. The plan had become suddenly, deadly, obvious to her, because of Troy's words and the things she could see in his face and the way he had smiled. *The network plotted this. Mark Troy was in it from the beginning. He had probably planted that story in the paper and waited to let events take their course.*

Gabrielle Cohen rose from her seat beside him. "We're also introducing new story lines geared toward a young audience. Let's begin with the character of Lisa Radford. A few minor script changes for you, Shannon. You're going to have a fifteen-year-old son." Gabby shot her a Cheshire cat grin. "Surprised?"

Shannon's face was expressionless.

"We're going to push her age up a year or two. And the baby was born when Lisa was very young. Her parents have been raising him as Lisa Radford's brother. And—" she looked directly at Shannon "—you will have a new love interest. A young doctor at the Vermont hospital. He's going to fall in love with you while he's treating you. He's going to be the one who finds out that Roger Radford is having you drugged."

"But I thought Eddie—"

"No. That has been changed. We like this story line better. It's much simpler. It will appeal to a teen audience. We've cast Thomas Hansen for the role." Scattered applause broke out in the room. "Yes, an excellent actor. Very handsome. And he has a fan club that follows him to every production he appears on. Shannon, we're going to milk that Viewer's Choice award you brought home for us. You're going to need everything you've got to pull off these new scripts. Do you follow your loyalty and return to the husband you think has been true to you? Or do you do what the viewing audience wants you to do with the young, handsome Thomas Hansen? Once again, duty versus the heart. A slight... change of direction."

Peter's voice rose up from nowhere, rich and warm, the one thing steady within her. *I'm not asking you to give up. Giving up is not the same thing as changing direction.*

Shannon stood, her sober face swept the group of VIPs, while Eddie grasped her hand from down low beside her. "I do not respond to power plays, Mr. Troy. This does not impress me."

"Miss Eberle," Troy's voice was stern. "Please. Don't make a scene. Be seated."

"No. I'm sorry." She turned regretful eyes toward him, and he was surprised by how beautiful she was. There was something about her, an intensity and an earthiness, that the cameras did not do justice to. "You owe me this much. You've let me become an integral part of this show." Shannon was trembling but only Eddie knew it as she sat below her, still grasping her clenched fingers. "You misused something that is very dear to me. You took the things I said about BEAT and twisted them to serve your own purposes. You've hurt me. You've hurt a hundred kids in a high school thousands of miles from here. I'm not prepared to continue acting for you under these circumstances."

"Perhaps I should remind you that you're bound by a contract to this network. You do not have a choice."

Shannon's chin was high with pride, her hair a mantle against her shoulders. "How can you do this? How can you choose ratings and money over people who have worked well for you and been loyal to you?" This was something Shannon hadn't had to face before, because she had been lucky—her Q Rating had always kept her safe from it—and because she was a star.

"Advertising revenue governs the choices I must make." Troy was not afraid to be honest. Things like this happened every day in the television industry. "Do I need to remind you that you are replaceable, Shannon? Despite the golden Viewer's Choice Award you so proudly accepted?"

Shannon held her breath for a moment, her eyes closed, and in her mind she saw a white farmhouse with a rickety porch and a light coming from the window. Her home. Her strength. Everything she had run away from for so long. "I am aware of that. But I believe in a way of life where people aren't so easily scattered by the wayside." She thought of Peter and of how he had cared for her and of the pain he had been incapable of hiding when he had let her go. And this time, when she spoke, her eyes were wide open, with the contained glimmer of tears and anger in them, and she was smiling. "I don't think—" her chin was firm against all of them "—that I want to do this show anymore."

The new head writer jumped out of her chair. "You can't get out of your contract. You belong to us." She wheeled toward Mark Troy. "Lisa Radford is our main story line for the next few months."

"A change of actresses might work, but I doubt it," Troy said. "Shannon, you know the fan support you bring this show."

"I do."

"Call in your agent," he told her. "We'll talk about this further. I'm prepared to placate you. We'll draw up a new contract. One that involves more money. Or—" he was tantilizing her now, dangling a career before her that, by his standards, should have meant more to her than anything "—I can release you. I'm a fair man. If you feel this strongly about this, perhaps you'll decide to forfeit your acting career." Troy was certain she didn't dare quit the show. He was calling her bluff. "Say

---

the word. Yes or no. Now." He had the power to rip it all away from her, and he was having a wonderful time wielding it. "I won't keep you against your will."

"No," she said. "You won't do this to me." She looked down and smiled at Eddie and then she felt her composure returning. She turned back to Troy. "When the BEAT program was born several months ago, I tried to use my own salary from this show to help it. But the people wouldn't take my money. All I had to give the people I cared about was a portion of the monstrous salary you pay me. And they were afraid it had too many strings attached. Money means nothing to me, Troy. Integrity does. And now BEAT will continue to help students in Wyoming no matter what I decide to do." Shannon stood firm, her feet planted apart, her eyes blazing, reflecting the varied colors of her victory, while Eddie gripped her hand. "Release me, Troy. I'm going home."

WHS Senior Float Trip
Saturday, June 15

Dear Mr. Barrett:
Thank you for helping our new teen program get off the ground.

We would like you and Mr. Gleason to join us for our senior float trip down the Snake River. This is something the senior class at Washakie does every year. We would like you to come.

You have helped us more than we can repay. If not for your belief in us, six of us would not be attending college next fall.

We will ride school buses to the river raft launching area west of Hoback Junction. We

expect to launch the rafts at noon. This will be the last time we will be together as a senior class. Hope you can join us.
Sincerely,
Tommy Eberle

Peter stared at Tommy's Signature scrawled beneath the letter, and picked up the telephone to call BEAT's first benefactor.

"It does sound like a good time," Cal Gleason's voice boomed at him over the wire as Peter relayed the invitation. "I haven't been white-water rafting since Marty and the children were here two summers ago. I'd enjoy meeting more of these kids."

"They're a great bunch," Peter agreed. The point they were rafting was not more than a half hour's drive from Jackson. But these were Shannon's kids, a group of seniors she had given her soul to save, and Peter didn't feel he had any right to accompany them. Everything he had done to help them, he had done for her.

Peter knew himself well enough to know it would hurt him to see Shannon's younger brother. Tommy and Shannon looked so much alike. The huge dark eyes. The cocky grin. Even Tommy's lanky limbs would remind him of Shannon's coltish ones. It had pained him just to read Tommy's name on the invitation.

In a way, Lorilee's death had been less wrenching than this. It had been final. He had been able to release his feelings for her in pieces, until all that remained were the ones he wanted to treasure. He had experienced in his own life how the movement of time could take an edge off the pain when you were missing someone. But Peter was impatient with himself this second time. He didn't want to wait; he didn't want to ache for Shan-

non. Yet he did. Over and over again, he relived the
night she had given herself to him. "It's just going to be
us, kid," he told Taylor so many times, trying to chase
his thoughts of her away. "Just us. Just you and me."

"What's your hesitation, Barrett?" Gleason demanded. "I won't go if you think it's bad for your
banker image to go rafting with a bunch of high school
rowdies. But I have to admit, I thought I knew
you . . . I'd have thought you would enjoy this."

"We'll both go. I was trying to work out my schedule," Peter lied. "I'll have to find someone to keep
Taylor."

"I'll talk to Martha. It's been a while since the
grandkids were here. She might enjoy baby-sitting that
day."

"I wouldn't impose on her. I'll call my housekeeper.
She cares for Taylor every day." Peter hung up. "I'll do
this," he said aloud to himself. And then he hated himself for his thought. *Maybe Tommy knows how she is.
Maybe he can tell her—*

He stopped himself. There was nothing more he could
say to Shannon. He had laid his heart out for her the
way he would have spread out a deck of cards on a table. He had to make himself let her go. It was simple.
Simple. His entire day had been spent letting go. And
he marvelled, as he tromped downstairs to pack the remainder of Lorilee's things, at how painless saying the
final goodbye to his wife had been.

He walked into his bedroom and stood beside the
open cardboard box on his bed. The box had seemed so
big yesterday when he'd brought it home from Farmer
Jack's, but it was almost full now, of pictures and a
woolen shawl and a nightgown, things that had been
Lorilee's that he hadn't been able to part with before.

The guilty verdict in Jim Brown's trial had finally brought him peace. But it was the gnashing pain he felt at Shannon's leaving that had served as a final release for him. He had not thought another woman could come into his life and make him feel so alive, so certain of himself. Although painful, loving Shannon and releasing her had served him as a final severing from his old life.

Peter opened the closet and searched the shelves. He didn't want to miss anything. His eyes rested on the eggshell satin wedding dress hanging there beside his suits.

He remembered Lorilee, how beautiful she had been on their wedding day as she'd stood beside him beneath the trellis woven with flowers, the satin of her dress and the joy on her face glimmering in the candlelight. If he counted his wealth in memories like that one, he was a very lucky man. And he realized, as he thought of his wife, he didn't think of the sad things anymore, only the happy ones, and he smiled to himself as he reached for the gown with the little pearls on it. Peter spread it out flat on the bed so it wouldn't wrinkle, and then folded it into the box.

THE CORRAL SWARMED with bleating sheep, their woolly backs huddled so closely together that only an occasional black-velvet muzzle came into view. Daniel Eberle grasped Shannon's hand as the two of them pushed their way through the animals. He had to shout to her to be heard over the bleating cacophony. "And you thought you were coming here for peace and quiet."

"This *is* peace!" Shannon shouted back at him with a grin. She shoved yet another fat body the color of rich cream out of her way. "But maybe not quiet."

This was Shannon's favorite time at the Eberle ranch. Shearing time. For three weeks out of every summer, the usually deserted corrals were filled with animals waiting to be shorn, bleating about the indignities of it. The bunkhouse filled with temporary men, a crew of a dozen or so of them, who made their way from Mexico to Canada each year, helping the ranchers along the way separate the herds and tie the wool and trample it into bags.

Daniel Eberle scheduled his shearing for June, early on, so the sheep had enough time to grow another base coat to protect them during the frigid Wyoming winters.

Shannon had forgotten about shearing season until she arrived at the house in her father's old pickup truck and heard the sheep calling to one another in the corrals. A sense of well-being had swept over her then, one that had been growing within her ever since, as she participated in the routine chores of the season. Everything remained the same as it had been when she was a child, well worn and comfortable, a life where she had always been welcome, no matter how many times she had gone away.

"I need to go back to the house," she told her father as they reached the far end of the corral together, away from the woollies, where they could talk. "Mother and Melissa have been working in the kitchen all morning." Melissa had taken time off from the café to help on the ranch while Nolan helped with the shearing. Feeding a dozen extra men each day was a full-time task for both the women, and Shannon was glad she had come at a time when she could help, too. She had baked four loaves of bread this morning while Melissa cleaned up from breakfast and her mother prepared stew for the crew for lunch.

"Don't go back just yet." Her father hugged her against his side as they both leaned out against the fence and his eyes scanned the horizon. "Let's talk."

Shannon stared at the horizon, too. She could barely see a herd of sheep grazing a mile away. She could just make out the silhouette of the herder's wagon atop a knoll nearby. "I thought we had already done that."

"Not enough of it."

"Daddy." Shannon felt the familiar sense of guilt settle in her stomach. "I'm sorry."

"What are you sorry for? The television set?" The only reason he had bought it was so that the family could watch "Wayward Hopes." And he paid twenty-five dollars each month above that to have the cable. But that wasn't what Shannon was sorry for. It was more than money and television sets. She still felt as if she had let them all down. "We'll sell it one of these days when the budget gets close. There isn't any reason to keep it."

"I've come down in the world, haven't I?"

"That depends on how you look at it." Daniel smiled at his daughter, and his eyes held a gentle challenge. "You could also say you have moved up. You're here with us. Elevationwise, we're at 6,334 feet above sea level. New York City is only—"

"Right." She leaned her head against his shoulder. "After all the times I cried to you at the dinner table about my dreams and feeling trapped here. I was never grateful enough, Dad. You and Mom gave me everything I ever needed when I was a kid."

"I'm starting to believe that," he said with a chuckle. "You keep coming back."

She laughed and then stood on tiptoe to kiss him on the cheek.

"Your mother and I are proud of you. We know it took great courage to stand up for what you believe in the way you did, sacrificing something you worked so hard for." He faced her then, his concern for her reflected in eyes the same color as the soil. "Yet I wonder why you're not happy."

"I'm okay, Dad."

"I don't believe you."

"You should. Everything's fine. I'll find a place to live soon and then I'll be out of your hair." Shannon laughed then, as she looked around the corrals again, at the bunches of sheep. "Or should I say 'Out of your *wool*?' And I'm excited about my job with BEAT. I'll finally be able to really help the kids." She was desperate suddenly to convince him of her words. And she was trying even harder to convince herself. "I just won't be famous anymore. Lisa Radford is gone. That's the only difference."

Shannon had talked to Jim Clarkson three days ago when she'd arrived from New York City. She had agreed to act as interim administrator for BEAT as soon as shearing season was over. Clarkson needed someone to sort through BEAT donations and cull finalists for next year's scholarships, to handle paperwork and admission forms for the recipients. He had offered Shannon the job permanently, and she was considering it.

"You'll always be famous in this family." Daniel Eberle stared out across the sagebrush and the sweeping native grasses as he pondered the glimpses of guilt and loneliness his daughter had unwittingly shown him.

She reminded him so much of his wife, Agatha, sometimes. *She's always trying to be brave.* "You know," he
said softly, and the tenderness in his voice beckoned to
her as she turned to study his face, "your mother always dreamed of being a teacher."

"She *did*?" Shannon had never heard this. "I didn't
know."

"She quit talking about it after a while."

Shannon saw just a trace of sadness touch his face.
Then it was gone. "Why didn't she do it?"

"She married me instead."

"But she still could have been a teacher."

"I don't suppose that's what God had in mind for
her." He hugged his daughter closer. "She was planning to go to the community college in Rock Springs
and work toward her teaching certificate. She wanted to
teach mathematics. We sold extra ewes that year. The
shearing was going well and we had lots of lambs, and
it was the first year we could afford school. She had
only been enrolled in classes two weeks when she found
out she was pregnant with Nolan. Nowadays a woman's pregnancy doesn't have to stand in the way of such
things. But it did then. Even if she had been making a
teacher's salary, we couldn't have afforded to pay for
someone to take care of a baby for us. She didn't want
it that way. And we needed the money from those ewes
to pay for the doctor.

"Since it was still early in the semester, she could
drop out and get our money back. So she did." His
voice quavered with emotion: the pride in his family,
love for his wife. "That was one reason she gained so
much from having you as a daughter, Shannon. Every
time you got angry with us for holding you here, you
reminded us of the past. And when you went away to

follow your career, she told me it was as if she was seeing her dreams come true at last, too. Your mother took so much pleasure from that. And her pride isn't diminished by the fact that you love her enough to come home when you think it's time to start something new."

Shannon kissed him in the corner of the corral as the great mass of sheep moved toward them again and bumped against their legs. "Thank you, Dad. You understand so much."

"But I don't understand the loneliness I sense in you, Shannon. I know that you're missing someone."

"I should go help with dinner."

"No. Not yet." He was grinning again, the melancholy in his voice replaced by mischief. "One more project for you before lunch."

"I'm afraid to ask."

"Remember when you were five and I taught you to shear sheep?"

"Oh, no."

"Can you still do it?"

"Of course."

Daniel Eberle insisted his sheep be sheared by hand. Tommy and Nolan could both do many of them in an hour. "Although I'm not very fast at it."

When they entered the barn, Tommmy and Nolan were both shearing, each animal and each man on a separate platform, while temporary workers milled about the barn, preparing the animals and taking the shorn ewes back to the corral. "All right, big sister," Tommy called out to her as Nolan grinned. Shannon watched them both for a moment, her brothers, every sweep of the shears and their hands meticulously planned, as the cream wool fell away in clouds around them. "You can use the platform and I'll get ready for lunch." A man led Tommy's sheep away while he tied the wool into bundles and jumped down. "Oh," her brother said, "I wanted to make sure you were planning on coming on the float trip tomorrow."

"I thought it was just for seniors." Shannon climbed onto the platform and knelt to retrieve the shears.

"It is. But we added all the people who have helped with BEAT this year. Since you're the new administrator, I think you should be there."

A temporary worker led a ewe into the barn and lifted it up to her. Shannon held the animal in a loose grip around the neck, clipping the shears against the wool in a pattern across the animal's back and down its side. She met Tommy's gaze. She had to ask him, she had to know, and her hand was shaking so hard that she was afraid she might cut the ewe's skin. "I suppose Peter Barrett is invited, too."

The sheep jumped against her grasp and it bleated. "Shan, don't hurt that sheep."

"Perhaps I shouldn't do this. Tommy..."

"It's okay," Nolan encouraged, but Tommy was frozen, watching her face. "Every ewe gets nicked in one place or another. You're doing fine."

But she wasn't doing well at all. Saying Peter's name aloud had sent tiny tendrils of sadness and longing through her. Tommy was still watching her, for he knew her moods. Shannon didn't know what to say to him. It had taken every ounce of her strength to keep from going to Peter when she'd arrived home in Wyoming. But when she'd left, she had taken the one thing from him that mattered most. She had taken his trust. And she knew she couldn't ask him to trust her again.

She bent over the sheep, trying to concentrate on the ewe and the wool, doing her best to forget her longings for Peter, her right hand moving in strokes along the animal's side. Lanolin coated Shannon's hands and the wool fell off in slices, leaving only fuzz and pink skin beneath it. It was the way she felt, too, as if someone was cutting off huge masses of protection she had garnered herself with, leaving only the vulnerable places of her heart exposed, parts of it raw, nicked.

"Shan." Her father moved toward her on the platform. He wasn't certain what was wrong with her. He was incapable of helping her when she was like this, and that frightened him. "Let me finish that for you."

"No. I'll do it." Her strokes became certain again. She had come here at last to follow her own soul's bidding. Peter had been so right about the things she needed. Perhaps she owed him the courtesy of telling him so. *My wars have all been intermingled,* she thought. Now might be her only chance to tell him about the courage his caring had given her. She knew he would never trust her again. His love for her had been such a gift, one that she had turned away from, and now she was home, leading a part of the life he had told her she would never be able to let go of. After all the miles that had twisted between them, the ones that had pulled them hopelessly together, the ones that had torn them apart, there was nothing left to come between them now but the pain she had inflicted on him.

Shannon knew she couldn't expect Peter to forgive her. She only wanted to make him understand how much he had given her. If she went on the float trip, she could see him one last time. She could tell him how needing him had helped her grow. She owed him that much.

A worker lifted the ewe off the shearing platform. "Tommy, I'll go."

"Good. It's settled. You can ride on the school bus with us."

"Just like passing back through time."

Tommy jumped and gave a triumphant smile as he reached for his sister to tickle her. She laughed at last and Nolan came, too, as their father stood behind them observing his children, two tall sons and his daughter, all of them so very different yet so very much alike, their arms linked, their voices braiding in and out of earshot, as they walked toward the house.

CHAPTER SEVENTEEN

THE MORNING of the Washakie High School senior float trip dawned flawless and still, a day that was typical of hundreds of mid-June days, the sky a crisp sailor blue that slashed against the backdrop of the mountains.

Peter did not notice the brilliance of the morning. All his attention was focused inward. For days now, since he had mailed the box of Lorilee's belongings to her mother, his existence had been one of cutting off feeling. He wanted to stop hurting over Shannon. Thoughts of her cut him like glass. So he controlled them the same way he would control a car. He downshifted gears, turned a corner, kept his eyes forward.

Today was going to be difficult for him and he knew it. He should never have told Cal Gleason he would accompany him on this float trip. But he was facing it now as he had faced the past few days. Today would represent the final purging of Shannon from his life. Almost all Shannon's Wyoming life would be there before him, floating down the Snake River in a multicolored series of rubber rafts. He would see them and he would bid them adieu. Grand finale. The end.

Camille had insisted on coming to the house to care for Taylor. Her husband was working long hours driving a stagecoach for tourists around the square. The

baby was awake and fed when Peter joined them upstairs. Peter allowed himself to feel pleased as he gulped
down an icy glass of orange juice.

"You should eat more breakfast." Camille was gen-
tler when she spoke to him now. Her motherly bantering had stopped the day she had told him she thought
Lisa Radford loved him. She had watched as a fine layer
of lifelessness glazed his eyes. The control in his voice
made her afraid for him.

"This is all I need. Thank you."

"I made you biscuits."

"Thank you." Again she saw that false, mechanical
expression of satisfaction on his face. "I'm just not
hungry."

"I'll wrap these in a napkin."

A car horn sounded from the driveway. "There's
Gleason." Peter turned to his housekeeper, and he
softened a bit as she scurried around the kitchen gathering up things for him—a knife and some jam and
several extra napkins besides the one she had bundled
the biscuits in. "I'll see what I can do." He took them
from her.

Camille lodged herself between Peter and the front
door. "Peter Barrett. Learning to wait is one thing.
Killing off your emotions is another. For mercy's sake,
you won't even let yourself feel hunger."

"I have to do things my own way." It was the first
time he had seen her look fierce in days.

"Your way is dead wrong."

"Camille, Cal Gleason is out in the driveway waiting
for me."

"I love you as if you were one of my own sons."

Peter bent to kiss her. "What would I do without you to lecture me?" But her concern for him had warmed him, and he was smiling in earnest as he closed the front door and climbed into the car beside his colleague. He handed the biscuits across the front seat to Cal. "My housekeeper made these for you, Gleason. Eat up."

THE SCHOOL BUS had already unloaded when Peter and Cal Gleason arrived at the raft put-in point. The school's equipment was already in place, three trucks piled high with colored rafts, blue ones and yellow ones and gray ones, and another flatbed truck was piled with bright orange life jackets and yellow slickers and oars.

"Mr. Barrett! Mr. Gleason!" Tommy yelled at them as he bounded up beside them, with Sandy in tow, and shook Cal Gleason's hand. "Now everyone associated with BEAT is here!" Tommy thought about his sister, who had bounced along beside him in the school bus this morning, all the way from Wind River, singing "We're the Washakie girls, we wear our hair in curls, we wear our dungarees way up above our knees..." "I never thought it would work out so well. My sister is here, too. She's going to be the new administrator for BEAT."

Peter stared at Tommy. "Your sister? Shannon?"

"She's here."

"Why? How? I'm sorry." He seized the boy's arm. "Tommy, I don't understand." He felt a barrier within him begin to give way, like a dam with an overflow spillway, and he wanted to ball up his fists and slam into something. He wasn't strong enough for this.

"You haven't been watching 'Wayward Hopes,'" Tommy said, laughing. "They announced it on the show just yesterday. She quit. She's moving home."

She's moving home. But to her family, not to him. It was the worst blow Peter could have been dealt, and it sent him reeling. "Where is she?"

"Over there." Tommy pointed to the left, and he saw her standing beneath a giant lodgepole pine, away from the rest of the group, her eyes on him. When she saw him see her, she started to move forward, as if she wanted to join him, and then she stopped.

Tommy was introducing him to someone. Peter nodded politely. His thoughts were whirring away from him like birds. Shannon had quit the show. All the things he had urged her to do, the things she had been angry at him for, she had done them all anyway, on her own, without him. He didn't know whether he should applaud her or hate her for not needing him.

She glanced up. Their eyes met and held. "Peter?" she called out to him, and he didn't know if her voice was shaking or if the wind had taken his name and had hurled it toward him.

Instantly he was moving forward. And when he stood in front of her, it took all his reserve to keep from reaching out to her, to keep from gathering her against him in his arms, despite his hurting. "Hello, Shannon."

"Peter. I'm so sorry… I probably shouldn't be here. Tommy wanted me to. And I thought I could see you—" she hesitated. "—one last time."

"It's a surprise to run into you," he said coolly. "Somewhat painful."

Shannon winced. She sought his eyes, trying to read them, trying to know what to say to him. She had been praying she would find some hint of hope there, but she saw nothing, only a lusterless darkness, like an overcast sky. "I'm so sorry..."

"I don't want you to apologize to me."

"Maybe I'm apologizing to myself."

Tommy waved at them. "We're filling the last rafts. You two had better come on."

Peter looked at her. "We had better select our life jackets."

Cal Gleason was already in a raft on the water. Peter saluted his colleague as the man floated by. Without speaking again, he and Shannon tried on life jackets and measured the length of their oars beneath their chins. They boarded the raft as the waves lapped at it.

Shannon waved at her brother. Tommy was in the raft that had pulled into the water just ahead of theirs. Sandy was right beside him, holding his arm. They were still best friends, and in fact, they had become even closer since Sandy had told Tommy about her father's petition. Now that Tommy was going to college, too, they had had fun together, picking the classes they would take, planning to be famous writers someday.

For now, the water remained calm. The river had widened and it was clear, the rocks beneath it iridescent in the midday sunlight. A bald eagle perched on a ledge high above them while its mate wheeled lazily in the updrafts overhead. Peter willed himself to relax as the raft bobbed along with the crests of the current. He couldn't. He could only think of Shannon beside him, wearing cutoff denim shorts and a T-shirt that said I Love New York, looking beautiful and sad.

He glanced at her but she was staring out at the river, thinking her own thoughts, her body turned away from him.

From up ahead, they heard the water roaring. "Everybody row!" somebody shouted.

The front of the raft tipped down crazily as the passengers in the back rode high. The raft was a bucking animal, as water rolled over the front of the boat and drenched them all. They were all laughing and cheering as the raft reached smooth water again, and without thinking Shannon clutched Peter's arm, grinning, as water rolled in little droplets down her nose. He looked down at her, and he forgot to fight his feelings. He forgot everything except the fact that she was sitting there, so close to him, trembling from the shock of the cold water. "You look gorgeous with water running down your nose."

Her voice rose in a tinkling laugh. It was the first time today that Peter had given her any hope, any indication that he would be willing to listen to her, so that she could thank him. She bowed her head then, almost as if she was praying. "I was hoping we'd have a chance to talk."

Her hand was still on his arm. He cupped his fingers around hers. "Tell me why you left the show, Shan."

She was silent for a moment, staring at another rocky ledge that rose high above them. "I guess I decided it was time I started living my own life and quit trying to live everyone else's. I got . . . brave." She was searching for the right words, trying to make him understand how it had happened. "I have you to thank for that, Peter."

"I don't understand, Shannon. The things I said to you made you so hurt and angry."

"That's why I had to come with Tommy today. To tell you...you were right, Peter...right all along." She gave him a melancholy smile. "I wanted you to know that. Even though I knew it would be difficult to see you."

"Tell me, Shan." He willed the harshness and the hurt from his voice.

She told him about Eddie and the Viewer's Choice Award on the mantel. She stopped talking to laugh when the raft splashed through two sections of white water and then she began again. He listened while she told him of Mark Troy's involvement with the newspaper story, how the network had planted it so they could oust Al Jensen. "Al is like my second father," she said to him, and he could see she was still unsure of herself because of the blow that had been dealt her. "He taught me so many things about acting. Eddie and I have been waiting for the scenes where she rescues me from the hospital for months now. They were so good and *real* and they were so good for *us*, and this new writer comes in and steals it away."

"I'm sorry."

"I had to find out the hard way, didn't I?" Shannon leaned her head against his arm. "And the funny thing is, when I started to talk about getting released from my contract, Mark Troy offered me *more money*. As if money would change anything."

"I'm so proud of you."

"So you see, I changed directions like you said I should," she said softly. "Only I did it my own way."

Peter's features hardened. Obviously her own way did not include him.

"And so you came home."

"The things you said to me gave me the courage I needed," she told him tentatively. "Thank you."

Peter was angry again. He didn't want her gratitude. He wanted her. Here she was beside him, and tonight he would go home to the big house, still loving her, knowing she had come full circle, back to her home, without coming to him.

Shannon read the pain that swept across his face. She saw it spread everywhere, so that it was in the rigid stance of his body and in the sharp square of his jaw, in his eyes that seemed to bore down to the very center of her. She knew all was lost to them then, for she couldn't ask him to trust her again, not now, after she had taken something so precious away from him.

She averted her gaze so he wouldn't see the grieving in her eyes. Ahead of them lay another swirling mass of wild water. "Everybody row."

"Watch the raft ahead of us," a student commanded. "They're really going to get wet. They're hitting that big wave sideways."

The journalism teacher was sitting on Peter's other side. Peter heard her gasp. "They're going to hit it wrong."

Peter's eyes shot forward and, instinctively, he grabbed Shannon's arm. "Use your oars!" he shouted. "Keep paddling or we'll go astray, too!"

"Peter? What's wrong?" It was a relief for Shannon to row so hard, to pull back against the water with a force that eased the gripping pain caused by Peter's nearness. The current had a force of its own now. She wanted it to sap her strength. She didn't want to feel anything. And then she saw the raft ahead of them, twirling around as if it was going down into a drain, as the first spray hit it and a countercurrent grabbed it, just before it rammed into a rock ledge on one side of the river.

One side of the craft shot up and Shannon cried out. They were in the rapids, too, and Peter was making her hold on. And she could only watch everything happening in roaring...no, silent...slow motion, as the raft ahead of them began to flip over, as Tommy and Sandy and ten other students disappeared beneath the roiling surface of the river.

"Grab the rope!" Peter shouted at them as their raft began to spin, too.

"Someone has to help those kids!" the journalism teacher bellowed.

"They've got life jackets!" someone else called out. "We can't do anything for them! It's murder to jump out of a raft in water traveling this fast!"

The upset raft was far ahead of them now. It had already shot the water far below them, and it was twisting in a quiet pool at the base of the rapids.

"Where are they?" Shannon was crying but she didn't know it. "I don't see *anybody*."

"That may be a good sign," Peter reassured her as he gripped her arm. "They may all be caught in the air bubble beneath the raft. They can wait until they get their bearings and then they can all swim out together. I rafted this river many times when I was a boy. That's the way it usually works."

Even as he spoke, heads appeared in the water. Almost immediately, the raft was circled by upright bobbing heads and orange life jackets. One teenager climbed atop the upset raft and held out an oar to others. One by one, the Washakie students climbed out of the water. The other rafts, still full of teenagers, floated quietly by, waiting to rescue any stragglers.

Frantically Shannon took inventory of the teens who had been in the boat. One head still in the water. Five atop the raft. One more climbing up. Ten. She only counted ten. There had been a dozen kids in that raft. They floated closer now, close enough to see faces. Shannon recognized them, all of the faces familiar, all of them students she had fought for. Sandy was not among them.

"Peter!" she cried to him. "Sandy isn't there!"

She continued to search through the bobbing heads. She was looking for her brother, his familiar tousled wet dark hair, the strong, broad shoulders gleaming in the water. She counted once again and didn't see him. And when the reality of Tommy's absence hit her, Shannon felt her bones turning brittle, like ice. "It's my brother! Peter, please!" she screamed and suddenly she was clutching at him like a terrified child as he gripped her arms. "It's Tommy!" she shrieked at him and he felt his heart go up into his throat. "I can't find my brother!"

TOMMY FELT the pressure of the water against his head and his life jacket, pushing him down, and he knew he must be going deeper with the current. The water was murky from the rapids and he was moving so fast beneath it that he had no way to gauge his direction. For endless minutes, he didn't know if he was going up or down or sideways, the pressure was so fierce against him. He opened his eyes and he could see nothing but darkness, and his lungs felt ready to explode despite the instinctive gulp of air he had taken just as he hit the water.

Tommy knew the water was turbulent on the surface, almost dancing, as it crashed down upon itself, wave upon wave, but now he could only hear the dull roar of silence, a deafening stillness, as the current around him began to slow.

He opened his eyes again. He had no idea how long it would take him to reach the river's surface. He had no idea how fast he was traveling. The force of the water had been so strong, it had counteracted the buoyancy in his life jacket as if he wasn't wearing one.

Tommy let several bubbles of air escape through his nostrils. He followed them as far as he could in the darkness. *Air bubbles rise.* It was the only way he could be certain of his direction. He gave a powerful kick and followed them. Up, up and then, after what seemed like forever, he could hear the river singing again, and he knew he had almost made it.

Tommy surfaced. The light blinded him. He was lost again, disoriented, and then he realized he was in the center of the rapid. The capsized raft had long since moved downstream from him, followed by the others. Several rafts had pulled to the shoreline, and the rocks that lined the river were teeming with his classmates.

"Up here..." He tried to wave his arms but he couldn't. Lifting his limbs was like lifting iron rods into the air. He was weakening fast. And no one could hear him shouting above the waves.

He decided to lie back and let his life jacket carry him through the water. But if he got sucked under, he knew he didn't have the strength to surface again.

Suddenly he heard a scream from upstream. It was piercing enough to penetrate the fury of the water and the numbness of his body. *Sandy.*

Tommy could see her above him, her arms flailing against the current. She was trying to swim, and Tommy realized that she was going to shoot past him. He pushed off against a boulder, trying to move far enough in the water to reach her, but he couldn't. The current was moving too fast. He watched futilely as her head disappeared beneath the surface.

His first instinct was to dive for her. But he knew he would never be able to find her. The water was too murky and the current too strong. He held his position, fighting to remain beside the rock long enough to see her resurface. "Come up! Sandy..."

Downstream, Peter straightened his back. "I heard something." He shielded his eyes from the sun with one hand and turned upstream. The wind and the crashing water made it impossible for him to be certain. But it could be. Sandy and Tommy could be trapped somewhere upstream, still fighting for their lives. And then he saw a solitary figure, caught beside a boulder in an eddy, just below the spot the raft had flipped over.

"One of them is up there!" Peter started up the shoreline at a dead run, three of the students with rescue equipment behind him, and Shannon ran, too, praying as she stumbled over the rocks, her tears streaming back into her hair as she lurched forward.

As soon as she was close enough to see the familiar tousle of wet hair, she felt her knees weaken below her. Tommy was alive!

"He's been in the water too long," Peter said quietly. "His body isn't going to tolerate that cold much longer. We've got to get him out. Immediately."

"Sandy!" Tommy was hollering to her over and over again, but no one shore could hear what he was saying. Even so, one of the students on the riverbank saw her. Sandy had appeared upstream again, at the top of the rapids, where the water was churning white.

"She's caught in the counter current!" another student shouted. "All rapids have them but this one is the worst! If Sandy hits it again just right, she'll go under and then she'll be swept upstream again!"

"Tommy must know she's there!" Shannon cried. "That's why he isn't trying to swim out of there."

"She must have passed by him before. And she's going to go by again. But I don't think he knows she's above him."

Peter was running, sending pebbles flying up from his feet as he made his way along the shore, gauging the current so he would hit it in the right place when he entered the water. They didn't have much time. Even if Sandy did move past Tommy again, the boy wouldn't be strong enough to pull her out. It could be deadly for both of them if he tried.

"No! Peter!" Shannon screamed at him as she saw him make ready to dive in. But it was too late.

"Get down below and get ropes out to pull us in!" he called back. And then, while Shannon watched helplessly, he dived headfirst into the Snake River.

As the icy darkness closed around Peter, he felt the current tug him. He was glad he had trusted his instincts. He had jumped in at the right location. He surfaced as he shot downstream at an angle, and he aimed his body for the eddy where Tommy was. Peter held his body rigid and felt the waves twist against him as he stroked against the water with his limbs, every muscle in his arms straining, his mind just as taut, until, as if by a miracle, he felt calm water surround him.

"Mr...Barrett." Tommy smiled but it was halfhearted and Peter knew the boy was struggling against exhaustion. "I'm glad someone in the senior class thought to invite you...to this party."

"Yeah." Peter cupped his arm beneath Tommy's head so the boy could rest. "Me too. How do you feel?"

"Not very sharp. I'd like to go to sleep."

"You can take a long nap soon. We're going to get you out of here." It was just as Peter had expected. Tommy was already showing symptoms of hypothermia.

"Sandy is here...downstream...I thought I had her...."

"We know where she is. You helped us find her." The cold was beginning to sap Peter's strength, too. They had no time to waste. "She's upstream again."

"Thank God...I tried...not far enough..."

"We have to get both of you out of this water."

"I could go for that."

"I'm going to help you up onto this rock. When I get Sandy, you'll have to come back in. We'll hang on to each other and try to break the current." Tommy could only nod as Peter helped him out of the water. "If we go together down this way, the current ought to shoot us straight downstream."

"Are you...strong enough...for this?" Tommy's words were slurred.

"I have to be. Tell me when you see her moving toward us." Peter positioned himself to spring.

"Now!" Tommy shouted. "Move...now."

Peter shot forward, his body straining again, as he saw Sandy thrashing against the water. She didn't know anyone was near. She could very well fight against him. He steeled himself for the struggle. He reached out to her and, for moments, she was still too far away, inches, one inch, and finally he grasped one wrist as she strained against him, an arm, kicking her legs. "Sandy! I'm helping you. Don't fight me."

She was whimpering like a puppy and he yanked at her with all the power he possessed, and then she was rolling over him and he felt Tommy grappling to help him, as the boy slid back into the water and they were together, all three of them, weakly clinging to one another. Sandy's teeth were chattering, as Peter shouted at them to hold hands, to make ready to plunge into a different current that would take them downstream.

SHANNON STOOD BESIDE the water on a tiny beach. The little surges of the river lapped at her feet like something alive and gentle.

Six students had taken a raft across the river, stringing a cable along behind them at the bottom of the rapids. They were waiting beside it, in still water, to help the three swimmers to shore.

Shannon felt as if she was swimming, too, alone and buffeted by the huge rolling waves, sucked down by a current that would never release her. "Dear God," she was praying aloud, but she didn't know it. "Give them strength." For a fleeting instant, she imagined what it would be like to lose one of them. If she had to lose Tommy... if she had to lose Peter...

The burning tears on her face mixed with the cold spray from the river. She couldn't lose either of them, either of them. They were both what she'd been fighting for in her life; for Tommy's future, for Peter's trust and love. If only God would let Peter look past the pain of her leaving, if only he could let Peter love her enough.

"He's got them!" A cheer went up among the students. "Here they come!"

The three of them were together in a new current, one that dashed down into the trough of a wave and plummeted them to the bottom of the rapids. She saw Peter's torso jerk to one side as they rushed across a patch of underwater rocks. "Sandy!" he called to them. "Tommy. Lie flat." And when they did, the collar of each life jacket came up beneath their necks and protected them as they shot into the pool below. The students along the shoreline applauded. Tommy's fist shot out of the water in a wordless symbol of victory.

Shannon raced along the shoreline to get to them. Sandy's hair was a trail of wet, muddy yellow as the students lifted her into the waiting raft. She tumbled in and sat huddled against the edge of the boat as another teacher reached for Peter's hand. He did not respond.

"He's hurt," Tommy called out from the water. Shannon felt her insides collapse again. She loved him. God, she loved him. He had to know. She had to tell him. What if she lost him? After everything he had been willing to give to her, what if she lost him? Everything inside of her seemed to collapse as she stared at him, unmoving, in the water.

"Someone get to a radio or a telephone!" a faculty member shouted. "This man needs an ambulance!"

Cal Gleason was in the water now, and several more students, swimming across the quiet place in the river, to help hold Peter's unconscious form rigid, as the Washakie High School seniors lifted him out of the icy water and into the raft.

CHAPTER EIGHTEEN

"BLOOD PRESSURE...heart rate..." The Teton County emergency medical technicians bent over Peter as the ambulance raced toward Jackson. "Do we have reflexes in the hands?"

"Yes."

"He's going to make it, Shan." Tommy was in the ambulance, too, wrapped in blankets on a stretcher, but he was fine.

"Shh." Shannon squeezed her brother's hand. "Don't try to talk." She was sitting on a narrow seat, pressed up against the wall of the vehicle, while the EMTs monitored Peter. He was still unconscious. "I love you, Tommy."

"I know." Tommy did his best to smile. "I'm glad Sandy's okay." His friend was following them, in a sheriff's car, accompanied by one of the teachers from the high school. The other students were going back to Wind River on the school bus.

Shannon turned back to Peter. She was still praying for him silently, afraid to voice her fears aloud.

Tommy followed her eyes. "I think he must have hit a rock or something."

There was a gouge on his side. Shannon had seen it as the kids had pulled him out of the water. He was unconscious from the shock, and the EMTs couldn't make the wound stop bleeding.

She nodded. "I saw how his body jerked right before he yelled at you to lie back flat in the water when you were going over those rocks."

"He told us what to do before he passed out. He yelled at us so we wouldn't get hurt the way he was."

"Yes." Shannon closed her eyes, burying her face in her hands, thinking of all the times Peter had exhibited the same style of self-sacrifice for her. "He does that."

They were nearing town now, and the traffic lights were green. It seemed as if hundreds of recreational vehicles and campers had pulled off the road to let them pass. The ambulance made one last turn into the emergency entrance at St. John's Hospital. The doors flew open and new EMTs rushed out, while a nurse helped Shannon down and pointed to a waiting room as someone else ordered Tommy to sit in a wheelchair.

A male nurse lifted Peter's stretcher from the vehicle, engaged the frame and wheels and ran with it toward the emergency room. Then, as quickly as everything had happened, everything stopped. Shannon sat alone in the waiting room, crying quietly, praying for Peter to be all right.

The minutes crawled by. Every time the secondhand moved around the clock, it seemed like forever had elapsed. She wondered if she should call someone for him. But she didn't know who. Peter's parents lived in Idaho. Perhaps someone at the bank would know their number. But for some reason, Shannon didn't want to call the bank first. The bank wasn't his home. The bank didn't love him.

Camille. Peter's closest family. Shannon gave one sad little smile. Camille wouldn't be at a loss as to what to do. Camille never was.

The housekeeper answered the telephone on the third ring. Shannon could hear Taylor playing in the background.

"Well, Miss Lisa Radford, it's about time," Camille chortled. "Thank heavens you have come back from the big city. Maybe now my life will become tolerable again. Peter has been so unhappy. Reasoning with him has been like reasoning with an ogre. He won't even eat my cooking."

Shannon winced. "Camille. He's been hurt. Badly, I think." She was crying again and furious with herself for not being stronger as she explained the day's events in as few details as necessary. "I'm at the hospital with him now. The doctors haven't told me anything. I thought his family should know, but I didn't know how to reach them."

"I'll telephone his mother right now," Camille promised. "They're only two hours away. I'm sure they'll want to come to the hospital to be with him. I'll call the Saunders, too. Lorilee's parents. They'll want to be praying. And Taylor and I will come to the hospital as soon as we can get there."

"Camille, thank you."

Shannon hung up the telephone and turned to see the doctor standing with Tommy at his side. "This young man—" the doctor motioned toward her brother "—is going to be fine. He's weak, but his body temperature is back up where it needs to be. All he needs is sleep."

"Thank you, Doctor."

"Mr. Barrett is being moved to a room," the physician told her. "He's still unconscious."

Shannon was shaking, and she wanted to grab on to Tommy but she couldn't move. She felt so alone, clenching her fists against her sides, in a hospital waiting room, and for the moment, she was all that Peter had.

"His condition has improved considerably. Are you a member of the family? I don't want him to be alone when he awakens."

"Neither do I," she said, nodding, tears of gratitude running down her cheeks. "I'm staying with him."

"We've stopped the bleeding and sewn up the wound, but I do want to give him several units of blood to get his blood count back up."

Shannon nodded again. She felt Tommy's arm around her. Her brother supported her in silence as a nurse led them into Peter's room. They waited there, Shannon pacing, Tommy resting in a chair, until two nurses and the doctor brought Peter in.

The medical staff settled him and left. Tommy got up from his chair. "I'm going to call the sheriff's department in Wind River. I hope I can find somebody who'll be willing to drive out to the house to tell Mom and Dad that everything's okay."

"I should go. You should rest."

"No." He shook his head and then he grinned. "You're just as exhausted as I am. But you need to stay with him. I'd like to check on Sandy. Her parents are driving up. She just called them. And I'd like to have a little time to talk to her before they get here."

After Tommy left her and Peter alone, Shannon edged closer to the man in the hospital bed and tentatively traced one of his eyebrows with her fingers. His torso was bare except for the gauze bandage wound around him. The color was gone from his cheeks, but he looked wonderful and handsome to her all the same. "I love you, Peter Barrett," she whispered as the tears came again. "Thank you for bringing me home."

Peter did not move. She ran her hand along the cottony spikes of hair on his chest and then she pulled her hand away. She felt alone again, as if she shouldn't be touching him, as if she wasn't a part of him now. She knelt beside him, watching his face, drinking in the knowledge of him, of how he had cared for her once and of how brave he had been. And as she leaned toward him, only a breath away from his face, he whispered her name.

"Peter?" He didn't hear her. He was still unconscious. But he was calling out for her as she grasped his hand. "I'm here. Oh, Peter... I'm here."

"Shan. Don't leave. Please." He tossed his head, still unconscious, his voice groggy. "Shan. Don't."

"I won't. Oh, Peter, I won't." She stroked his jaw with outstretched, delicate fingers. "I promise."

His lashes cast a flicker of a shadow against his face as at last Peter responded to her touch. His eyes opened and he lay silently looking at her.

"Hello, Mr. Barrett." Shannon traced his nose with one featherlight motion.

"You're here," he said slowly. "Why are you here?"

"Let me tell you."

"You're here," he repeated.

"Do you want to know what's happening?" Her question was soft, as gentle as her touch.

"Yeah."

"You rescued Sandy Budge and my brother. Do you remember that part?"

Peter nodded slowly. His head still ached, but Shannon could see some of the color coming back to his face.

"They're both safe. But you got banged up a little bit."

"I feel banged up."

"You're in St. John's Hospital. The doctor tells me you're going to live."

"That's nice." He did his best to smile at her.

Shannon grinned down at him. "I thought you'd want to hear that right off. I called Camille. She's on her way. She's bringing Taylor. Your mother and father have been notified in Idaho."

Suddenly Peter realized why Shannon was here. She had only stayed so that she could notify his next of kin. "Well, you've been kind enough to take care of everything." His face screwed up against the pillow, and Shannon wasn't certain why he looked so desperately sad. His voice was flat, devoid of emotion, when he spoke to her again. "You can go then. You've notified everyone of any importance in my life. Go back to Wind River with your team of dreamy teenagers. Go shear a sheep."

Shannon reached out to touch him, but he pulled back from her. And she wanted to cry again but she didn't. "What's wrong with you? Why can't you just accept the things I have to offer you?"

"I tried." He tried to sit up and flinched. "I'm the one who told you that you didn't have to give every part of yourself to something. But I love you so much that I find myself wanting you to give all those things to me." He lay back against the pillow and looked lost. "I suppose I should be angry with myself, not you."

Shannon sat without speaking, aching, for she would have given anything to take his hurting away.

"I'm glad you came home to Wyoming, Shannon. I know you. I've known for a long time that coming home was what you needed. I'm not sorry you returned to your parents' home. I only wish you had come to mine."

"Peter." If only he knew how wrong he was. "You don't know why I stayed away. And you don't know why I'm here now."

"I do," he said, ignoring the first portion of her statement. "You didn't want me to wake up here injured and alone. And you probably feel gratitude because I happened to be in the right place at the right time to help your brother. And that's the gist of it." He dared her to prove him wrong with his eyes. "Isn't it?"

"Oh, Peter," she whispered. And then she smiled at his tone of voice. So many people had been daring her and baiting her, and all she felt inside now was peace. "I'm here because I love you."

He looked at her for a long time then, his eyes dull, his mouth in a half smile. He wasn't thinking clearly. He had to concentrate on the things she was saying. "Would you mind saying that again?"

"Okay." Her smiled broadened a touch. "I . . . love . . . you."

"But," he said finally, "when you were with me, at my home . . . we made love . . . you said it wasn't enough."

"*I love you*, Peter Barrett. That's enough for me." Shannon was trembling so violently that she was shaking the bed where he lay. And then she wasn't smiling anymore. She lost all control of her face as her lips quivered and her features contorted with pain. "It's too late for me to pull away. You're too much a part of me, Peter. I'm not anything anymore unless I give myself to you. I've hurt you so much. I returned to my parents' home because I knew I couldn't ask you to trust me a second time. I don't even know if I trust myself yet."

Peter reached for her hand and clutched her arm. "Shan." She was here beside him and he never had to let her go again and he knew it. "Trust me. Trust yourself. Trust the power in life that gave me a second chance...to be happy...to love you."

She buried her head in the blankets beside him. "Do you? How can you still love me?"

"It's very easy, Shannon." He raised his hand to her neck and his thumb brushed against her skin there as he gathered her hair into a bunch. "It's one of the easiest things I've done my entire life."

"Thank you," she whispered.

"Now—" his voice was quiet as he lay beside her, but she caught just a tinge of mischief in his tone "—we have one more thing we both need to consider."

"What's that?"

"My image as a banker in this town." He couldn't resist teasing her. "I have to be extremely careful, you know. If all the rich little old ladies here didn't approve of me, they wouldn't put their money in First National." If he had been stronger, Peter would have been chuckling, but as it was he could only say, "My image is very important. How I dress...the things I say..." He grinned. "So I probably should do right by the woman I love. If I don't, there's no telling what that would do to the interest rates. I think it would be best, Shannon, if you would agree to marry me."

Shannon stared at him in disbelief. "You crazy man."

"I'm crazy about you." He gripped her hand as she knelt by the bed. "I need you beside me."

She gazed at him, loving him, thinking of the future that lay ahead, if he really wanted it, with Taylor, and with their other children, too.

"Shannon Eberle. I'm asking you to marry me. What do you say? Out with it. I can't wait all day."

The door creaked open and in walked Taylor, his tiny arm stretched high to reach Camille's hand. "Look who's here." Shannon winked at Peter. "Taylor the Toddler Extraordinaire." She jumped from the floor beside Peter's bed, grabbed Taylor from an astonished Camille and whirled the tiny boy around the room. Her heart swelled as she thought of it. She would be his mother now and she could cuddle him and feed him bananas and pick him up when he fell. "Taylor," she said as she hugged him to her. "I'm going to marry your father. What do you have to say about that?"

"Dinosaur kiss!" Taylor shrieked.

"Wonderful," Shannon responded, giggling. "I think he wants to invite dinosaurs to the wedding. I wonder where they're going to sit? We'll have to put them on your father's side."

"Well, alleluia!" Camille exclaimed from the doorway as Peter shot her an Okay sign from the bed.

"Son...thank you," Peter chuckled. "I think I just got my answer."

SHANNON AND PETER'S wedding day was one of those golden ones in Wyoming. It was one of the days that makes the state one of the best for ranching, a burnished morning in August, the sun still arching to almost its highest point across the sky, curing the native grasses into hay while it stood, still growing, in the fields.

Inside the Eberles' white clapboard house, all was ready for the onslaught of guests. The white crocheted tablecloth was spread out on a table that stretched the length of the room. There were pies and cookies, and

there was a massive carrot cake, three tiers high, that
Melissa had made herself, decorated profusely with icing and with live wild daisies.

Sandy had come to the house for the past three days
to help Agatha Eberle make mints out of candy molds
and cream cheese and powdered sugar. They had made
hundreds of them. Both females wanted to be prepared
for the entire student body at Washakie High School to
attend the wedding ceremony. And they had been right
in doing so. Many of the students had come.

All the preparations were over now, and the little
house stood empty, the only motion there the movement of the curtains, white lace lapping gently against
the screens in the living-room windows.

Outside in the native grasses beside the house, Shannon stood beside Peter, her ankle-length eyelet skirt
lapping against the tops of her dainty white laced boots
in the same delicate dance as the curtains. She tilted her
face ever so slightly so that she was still turned toward
the preacher standing before them. Only now she was
gazing at the man she loved, too.

Peter beamed down at her. Her face was covered with
a layer of gossamer lace trailing down from a dainty
straw hat. She looked so beautiful to him that he wanted
to cry out to her. He kept having to remind himself that
the kindly old Baptist preacher standing before them
was not a fantasy. He was not watching this celebration on television. Shannon was standing beside him.
This was the real thing.

Agatha Eberle moved forward and took the bundle
of wild daisies Shannon was holding as the preacher
motioned for them to face each other. They exchanged
vows, Peter's voice firm, occasionally quavering with

emotion, Shannon's voice quieter, just as certain. "I do," the couple repeated.

The preacher smiled down at them and raised his arms. "I take pleasure in introducing to you ... for the first time ... Mr. and Mrs. Peter Barrett."

The yard exploded with sound, and out back in the corrals the sheep near the house echoed it with bleating, as students surrounded the newlyweds and Shannon hugged Peter's father and Lorilee's mother and then her own mom and dad.

"Oh, gad!" A familiar voice, louder than the others, rose above the din of the guests. Shannon recognized the nasal New York twang immediately. "So this is what Wyoming looks like."

Shannon spun around to face the voice and there stood Eddie, grinning, her fingernails painted so pink that they glowed, with a huge silver-wrapped package in her hands, wearing a pink leather miniskirt and matching jacket straight from the designer department at Saks Fifth Avenue.

"You!" Shannon squealed as she ran to her best friend and embraced her. "Oh, Eddie." And when she hugged the actress, she saw the rest of her New York friends, too—Al Jensen, standing just a step back, and Larry Wills. "You came! I didn't dream you would come all this way!"

"We had to bring you your wedding present," Al said, laughing.

"Here." Eddie tossed the package at her. "Open it. Now. We can't wait."

Shannon ripped open the paper as Peter stood beside her, watching her, grinning, and when she tore open the lid, she shook her head at them and she was laughing so hard that she couldn't talk. She reached into the box and pulled out a wrinkled hospital gown, white with little blue designs on it that looked like tiny eggs. It was the gown she'd worn on "Wayward Hopes" for months.

"I absolutely *hate* this thing," she said, giggling.

"It's okay," Eddie interjected. "We have a more traditional gift in the car. A silver punch bowl."

"But we thought Peter might find this...appealing," Larry said, grinning.

"We stole it from Gabrielle Cohen's discarded wardrobe box," Al told her. "We thought you might want to give it a proper burial."

"I do." Shannon tossed it across her shoulders. "Thanks."

"Actually, Shannon..." Larry Wills stepped forward as the others moved away with the crowd. Shannon stopped short, Peter beside her. "One of us in the group came today to see if you might be interested in an audition I set up for you."

"Larry, it means a lot to me that you're here. But no. I don't want another acting job."

"You may not want it, Shannon, but it wants you. I've had three prime-time shows out of L.A. call because they were interested in you. And I turned them down like you told me to. But not this one. I won't tell them no until you hear about it. And I know you don't have a telephone on this confounded sheep farm."

Shannon frowned. "So that's why you flew all the way from New York to come to my wedding."

"Partially. And partially because I wanted to share the momentous occasion."

Peter hugged his wife to him and pressed one finger over her lips. "Let's hear about it, Larry."

"It's going to be filmed in Wyoming this winter. They've already contacted the film commission, and I think they're going to house all the crews in Jackson. It's a made-for-television movie about a young ranch woman who opens a riding school for handicapped kids. It's a true story. A beautiful script...."

"Larry, no." Shannon felt Peter's arm supporting her waist, and she leaned against him.

"Shannon, I'm just talking about one movie."

"And I'm talking about one lifetime. I've accepted another job, Larry. I'm the permanent director for BEAT. I'm happier than I've been in a long time. Stop bugging me."

"Fine," he said glumly and frowned. "I get the point." And then he couldn't resist teasing her just a bit. "But I was going to get rich off this one. And you were going to be *so* famous."

"No," Shannon said, laughing. "Nobody will ever get rich off me again. And I've had enough fame for a while, too, thank you."

Larry left them then and Peter pulled her closer. "Are you certain? Shannon, it's just like you to give this up for me. I don't want you to do that."

"I'm not doing it for you," she told him. "This time, I'm doing it for myself." She hugged him tighter. She couldn't pull him close enough as she rested her head against his shoulder. "This is what is called 'a change of direction.'"

Peter couldn't resist pushing back the little hat she wore and kissing her on the top of the head. "You've taught me how to fight for what I believe in, Mrs. Barrett." He held her away from him for a moment so he could watch her face as he spoke. "You've taught me that sometimes, when you believe in something enough, life will be willing to change its direction for you."

"Are you giving me a speech?" Now Shannon was laughing again. "Are you trying to tell me about the goodness of life?"

"Shannon! Peter!" One of the cousins screeched from the house. "You two get in here. Melissa's all mad because somebody put a green plastic dinosaur on the cake and smushed the icing."

Just then, Taylor toddled by them, with Peter's mother and Camille both in pursuit. "Come here, Taylor." Peter pulled one arm away from Shannon and scooped up his son. "You're in luck, kid. Somebody *did* bring a dinosaur to the wedding." Peter lowered his mouth to his son's neck and gave him a series of gentle nips and kisses that made Taylor throw his head back in an outburst of giggling. "Dinosaur kiss," Peter teased him. "Dinosaur kiss."

"Hey." Shannon pretended to pout. "I want one of those, too."

Peter encircled his wife and his son with both of his arms. "Sure thing, ma'am. Dinosaur kiss . . ."

"Aug!" Shannon laughed and threw her head back, awaiting more, but she stopped when she realized Peter was standing over her, only watching her.

"What a family we make," he said softly, and then he touched her lips with one finger. "What a beautiful new wife I have."

"I love you, Peter," she whispered against his fingertips, and then she kissed them. She was oblivious to the crowd around them then, the students and her friends from New York and both their families. She only had eyes for Peter, her new husband, and bundled between them, her new son. "And that, guys, is all I'll ever need."

Peter proudly pulled her to him and gave her a quick, hard kiss before he took her hand and guided her up the steps onto the porch of the little house that, in her heart, had always been her home.

Shannon followed him, her hands clutched together around his wrist, laughing again, because she was so certain of everything now...because, at last, she had learned how to hold on to love.

**There was no hope in that time and place
But there would be another lifetime . . .**

---

*The warrior died at her feet, his blood running out of the cave
entrance and mingling with the waterfall. With his last breath
he cursed the woman. Told her that her spirit would remain
chained in the cave forever until a child was created and born
there.*

So goes the ancient legend of the Chained Lady and the curse
that bound her throughout the ages—until destiny brought
Diana Prentice and Colby Savagar together under the influence
of forces beyond their understanding. Suddenly each was
haunted by dreams that linked past and present, while their
waking hours were fraught with danger. Only when Colby,
Diana's modern-day warrior, learned to love could those dark
forces be vanquished. Only then could Diana set the Chained
Lady free. . . .

Next month, Harlequin Temptation and the intrepid Jayne
Ann Krentz bring you Harlequin's first true sequel—

DREAMS, Parts 1 and 2

Look for this two-part epic tale, the

Temptation

"Editors' Choice."

Harlequin Temptation dares to be different!

Once in a while, we Temptation editors spot a romance that's truly innovative. To make sure *you* don't miss any one of these outstanding selections, we'll mark them for you.

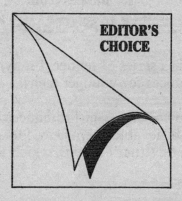

EDITOR'S CHOICE

When the "Editors' Choice" fold-back appears on a Temptation cover, you'll know we've found that extra-special page-turner!

THE

Temptation

EDITORS

Harlequin Superromance

COMING NEXT MONTH

#334 WORKING IT OUT • Patricia Rosemoor
Fitness expert Leila Forester knows men are drawn to
her beauty—and too often for the wrong reasons. So
when journalist Wynne Donegan approaches her, Leila
is suspicious. She considers his magazine article a ploy
to get near her. But Wynne is so charming she decides
she just might play along....

#335 SPRING THUNDER • Sandra James
Brody Alexander is no ordinary hired hand, as Jessica
Culver quickly learns when she offers him work in her
fledgling nursery business. He's gentle, caring and just
plain irresistible. But Jessica has a nagging suspicion
about Brody. And when her worst fears are confirmed,
only their love will protect them from the nightmare....

#336 ANYWHERE ON EARTH • Kelly Walsh
Teri Manzoni's wildest fantasies come true when she is
reunited with her first love, Kevin O'Shea. Now a
widow, Teri can't forget how Kevin forsook her. Still
madly attracted to him, she can only hope that this time
their fairy-tale affair will have a happy ending....

#337 A PATCH OF EARTH • Bobby Hutchinson
Fiery dance hall girl Liz Morrison isn't the kind of
woman to envy her best friend's happiness. Liz just
wonders why she's always a bridesmaid and never a
bride as she's overcome with loneliness at the wedding
of Chris Johnstone to Michael Quinn. As the ceremony
ends, Liz lifts her tear-filled eyes and meets the piercing
blue gaze of Tony Van Fleet. Suddenly Liz knows,
without a doubt, she need never be alone again....